Brutal
Diplomacy

A Clay Warrior
Stories book

J. Clifton Slater

This is a work of fiction. While some characters are historical figures, the majority are fictional. Any resemblance to persons living or dead is purely coincidental.

Brutal Diplomacy takes place in late 264 B.C. when Rome was a Republic and before the Imperial Roman Empire conquered the world. While I have attempted to stay true to the era, I am not a historian. If you are a true aficionado of the times, I apologize in advance.

I'd like to thank my editor Hollis Jones for her work in correcting my sentences and keeping me on track.

Now... Forget your car, your television, your computer, and smart phone - it's time to journey back to when making clay bricks and steel were the height of technology.

J. Clifton Slater

Website: www.JCliftonSlater.com

E-Mail: GalacticCouncilRealm@gmail.com

FB: facebook.com/Galactic Council Realm & Clay Warrior Stories

Brutal Diplomacy

Act 1

Flash point Messina, 264 B.C.

The Empire of Carthage (Qart Hadasht) - manipulative and arrogant, the only diplomacy Carthage understood was their way or the tip of a spear.

The Republic of Rome - direct and efficient, the only way Rome could get vicious enemies to sign peace treaties was brutal pacification.

The Kingdom of Syracuse – economic power on the southern tip of the island of Sicily. Grown tired of raids on his inland cities and on his merchant ships at sea by the Sons of Mars, King Hiero II threatened retaliation on the residents of Messina.

The Mamertines (Sons of Mars) - pirate rulers of Messina and the harbor. A nonentity in the power struggle for Sicily (Sicilia) until they broke faith with Syracuse. Their call for help against King Hiero II caused the Republic and the Empire to clash. The conflict started the first Punic War.

Brutal Diplomacy is far from a scholarly work. This is an adventure story. Some of the characters were real people, the settings are as close as my research allowed, and the action follows historical events. However, the story is mostly fiction.

Chapter – 1 Gladiator Games

The Insubri warrior's sword slashed towards the Legionary's torso. Jerking back saved the Legionary as the steel tip miss his bare chest and hip by inches. As the sword dropped below waist level, the Legionary surged forward crowding inside the barbarian's guard. The hilt of the gladius slammed into the solar plexus of the Insubri. The warrior bent, collapsing around the pain. With his face screwed up in agony, and his mouth open to grunt from the blow, the northern tribesman attempted to shuffle back. But his attempt at putting a safe distance between him and the Republic's fighter failed.

Driving with his right leg, the Legionary propelled his body forward while raising his left knee. It smacked into the forehead of the retreating barbarian. The hard bone of the patella impacted the barbarian's head as loudly as a hand clap. When his head snapped back, the movement exposed the Insubri's throat. Instead of using the Legion short sword, the Legionary lashed out with his left fist and tapped the Adam's Apple of the tribesman.

Gasping to pull air through his windpipe as he rocked back and over, the Insubri smacked his head and shoulders into the sand. Semiconscious, he lay staring at the sky with glassy eyes while choking.

"Very impressive," commented Senator Spurius Maximus. He let his eyes run over the two other warriors recovering from bouts with the Legionary. "Can they win?"

It was a weighted question. The Legionary could train the northern slaves with the aim of them winning. There was no doubt he would teach them because nobody refused the powerful Senator, especially, not a lowly Lance Corporal. After that, the winning was up to the individual Insubri warrior.

"General Maximus. They're experienced fighters. And, all three have good and bad habits. I can enhance the good and tamp down the other, maybe," replied Alerio Sisera using the Senator's preferred term of address. When two of Maximus' house guards roughly jerked the choking Insubri to his feet, Alerio warned them. "Break the merchandise and you'll take his place on the training sand and at the funeral games."

The guards had witnessed the three large and muscular barbarians fall, unbloodied, to the armed weapon's instructor. Neither wanted to fight the Lance Corporal or fight in the death matches of the games. They loosened their grips and slowed down as they dragged the warrior over to a bench. There, they deposited the warrior beside the instructor's other groggy students.

"If these aren't adequate, I'll go buy three more," General Maximus declared. "Flaccus sent back sixty from each tribe when he shipped back the spoils from Volsinii. As enthusiastic as our Consul is, I'm surprised he stripped the town before razing it to the ground. You were there, weren't you?"

"No, sir. I was in Volsinii with General Fabius Gurges' Legion," explained Alerio. "I missed General Flaccus' campaign. When he marched north, the Legion sent me to Sicilia."

"Oh, that quagmire," Senator Maximus moaned. "Between Syracuse, the Qart Hadasht Empire, and those accursed Sons of Mars in Messina, we should just beef up our Southern Legion. Let them wear each other out. Now, about those replacement Insubri?"

"These will do, General," exclaimed Alerio. "But they were starved during the march to the Capital. If you want them to have a chance against the Etruscans, they'll need to be fed."

"It'll be worth the price of the rations to take Consul Caudex's coins and put him in his place," Senator Maximus stated. "What else do you need?"

"Time for them to strengthen up," Alerio said. "And time for me to teach them."

"Junius Brutus Pera lies in state until tomorrow and the funeral games are two days after that," replied Maximus. "You've got three days to work your Legion magic on the barbarians. Don't let me down."

As the Senator strutted towards his Villa, Alerio called the four house guards over.

"Did you serve in a Legion?" he asked. All four confirmed they had and he continued. "I saw good men run down by Insubri cavalry. And more butchered by the Etruscans warriors. I don't hold any love in my heart for either tribe. But General Maximus wants victory. When you're tempted to mistreat or short ration those three, remember this..."

Alerio pointed to the three warriors slumped on the bench.

"Across the city, three Etruscans are being fed, watered and trained," the Lance Corporal explained. "Forget they're enemies of the Republic. Think of them as prized, and yes dangerous, race horses. Guard them, care for them, and during the games, bet your coins on them. Do that and they'll kill three Etruscans for us. And, you'll make a profit."

"You really think they can win?" one of the house guards asked. "The Etruscans are being trained by Corporal Daedalus of the city guard. He's a great swordsman. I saw him destroy every opponent in the harvest games last year."

Alerio turned so his right shoulder faced the guards displaying a row of scars. Then, he reached across his chest and traced the two lines on his shoulder cap with the tips of two fingers.

"See these scars? Corporal Daedalus tattooed them on me," Alerio informed them. The faces of the house guards fell as they peered at the marks left by Daedalus' gladius. "Yes, he stabbed me. Just before I beat in his helmet and knocked him out. If the marshal hadn't pulled me off, I'd have killed him. You see, I was upset with him for marring my perfect skin."

The house guards studied the crescent shaped scar on the Legionary's head, the line on the back of one arm, the scars on his forearms, the top of one hand, and on his right hip. All from blade attacks. Then, there were the sunken holes in his thigh and side from where arrows passed through the muscle and flesh.

"Excuse me," one of the guards expressed his puzzlement. "I don't understand what you mean? No offence Lance Corporal but, your skin is far from perfect. You've got battle scars."

The other three guards groaned.

"What he means is, he's better than Daedalus," another guard explained.

"Oh, then why didn't he say so in the first place?" asked the confused guard.

"Weapon's instructor, the Insubri will be well cared for," another guard promised ignoring the thick-headed guard. "When do you want to start the training?"

"Feed and water them and let them rest tonight," answered Alerio as he slipped a tunic over his head. "I'll be back before dawn."

Alerio left the sand pit area, crossed the Senator's manicured lawn and took the clay brick path around the Villa.

Once past the front gate, he paused to bow respectfully to the statue of Bia, one of Jupiter's winged enforcers. After a silent prayer thanking her for his bodily strength, Alerio turned south and headed for the Chronicles Humanum Inn.

Chapter 2 – Tangled Up in Politics

The great room of the Inn held a full complement of junior officers, senior NCOs, and a few lady friends. Every table was full of food and drink. Two waitresses scrambled to keep the customers happy. Behind the granite counter, Thomasious Harricus busily filled mugs with vino.

"Give me a mug of wine, Master Harricus," Alerio ordered as he approached the innkeeper. "I'm heading for the baths."

"I'm curious to know what Senator Spurius Maximus wanted with you," Thomasious replied as he slid a mug across the granite top. "But as you can see, my establishment is at capacity."

"Where did all the Legionaries come from?" Alerio asked.

"Still lingering in the Capital after General Flaccus' victory parade," explained Harricus. "They'll be heading out to new assignments in a day or so. Right now, I've got a bunch of them here and I need to make coins. Off you go."

"We'll talk later," Alerio promised as he walked to the double doors at the end of the counter and pushed through to the rear hallway.

***

The Lance Corporal soaked in the tub sipping his vino. It was the first chance he'd had to relax since the trip from his father's farm. When he reported in at the Legion

Transfer Post at the Capital, a letter from Senator Maximus waited for him.

'Lance Corporal Sisera. As soon as you receive this missive, report to my Villa without delay. General Spurius Maximus.'

With a slight detour to drop his gear and clean up a little at the Chronicles Humanum Inn, Alerio had taken a carriage to Villa Maximus. There he found three half-starved Insubri warriors and an impatient Senator.

"Consul Caudex wanted to see Insubri and Etruscī die on the wood," Maximus explained. "Probably as public revenge for Senator Gurges' death. My friend, Junius Brutus Pera, was deathly ill. I convinced his sons to hold a public gladiator fight in his honor when their father's strings were cut. As a result, instead of simply crucifying the Insubri and Etruscī, six captured tribesmen are going to entertain the crowd in death matches."

"Why am I here, General?" asked Alerio.

"You're going to train the Insubri, weapons' instructor," Maximus announced. "And when they win, I'm going to gloat in Appease Caudex's face while I take the whiny cūlus' coins."

Alerio shook his head to clear the memory. He couldn't get over the disrespect the politicians showed each other. When rivalry between units in a Legion arose, they settled it with physical games. Afterwards, they saluted the winner with drinks. In the Senate of the Republic, the rivalries took a darker turn. The games involved political maneuvering and mentally stabbing your opponent in the back.

Afterwards, the winners gloated while the losers plotted revenge. It was well over the head of a simple Legionary.

***

"Lance Corporal Sisera?" a man asked as he stepped into the bathhouse. Thick set and wearing the armor of a city guardsman, the man stood with his fist resting on his hips. Following closely behind, came another large guardsman. Their swords were sheathed but, due to their size in the confined space, they didn't require blades to be threatening.

"I'm Alerio Sisera," he responded while eyeing his sword and knife which he'd left on a bench, far out of arm's reach. "What can I do for you gentlemen?"

"Did you hear that, he called us gentlemen," the lead city guard exclaimed.

"He doesn't know us very well, does he?" the other replied.

"My friend is right, Sisera, you don't know us," the first sneered. "And you don't want to. Just be sure the Insubri die gloriously at the funeral games and you never will. If they win, you'll wish you'd never met us."

"Listen up, Sons of Coalemus," Alerio instructed as he climbed out of the bath. "Tell Daedalus, the next time he wants to talk with me, come himself. Don't waste the God of Stupid's time by sending the two of you."

They both bristled, swelled up like roosters, and took a half step to circumvent the bath. Then, a club's head shot through the door striking one of the guardsmen in the back. Spread-eagle, he splashed into the tub. Next a fist hammered the other guardsman in the back of his head and he joined his friend in the water. Erebus, Thomasious Harricus' barbarian servant, stepped over the threshold.

"Master Sisera. I'm sorry to disturb your bath," Erebus announced while ignoring the two men. They were struggling to shove each other out of the way so they could stand in the deep tub. "But I need to lock it up for the night to prevent unauthorized use."

"I understand," Alerio replied as he gathered his belongings and walked by the servant.

Erebus stepped out, slammed the door, and dropped a beam across the frame.

"I'm leaving to run an errand for Master Harricus," the big barbarian apologized. "The bath won't be open until I get back in the morning."

"I got the road dust washed off. And some merda from the city streets out from under my feet," Alerio proclaimed. "Thank you for your assistance."

"You are welcome, Lance Corporal Sisera," Erebus said as he lumbered towards the stables.

Alerio headed across the compound to the Inn's rear entrance. He'd had a busy day and needed a good night's rest to avoid Insubri swords in the morning.

***

Long before first light, Alerio pushed through the double doors and strolled into the great room. As he expected, Thomasious Harricus sat staring out the window at the dark street.

"Good morning. Care for some company?" Alerio asked.

"Please, I've been waiting for you," Thomasious replied indicating a chair, a covered platter in the center of the table, and a pitcher. "You owe me an explanation from yesterday."

As Alerio sat, the innkeeper poured watered wine into a mug, then he lifted the cover. Ham slices, cheese and a loaf of bread filled the platter.

"I suppose you mean General Maximus' summons," Alerio stated as he ripped off a piece of bread and piled ham and cheese on it. "He wants me to train some Insubri for a funeral game."

"Gladiator blood matches for the public," Thomasious corrected him. "For years the Patrician families have held private matches at the grave sites. Human blood, after all, helps purify the deceased soul. But, we've never seen the sacrifice as a public spectacle. And between hardened warriors, at that. It should be a great show. If you're training the Insubri, who is training the Etruscī?"

"Master Harricus. If you know it'll be between three Insubri and three Etruscī, I have to believe, you know that Corporal Daedalus is the other weapon's instructor," Alerio said between bites. "It's just a dressed-up execution. Why is everyone taking it so seriously?"

"There are many factions in the Senate. But two are very large. Appease Caudex controls one powerful group," explained Thomasious. "Can you guess who heads the other?"

"Spurius Maximus?" ventured Alerio.

"Exactly. When Maximus' man, Flaccus, rode triumphally through the streets of the Capital after draining the city's coffers to fund his Legion, Caudex lost his bearings. He uttered some very rude things in public," related Thomasious. "The gladiator game is more than a funeral rite. It's a proxy fight between powerful men."

"And powerful men don't like to lose," Alerio stated as he stood.

"Now, you go off and play with your savages," Thomasious advised as he stood. "I've got to call the city guardsmen."

"The city guards? Whatever for?" asked Alerio.

"I seem to have rats in my bathhouse," Thomasious replied. "And I'd like to have witnesses when I open the door."

Chapter -3 Villa Maximus

"Names!" demanded Alerio of the three warriors standing in front of him. When none spoke, he asked again and gave them something to think about. "Names? Did you eat last night? Were you beaten? I see full bellies and no new bruises. Except for the welts I beat into you last evening. Wouldn't you like a chance to pay me back?"

"Petrus," one replied with a grin on his wide face. "I would pay you back."

He was a solidly built man - thick of arms and legs with a neck like a bull. Alerio walked over to a weapon's rack and snatched up two spears. Tossing one to Petrus, the Lance Corporal carried the other as he walked a careful circle around the man.

The four, armed house guards shifted uncomfortably. They feared for the weapon's instructor's safety and their position in Villa Maximus if he was injured. When two began to draw their gladii and step forward, Alerio waved them off.

"You're a big brute, Petrus," Alerio observed as he circled. The Insubri turned with small steps, watching the Legionary closely. "But your hands? Little, with fingers like a girl."

Petrus glanced down to where his hands held the spear shaft. The glance was all Alerio needed. He dropped low, stepped forward with one leg, and swung the shaft. To better turn and face the circling Legionary, the tribesman had his feet close together. The shaft connected with the back of his knee and the blow folded his legs. The Insubri fell onto his back.

13

"Two rules for you, Petrus," Alerio instructed. His spear point was against the barbarian's neck, pinning him to the sand. "Never take your eyes off a foe. And, keep your stance wide. Big men are hard to take down if they are vigilant and balanced. Now get up and let me show you."

Alerio started to step away then stopped.

"You're mad at me. And you will try to kill me when I let you up," Alerio advised. "Know this. Every time you go for the kill while I'm teaching you, I'll make your head hurt."

Petrus waited for a heartbeat before he came up on his knees. Once he'd gathered his feet under him, he charged at the Legionary. Spear point forward and all of his body weight behind the attack, he yelled a war cry. The iron tip closed on the Legionary's side. But the iron head missed as Alerio twisted his hips away from the spear and stepped to the side. Petrus hurdled forward past his target. Alerio twirled his spear bringing the butt end around. He knocked Petrus in the back of the head.

The big man landed with his legs in the sand and his chest on the lawn. Alerio rested the tip of his spear between the man's legs.

"You are a bit of a cūlus," observed Alerio as he poked at the man's rear. "Maybe I should install a new one and have them send me another Insubri. No, not yet. Get up and this time listen to me."

Petrus struggled to his feet, picked up the spear and turned to face the Legionary. Then he stopped. The weapon's instructor had pulled off his tunic and the Insubri got a look at the scars. Yesterday, he was sick from hunger and couldn't focus. This morning, although his head ached, he paid attention.

"You are young for so many battle marks," Petrus stated. "Still, I will kill you."

"It's your headache," Alerio replied holding the spear diagonally across his body. "Well, fat man, I don't see anyone else with a spear and a chance to use it. Come on!"

Petrus shuffled forward. The muscles of his shoulders bunched and the veins in his arms bulged

Shifting his head to the side as if looking at the guards, Alerio spoke to them.

"Holy Goddess, it's like waiting for Morta to come and snip your life strings," Alerio complained to the guards. "I thought barbarians were fast."

With the Legionary's head turned, Petrus saw his opportunity and he sprinted forward. Suddenly, the spear held cross chested, flipped over the weapon's instructor's shoulder and before the tribesman could stop his charge, or block the spear shaft, the butt end came up and slapped the side of his head. Petrus didn't go down but, he did drop his spear to place both hands on his temples.

"Hurts, doesn't it?" Alerio stated. "If you're finished fooling around? Pick up your spear and let's begin."

"How?" mumbled Petrus.

15

"You were watching my spear and my head," Alerio instructed. "But you failed to look at my eyes. They were on you. That's another lesson for you."

***

When Alerio finally released Petrus, the big tribesman dropped his spear, placed one hand on the side of his head and another on the back of his head. Then, he staggered to the bench and collapsed.

"Name?" called out Alerio as he stowed both spears. "Let me remind you that in three days, you'll be fighting for your lives. I'm trying to help you stay alive. Name?"

"Eolus," declared a rawboned and wiry tribesman as he stepped forward. "The headaches, I don't want."

Alerio selected two small shields and two medium length swords.

"I fight with my tribe's sword," Eolus declared when Alerio offered the shield and the sword to the Insubri.

"You mean a shield smasher?" replied Alerio. "Fine. Set those aside and go get one. I'll keep these."

Eolus chuckled as he walked to the weapon's rack. Figuring the small shield and the short sword would hinder the Legionary, he chose a heavy iron sword. He swung it back and forth as he stalked back to the sand pit.

"I will attempt not to injure you too much," the tribesman stated. "When do we begin?"

"Attack me," ordered Alerio.

The controlled low to high arc was a good opening strike. It forced Alerio back to avoid the heavy blade. Plus, the reverse would be a powerful backhanded slash that should cleave the shield and the Legionary. Except, Alerio stepped forward and rammed his shield into the back of Eolus' raised arm.

Twisting away from the shield to free his sword arm, Eolus hopped back and spun in a circle. The sword led the arc of his turning body with the blade dropping towards the level of the Legionary's head. Eolus snapped his head around checking the angle of his blade for the most efficient kill. Then he stopped and let the sword fall from his fingers.

Alerio's blade rested on Eolus' cheek. The tip just below the Insubri's left eye.

"A heavy sword isn't always the best weapon for individual combat," instructed Alerio as he straightened his legs, still maintaining pressure on the tribesman's cheek with the sharp point. "A quick man can get inside a guard with a shorter sword."

"I will try the sword and shield," agreed Eolus. Only then did Alerio withdraw his sword from the barbarian's cheek.

***

"Name?" asked Alerio of the last Insubri.

"Eutropius. And I will not be struck in the head or fooled into allowing you inside my guard," the man announced. "What weapon do you suggest?"

17

Alerio studied the man. His frame fell somewhere between Petrus' mass and Eolus' taunt muscles. Two javelins and tribal shields were the choices. The weapon's instructor carried them to the center of the sand pit.

Eutropius accepted the shield and fitted it on his left arm. Then he hoisted the javelin over his head.

"Am I to throw it at my opponent and pray with an empty fist for the rest of my life?" Eutropius inquired. "For it will be a short life."

Alerio slammed his shield into the barbarian's. With their shields locked, the Legionary shoved the shields to his right. The movement exposed his left side, leaving it unprotected and open to Eutropius' javelin.

With a smile, the Insubri drew back the javelin and poked forward at the instructor's exposed flank. The iron tip never reached the flesh. While Eutropius focused on the advantage of the opening, he forgot how close they were standing. A foot hooked behind his front leg, lifted it off the sand, allowing a shove from the Legionary's shield to send the off balanced warrior toppling over backwards. Then he remembered but it was too late.

"There are no gifts in combat," Alerio stated, looking down at the Insubri from over the top of his shield. "If you don't cause the opening in your foe's defenses, be wary of a trap."

Eutropius ran his eyes along the bottom of the tribal shield and noticed the man's ankles were back and out of range from a quick attack by his javelin. At the top, the man's face remained behind the barrier. Even while instructing, the Legionary protected himself.

"We will listen and learn," Eutropius announced as he braced a hand on the sand and stood. With his shield forward and the javelin resting on the top edge of the shield mimicking the Legionary, he begged. "Show us how to survive."

Alerio spent the rest of the day having the warriors spar. Shield and javelin against shield and sword, and spear against both. By the time the sun lowered in the western sky, the three Insubri were bruised and exhausted.

"Can they win the games, Lance Corporal?" inquired a house guard.

"You've seen them progress during the day," Alerio replied. "Two more days and they should be able to stand against anyone."

"Even Legionaries?" asked another guard.

Alerio's stomach sank. Even Legionaries?

Chapter – 4 A Targeted Weapon's Instructor

"There are two groups loitering on the street," a house guard announced. He had come from around the Villa and walked to where the four stood with Alerio. "One group to the north and one to the south."

"It's a public street," another guard replied.

"It is. But too many of them are watching our main gate," the newly arrived guard informed him. "I don't like it."

The guards had served in General Maximus' Legion. Typical of combat veterans, they balanced caution with common sense. But, they never discounted the possibility of an attack.

"They may be waiting for me," ventured Alerio. "Two city guardsmen warned me off from training the Insubri. The funeral games are turning out to be more political than a sendoff for a nobleman. Would they dare invade the Senator's home?"

"I don't think so. However, they might come over the walls and damage the merchandise," another responded, referring to the Insubri warriors. "We'll bring in more of our veterans to protect the compound. I suggest, Lance Corporal, you either spend the night here or sneak out the garden gate."

"I have someone I need to speak with," Alerio informed him. "I'll use the garden gate."

**

The guards doused the lights near the garden gate and opened it just enough for the Legionary to slip through. Alerio crouched in the dark by the wall and scanned the street.

His goal was a few streets over and much farther south. At the end of the Senator's wall, two men stood in the intersection. If they were talking and looking at each other, they might have passed as friends having a conversation. But they stood silently, each watching a street - the two streets bordering the wall of Villa Maximus.

Alerio stayed low and crept closer to the pair. A loud fight would draw more of the watchers. Were they watchers or knee breakers? He wasn't sure and didn't want to find out. When he slipped as close as possible, Alerio noticed they were shifting their eyes from the streets to the top of the walls. This confirmed they were waiting for someone to leave, or for a sign to enter the compound, and not simply idling away their time by standing in the street.

Drawing his gladius slowly to avoid scraping the blade on the sheath, Alerio inhaled. As he exhaled, he sprinted at the two men.

They noticed the movement. Before either could make out the form emerging from the shadows, one got smacked in the face by the flat of a blade. The other folded in two from a shoulder in his stomach. As he was powered backwards, a gladius pommel slammed into his temple. The other man, holding a bleeding nose, was taken off his feet by a leg sweep. He also received a tap from the pommel. Then Alerio was on his feet and racing away from the two unconscious watchers.

Chapter – 5 Wisdom of a Retired Centurion

Tomas Kellerian opened the door to the Historia Fae and ushered Alerio over the threshold.

"When a farm lad shows up on my doorstep after dark, I know it can't be good," commented the armorer to the Gods as he threw the bolts securing the door. "Whose wrath have you incurred this time, Lance Corporal Sisera?"

"Apparently, the city guards, some street gangs," replied Alerio. "Oh, and possibly Consul Appease Caudex. I need advice."

"Advice? Sure. March yourself across the city and throw yourself from the Tarpeian Rock," suggested Tomas. "Better to kill yourself than wait for a Consul to have you pushed over the edge for treason. The fall won't hurt. It's the sudden stop at the bottom that gets you."

"General Maximus will stop any charge of treason. I hope," Alerio ventured. "I'm training the Insubri to fight at the funeral games for him."

"I've told you before. I've spent most of my life with the Legion defending the Republic from barbarians," growled Tomas. "I don't believe in teaching them our skills or how to kill Legionaries."

"I guess that precludes you from helping. I'm a marked man and my travels are restricted," confessed Alerio. "I was hoping you'd help with the training."

"By Hades! Absolutely not," declared the retired Centurion. Then he thought for a moment and a puzzled looked crossed his face. "You said the city guard is after you. Who is training the other gladiators?"

"Corporal Daedalus. If I'm disabled or not able to train the Insubri, his Etruscī warriors will win," Alerio reported. "But I'll figure something out."

The Armorer walked away and the Legionary thought he'd been dismissed. A short time later, as Alerio waited to be let out the front door, Tomas returned with his arms full of stacked armor and a personal pack.

"The day after General Flaccus' triumphant parade through the city, two drunken Legionaries came to see me," Tomas related as he placed the armor on a workbench. "They were broken up. Seems their squad leader must have been killed by the barbarians because he didn't come back for his armor and gladius."

"Cimon and Drustanus?" asked Alerio. "Where did they go?"

"They said something about finding a sacrificial bull," Tomas informed him. "Their Century is camped east of the city. Waiting for release orders to return to their Legion."

"Then I better go see them and break the bad news that I'm alive," Alerio said cheering up. He pulled off his tunic and began strapping on his armor. "Thank you for storing my gear."

"I'll see you in the morning at Villa Maximus," Tomas said.

"You're going to help?" asked Alerio. "Why?"

"On one condition. And to be sure the Etruscans die on the sand," the Armorer stated.

"What's the condition?" inquired Alerio.

"I'll tell you later," Tomas replied as he guided Alerio to the door.

Chapter – 6 Seventh Squad, 47th Century, Flaccus Legion

The squalor of Fireguard District had been reduced to ashes and most of the ash and rubble were gone. A newly constructed road cut through the area where flimsy buildings once stood. Alerio marched up the torch lined street and, at the top of what had been a steep earthen berm, he gazed down at neat rows of Legion tents.

At the bottom of the road, he asked a sentry for directions to the squad area of Forty-Seventh Century. Armed with the Legionary's instructions, he marched down the center of the Legion camp. On the far side, he turned down a camp street.

"Seventh of the Forty-Seventh?" he asked a squad guard.

"Two streets down on your left," the Private replied.

***

"Private Cimon. What's the turn!" Alerio demanded as he approached the campfire in front of the tent.

Without thinking who was asking, Cimon glanced at the squad's hourglass. Then recognition came to him and he jumped to his feet.

"Lance Corporal Sisera. Is that you or a ghost come to haunt us for not sacrificing a bull in your name?" the Private asked. "Because we tried. Do you know what a sacrificial bull costs? Even with Drustanus negotiating, we couldn't get a reasonable price."

"As you can see, no sacrifice was required," Alerio informed him. "I'd like to see Drustanus, but right now I need to speak with Centurion Seneca. Is he in camp?"

"He's taken Officer of the Day and Duty NCO so Meleager could take our new Corporal into the city," responded Cimon. "Come back later and I'll cook you some rations."

"I'll come back for your cooking and to sleep," admitted Alerio. "This is the safest place for me right now."

***

"Because General Maximus has me training the Insubri, I'm a target of the city guardsman," Alerio concluded his report to Forty-Seventh's Centurion. "I'm afraid, the political pressure will result in an attack on the warriors."

"Let me get this right, Lance Corporal Sisera," replied Centurion Seneca. "You want Seventh squad to protect Insubri warriors?"

"Just at Villa Maximus. And, to the funeral games," Alerio assured the Centurion.

"Do you really believe you'll have any of them left alive after the games?" challenged the old Legion Officer. "I hear Corporal Drustanus is an excellent swordsman."

"I do, sir," Alerio assured him. "General Maximus has a lot of political capital tied up in the games and he is depending on me."

"Sisera, this is lunacy," Seneca observed. "If it was for anyone besides the General, I'd throw you out of my tent with a kick to your cūlus. However, once a General's Senior Centurion, always one. Take Seventh squad and protect the General's property."

***

Before sunrise, there was a small commotion in the Legion camp. Seventh broke down their tent, packed it on their mule, and marched towards the Capital. The left, stomp, left, stomp of an armored squad of Legionaries echoed off the dark buildings and later off the walls of Villas. They passed a few city guard patrols, but the guardsmen stepped to the side of the street and let them pass unchallenged. Armor, big shields, javelins and the hobnailed boots of heavy infantrymen had that effect on people.

"Who goes there?" a house guard asked when Alerio pounded on the front gate.

"Lance Corporal Sisera and Seventh Squad of the Forty-Seventh," he called out loudly so the thugs mustered far down the street could hear.

"We could go and give them a taste of infantry shield for breakfast," Private Cimon suggested before the house guard could open the gate. He indicated the watchers on the next block.

"I promised Centurion Seneca that we'd keep damage to citizens to a minimum," Alerio answered.

"Minimum damage? Perfect, just a little toss with our shields," Drustanus added.

"Private, I've seen you knock down a barbarian and almost behead him with your shield," Alerio said.

"I would have," protested Drustanus. "If the other one hadn't begged for a chance to run his guts onto my blade."

The gate opened and Alerio ordered the squad to form up single file as they marched into the General's compound.

Chapter – 7 General's Inspection

Alerio blocked Eutropius' javelin to the side. Then dropping to his knees, he spun and brought his javelin up and jabbed under the warrior's shield.

"Don't over commit unless you have your shield in place," Alerio informed him.

From the porch on the back of the Villa, General Maximus cried out, "What's this?"

He stomped down the steps and marched directly towards Seventh squad's tent. At the tent, he returned the duty guard's salute before walking around testing the guide ropes. Then, he checked the stacked javelins, and the infantry shields propped against each other in squares of four. Finally, he raised an arm and motioned for Alerio to come to him.

"You run a tight camp, Lance Corporal Sisera," Maximus stated. "I haven't had the pleasure of inspecting a Legion camp in years. But, for Bia's sake, why is a squad of heavy infantry camped out at my Villa?"

"Thank you, General. I'll pass along your compliment to the men," Alerio replied. "I've had troubles with the city guard about training the Insubri. Plus, I feared for your safety. When I explained it to Centurion Seneca, he insisted I place a squad under your command."

"You never argue with experienced officers or NCOs. That's a lesson for you Lance Corporal," Maximus said. "Now tell me about my gladiators."

Alerio walked the Senator around the three Insubri warriors. As they circled, he explained each of their weaknesses and strengths.

"This is important to me," Maximus reminded Alerio as he headed back to the Villa.

"Yes, sir. We'll put on a good show," Alerio replied.

The Senator turned around and drilled Alerio with his eyes.

"I don't want a good show," he stated. "I want to win all three matches!"

***

Alerio was sweating and had a bruise on his arm from Eolus' shield. The tribesman was fast. Then, a hand cart came from around the side of the Villa being pulled by a Legionary. Behind the cart walked Tomas Kellerian.

"Are they going to fight naked?" asked the Armorer. "If so, fine. But a man should drill in the armor he's wearing to war. Bring those three over here so I can fit them with some protection."

A short time later, all three warriors had shin guards, forearm, shoulder armor and a helmet. Even Tomas wore armor.

"I'm going to work them to see if they learned anything from you," Tomas informed him. "Go sit on the grass."

"Yes, Centurion," Alerio said thankfully.

He strolled to the lawn and sank down. Tomas called out the Insubri warriors and bashed them one at a time to help them adjust to the armor. Then he called over three Legionaries and pair them up with the barbarians. By night fall, the gladiators were moving better in their new gear as well as a little stiffly from the work.

Chapter – 8 Game Day

"Tomas. I'm taking two infantrymen with me to secure our area at the games," Alerio informed the Armorer.

"Won't you be more secure with the full squad," suggested Tomas. "The city guard and the thugs are waiting for you to stick your head out of the compound."

"They'll have to recognize me first," Alerio replied as he slipped on a helmet, slid his arm through an infantry shield's brace, and picked up a javelin. "Private Cimon. Choose a left side man and gear up."

Cimon pointed to another private and the two of them armed up.

"Master Kellerian. The games start after the sun's apex," Alerio reminded Tomas. "Watch over the merchandise. I'll see you there."

***

Two city guardsmen loitered on the far side of the intersection. They straightened when the gate opened and three infantrymen appeared. To the south and north, thugs also turned and watched.

"You've got their attention," Cimon said out of the side of his mouth.

"Seems we do," confirmed Alerio. "Form up and let's see if they want to play."

With their left arms snug against their sides to support the weight of the shields, one stepped forward and began to march towards the city guardsmen. The other two fell in a half step back, flanking the lead. All three rested their javelins on their right shoulders with the iron tips level with the tops of their helmets. If necessary, the shields could rapidly be brought forward creating a wall, and the javelin tips lowered, adding iron points to the shield wall.

"You there! What's your name?" demanded a city guardsman as he fell into step beside the three. He was speaking to the unit's leader marching at the head of the formation.

"Private Cimon of the Seventh of the Forty-Seventh," Alerio's left-pivot replied.

On his right and a half step back, Alerio kept silent.

"We have an arrest warrant for Lance Corporal Sisera," the guardsman said as he fast walked to stay abreast of the formation. "He assaulted two guardsmen."

Barely turning his head to address the guard, Cimon inquired, "Are they dead?"

"No but…"

"We've just come from Volsinii," Cimon interrupted the guardsman. "If they are alive, Lance Corporal Sisera didn't assault them. Up north, when we assaulted, barbarians died. If they are alive then Sisera was just playing with them."

"Now see here," protested the guardsman but the unit had reached the next intersection. He decided on returning to his companion to resume their vigil on the Villa.

"I take it Sisera isn't in charge of the unit," the other guardsman commented when the first returned.

"No. Just some hard cūlus veterans from Volsinii."

"Good. That's three less we'll have to deal with when Sisera comes out," the second guardsman ventured. "Did they really level Volsinii after the attack?"

"Every building, right down to the pavers."

"That's extreme."

"That's the heavy infantry," the guardsman replied glancing up the street. Three blocks away, the three infantrymen were dodging traffic as they crossed the boulevard.

***

Cimon guided the trio down Viminal Hill and turned south on the low road. Villas on their right rose in tiers covering this side of Quirinal Hill. At the southern toes of the hill, they turned on a westward road.

"The stockyards are close," announced Cimon.

"What was your first clue?" inquired Alerio. "The merda on the roadside or the smell?"

Ahead of them, the Servian Wall loomed and on the south end of Quirinal Hill, they passed the last Villa. Small trees and grass replaced the walls and courtyards of homes.

The natural landscape continued around to the western slope of the hill. At the base, a road bordered the stockyards. Alerio shivered as he remembered a night of pain and confusion when he'd crossed the city. Injured and dodging the city guardsmen and the crime syndicate, Spilled Blood, he'd barely reached the Golden Valley trading house before passing out. Now at least, it was only the city guard after him.

Viewing for the funeral games was provided by the natural Amphitheatre of the slope. Rows of seating for important people had been constructed along the crest of Quirinal. On each end of the rows, dirt had been piled and flattened and platforms built. Obviously, these were for the Consuls and their guests. Lower down, commons citizens and visitors to the Capital would have to make do with sitting on the grass. Food and beverage vendors had claimed territory and were already cooking or setting out their wares. And placed around the hill for easy access, betting stalls were going up.

The three infantrymen wheeled to the north and marched up the road following the fencing for the stockyard. They passed penned in cows, bulls, sheep, goats, horses, mules, and ponies. Their destination sat at the end of the pens.

A raised area, usually for displaying livestock during auctions, had been heightened with a thick layer of sand. Behind the makeshift arena, two Legion command tents occupied most of the space between the sand, the Servian Wall, and the pens.

No livestock would be displayed and sold on this day. Today, the display was combat, death, and blood to honor the recently departed Junius Brutus Pera.

"Which tent?" asked Cimon.

Recognizing Belen, Senator Maximus' secretary, Alerio instructed, "The one on the left."

Chapter – 9 Pregame Diplomacy

"Cimon. I want one of you standing guard here at all times," Alerio instructed as they reached the tent's entrance. "And the other patrolling inside the tent."

"Lance Corporal Sisera, is the armor and Legion guards necessary?" asked Belen. "It is just funeral games."

"It maybe games to most people but someone is taking it very seriously," replied Alerio. "Haven't you noticed the people watching the Villa."

"The Senator did and he's been traveling with extra security," admitted Belen. "But this is…well, I'm not sure what this is. There's never been combat to the death as a public spectacle."

"A senior NCO once told me, in the presence of combat, your temper gets up and you want to lash out either verbally or with your sword," related Alerio. "The Legionaries are here to be sure nothing more dangerous than words are exchanged."

"There are refreshments on the table in the back," was all Belen had to say after Alerio's comment.

***

"That's a veteran Legionary," Senator Maximus bragged from outside just before he entered the tent.

Behind him came Consul Flaccus, and five men in gold and silver trimmed tunics. Alerio assumed they were Senators or wealthy supporters of Maximus.

"Consul Flaccus. Let's put an end to all this ugly talk about getting involved in Sicilia," suggested Maximus. Around him, the important men nodded their agreement. "Recent wars have cost us too much. Thanks to Consul Flaccus, our coffers are filling as we liquidate the spoils from Volsinii. But too slowly to support another war."

The group followed the senior Senator to the back of the tent. At the refreshment table, he picked up a piece of beef and waved it around as he continued.

"As much as I hate to agree with Consul Caudex, the Capital needs to enlarge. In your speech, Flaccus, throw your co-Consul a bone," Maximus urged. "Promise to support his roads and utilities bill. Maybe that'll soothe his frail ego."

"Nothing short of a bloodletting will pacify his damaged ego," Flaccus added. "Ever since my parade, he's been worshiping at the feet of the Goddess Invidia. Every time I see him in the Senate he gives me the evil eye. The man is eaten up with envy."

"Oh, for Vulcan's sake what does he want? A golden forge?" Maximus cried. "Tell him, we'll name a boulevard after him."

"That's not what he wants, Senator," one of the men in the richly appointed tunics explained. "He wants glory and fame."

From outside the tent, the Legionary's voice carried to them.

"Tribune, good morning, sir!" the sentry called out.

Alerio, who had been hovering near the group, immediately headed for the entrance. Before he reached the tent flaps, Consul Appease Caudex, followed by four men, strutted into the tent. One of them was a Tribune in ceremonial armor.

"Tribune, good morning," Alerio stated while slamming his fist into his chest.

"And who are you?" the Tribune inquired, glancing towards the back of the tent where Cimon stood at attention. His posture was correct except for his bulging right cheek. It was obvious, the Legionary had stopped chewing a piece of food he'd snatched from the refreshment table. "And what are you doing here?"

"Lance Corporal Alerio Sisera of the Southern Legion, temporarily detached to the Seventh of the Forty-Seventh," Alerio responded. One of the men in Caudex's group snapped his head around at the mention of the name. "We are security for Senator Spurius Maximus and his gladiators."

"Since when does the Legion protect only one citizen?" demanded the Tribune.

"I wouldn't know, sir," Alerio pleaded. "We are just following orders from our Centurion."

Before the Legion staff officer could question him further, Consul Caudex called to the Tribune.

"Gaius, come over here," Caudex ordered. "Gentlemen, this is Tribune Gaius Claudius. He's been keeping me abreast of the invasion of Sicilia by the Qart Hadasht Empire."

"It's hardly an invasion, Consul," Maximus corrected him. "They've occupied the northern edge of Sicilia for years. But Syracuse and the Sons of Mars have kept them on their side of the island."

"They did. But now the Sons have invited the Empire into Messina to protect them from King Hiero and his army," Appease Caudex replied. His eyes were open wide with excitement and his breathing rate increased as he argued his point. "The Empire is on the threshold of the Republic and we must slam the door in their face."

"We can send an ambassador to Messina," replied Maximus. "Diplomacy is cheaper than warfare."

"Tell them, Tribune Claudius," Caudex ordered.

"Sirs, I've been in communications with Southern Legion's head of planning and stratagies. One, Tribune Velius, who sent envoys to Messina to speak with Admiral Hanno of the Qart Hadasht," Gaius reported. "His reply was, and I quote: The oceans belong to the Empire. Don't even take a glass of sea water without asking permission. And remember, the only reason you, dirt farmers of the Republic, have foreign trade is the Empire hasn't gotten around to you, yet."

"That, gentlemen! That is their response," an excited Appease Caudex shouted. "The tip of a Legion javelin is the only diplomacy the Empire understands. I say we march on Messina."

"And I say we don't, co-Consul," Marcus Flaccus said reminding Caudex that he was only half of the Republic's leadership. "We need to improve the Capital. Even you, until recently, insisted on the importance of new roads and utilities for the expansion."

"And we won't have a Republic if this affront from the Empire goes unchallenged," Caudex growled. His eyes burned with lust for glory and he vibrated with a passion for his new cause. "I will lead a Legion to Sicilia and smash both the Empire and Syracuse."

"You'll drain the Republic's coffers to do what?" demanded Flaccus, "Capture a sea port across the Messina Strait from Rhégion. Where is the economic advantage in that?"

"You may be right, co-Consul," admitted Caudex, slumping. "Come, gentlemen, we have games to witness."

***

Once Caudex and his entourage departed, Maximus exhaled loudly. "That went well, I guess."

38

"He gave in too quickly," advised Flaccus. "He's up to something. I suppose we'll find out tomorrow in the Senate."

Their discussion was interrupted by the tent flap opening. Tomas Kellerian strolled in, crossed the tent and greeted the group.

"Consul. Senators. May I present your gladiators," he announced. "Legionaries, bring them in!"

The three Insubri warriors had to bend their heads in order to pass through the opening. In the confines of the tent, they appeared huge. One of the Senators, involuntarily steeped back. Only Master Kellerian and Senator Maximus matched the barbarian's girth, although Consul Flaccus was their height but lacked the mass.

Alerio inspected his students. They were armored but didn't carry shields or weapons. He would arm them just before they entered the sand. Even with a squad of infantrymen, it wouldn't be a good idea to have armed warriors sitting around.

"Win today," Senator Maximus informed the Insubri. "And you'll receive a pony, an escort out of the city, and a letter of safe passage to your homeland. Lose and we'll toss your dead body in the Tiber for fish food."

"Seventh squad," ordered Alerio. "Form double files. Face inward. Salute."

The seven Legionaries at the entrance separated into lines and turned to face each other. As Maximus marched down the lines, the Legionaries performed a cross chest salute.

"Nicely done, Lance Corporal Sisera," Maximus said before he left the tent followed by his group.

"Rest. Get something to eat from the table," Alerio told the squad. "And feed the barbarians."

Tomas sidled up beside him and commented.

"Senator Maximus is impressed with you," observed the Armorer as he shoved a pack into Alerio's chest. "You've found yourself a patron."

"It seems I have," admitted Alerio as he searched in the bag. "Unless my three barbarians die. Then, I don't know. By the way, thank you for your help. What was your condition again?"

"In good time, Lance Corporal," the Armorer said as he went to joined the squad at the refreshment table.

While outside, Consul Flaccus began his speech, Alerio walked to a corner and stripped off his armor. With the crowd wildly cheering the hero of Volsinii, Alerio reached into the pack and pulled out a military tunic and a scarf. He pulled the tunic over his head and draped the scarf over his shoulder. Smoothing out the wrinkles, he looked down at the insignias of his prior units and his expertise. Weapon's Instructor, Legion Scout, and Combat Rower were the medals. The units were sewn on strips of colorful cloth.

Once dressed, he walked to the tent exit and stepped into the sunlight. He wanted to get a look at the arena, the crowd, and the competition.

Chapter – 10 Funeral Games

Consul Flaccus, the Republic's hero, finished his speech to more insane cheering from the crowd. Then he guided two young men to the hillside and the three of them climbed to his platform. It was obvious, they were the grieving sons of Junius Brutus Pera, the honoree of the funeral games. Senator Maximus greeted them with hugs and whispers, no doubt of condolences, into their ears.

Glancing across the seating area and the grass, Alerio guessed there must be over five thousand people there to watch the games. He had no reference to gage if this meant the games were a success or not. At the other platform, Alerio noted Consul Caudex bent forward and in deep conversation with Tribune Claudius.

"Alerio Sisera. I'm surprised to see you," Corporal Daedalus of the city guard stated. He walked from the entrance of the other tent and stopped halfway to Alerio. "My lads have been searching high and low for you."

Daedalus hadn't changed since the last time Alerio saw him. His legs were thin, a small belly strained against his sword belt, and he wore the gladius on his right hip for a left-handed draw. Despite appearances, Daedalus was deadly with a sword.

Correction, Alerio thought, the last time he saw him, the Corporal and Recruit Sisera were bleeding as Alerio beat Daedalus' head and helmet with a sword.

"I told your fat men that if you wanted to speak with me, come yourself," Alerio replied. "I was training the Insubri to murder your Etruscī."

"You really think Legion training will compete with instructions from a master swordsman?" Daedalus inquired.

"Say, Corporal, why don't we start the funeral games off right by testing your theory," challenged Alerio. "You and me, in the sand, right now?"

"I don't think so, Lance Corporal," Drustanus declined. "I'm making some fat coin on this competition. No sense messing up a sure thing."

Alerio started to turn away. He wanted to walk the sand. But, being wary of Drustanus, he watched the man out of the corner of his eye. The guard Corporal glanced at the top of the stockyard building, nodded, and dropped his head.

"Private. Send Drustanus and Cimon out to see me," Alerio shouted to the Legionary guarding the tent's entrance.

Without waiting for them, he took the ramp up to the elevated livestock display area. When Alerio stepped onto the sand, the crowd cheered. Not knowing what else to do, he faced the slope and the throng and saluted. As he began testing the sand for soft spots or pockets that might collapse when a gladiator stepped on the covering crust, a murmur started from the crowd.

At the appearance of two armored Legionaries, Cimon and Drustanus, the muttering increased to rumbling until it broke into a thunderous roar. Before Alerio could speak, Cimon indicated for Alerio to face the crowd. About a third of the citizens were standing and even more, were chanting.

"Revereor Legion, Revereor Legion," rolled from the crowd. "Revereor Legion."

"Better give them what they want, Lance Corporal," suggested Drustanus.

"Stand by," Alerio ordered and the three Legionaries lifted their right leg.

And as they stomped the sand, shouted, "Standing by!"

"Salute!" called out Alerio and the three Legionaries slammed their fists into their chests.

Alerio lifted his eyes to Caudex's platform. The Consul was leaning forward in his chair, beaming at the impromptu display by the Legionaries. And standing next to him was Tribune Gaius Claudius, returning the salute.

Quickly, Alerio shifted to Consul Flaccus' platform. There was no saluting or smiles. Just tight faces and wrinkled brows.

"About face," ordered Alerio wanting to disappear. "Forward march."

The three Legionaries left the sand and were followed by the chant of esteem and respect for the Legion. Alerio wondered if a moment of glory was worth a Senator's patronage.

"Take two more of the squad and slip out the back of the tent," Alerio explained. "Daedalus was signaling someone on the roof and I want to know who. And why he has a confederate hidden up there."

"We're on it, Alerio," Cimon and Drustanus replied before marching into the tent.

***

A priest shuffled to the center of the sand. He stood stoically with his head down until the cheering died off.

Lifting his arms to the sky, he prayed, "Today we purify the soul of our brother Junius Brutus with human blood. We ask Mercury to fly his cleansed soul to the River Styx. A coin for Charon has been placed in his mouth to pay the ferryman. Be kind when you judge him Minos, Aenaeus, and Rhadymanthas. He was a good man who produced two worthy sons. May he be judged kindly and sent to his peace on the Plain of Asphodel. Let all who witness today's events forever remember citizen, Junius Brutus Pera."

The priest dropped his arms and shuffled off the sand. Taking his place was a city guardsman.

"Gladiators. I need the first pair of gladiators on the sand," he bellowed.

No one emerged from either tent. Corporal Daedalus and Lance Corporal Sisera were playing the same game. They wanted to see the competition before selecting the opponent.

Chapter – 11 Purifying Blood on the Sand

The guardsman called out, "Gladiators to the arena!"

He was looking at Alerio while he yelled and ignoring Daedalus. Suddenly, Petrus stumbled from the entrance. Cimon appeared behind the big warrior holding a spear.

"Two archers with short bows on the roof. They won't be a problem," he explained. "I figured they were for later. If they shot early in the matches, the gamblers would stab Daedalus in the heart. So, we decided he would send out his strongest first and hold the archers for his weakest."

Alerio nodded his approval and gratitude. He took the spear from Cimon.

Handing the weapon to the Insubri, Alerio advised, "Petrus. For your life and your freedom, kill the Etruscan."

"You teach well, Legionary," the big barbarian stated. Then he marched up the ramp and stopped beside the guardsman. Raising the spear over his head, Petrus shouted, "Perfututum the Republic and its Gods forsaken citizens."

"Nice speech," Cimon observed.

A round of booing came from the spectators but changed to cheers when a large Etruscan ducked out of the other tent. Alerio peered up at several of the betting stands. People were flocking to place coins on their favorite. Alerio knew it wasn't the Insubri warrior.

Armed with a tribal shield and a heavy sword, the Etruscī stomped to the sand. He raised his sword and saluted the crowd. A round of cheering washed over the gladiators.

The guardsman stood between the fighters. After waiting for the crowd to settle, he raised his arms for silence.

"Citizens of the Republic. Today we gather to honor the passing of Junius Brutus Pera," he announced. "To cleanse his soul and to keep his memory alive, we offer three battles to the death. All enemies of the Republic, all proven warriors from the north, and all fierce and brutal barbarians. Citizen of the Republic, I give you Insubri against Etruscī! Fight!"

The guardsman backed away and hurried down the ramp. At the bottom, he turned, crossed his arms over his chest and watched.

***

As soon as the guardsman cleared the space, the Etruscī lashed out with his sword. The blade, coming backhanded, swept towards Petrus' chest. But as he'd been coached, Petrus had his eye on his foe.

Releasing the spear with his left hand, the Insubri swung the shaft around his body and behind his back.

46

Continuing the arc, he spun away from the blade. The tip of his spear slashed across the Etruscī's ribs as Petrus completed the circle. With blood running down his hip and leg, the warrior shuffled back. Petrus let him retreat.

In the crowd, people jumped to their feet, made slashing motions with their arms as if they too were in the arena. Those weekend warriors, no doubt voicing their opinion of how they would have handled the first engagement, went unheard in the thunder from the crowd.

The warriors circled each other. Petrus always moving to his right and away from the blade. He kept his feet wide apart making his steps appear awkward. In reality, the big Insubri maintained his balance and options for advancing or moving away from his opponent. The Etruscī, on the other hand, kept his feet close together so he could use his thigh muscles to drive powerful sword strikes.

Petrus flipped his spear so the dull end faced the shield. Then, he smacked the shield with a jab. In response, the Etruscī hacked twice at the wooden shaft. Again, Petrus tapped the shield and the Etruscī chipped into the shaft. When Petrus pulled back, the end of the spear hung down, held by a few thin strips of hardwood fiber. Removing his left hand from the shaft, he raised the spear as if it was a fishing pole and pointed at the dangling piece.

The Etruscī took his eyes off his foe. Petrus whipped the shaft back and forward. The dangling piece broke free and flew at the Etruscī's face. He should have ignored the small dowel as his helmet would protect him. But human nature took over and the Etruscī flinched back as the piece of wood came at him.

With his opponent momentarily distracted, Petrus slapped his left hand on the shaft and pulled back. The spear rotated and Petrus drove his right arm forward bringing the iron head up. As the iron head came level with his foe, the Insubri bent his knees and surged forward.

The iron tip slid by the shield, cracking two ribs before it pierced the Etruscī's lung. As he staggered back, Petrus followed twisting the spear. Two more ribs broke as the broad head opened the deep gash.

Screaming at the blessed, human blood pouring onto the sand, the crowd cheered. They forgot who they placed their bets on as the Etruscī fell to his knees, gasping and dying. Petrus tossed his spear away, turned to the spectators, made a rude gesture, and marched from the arena.

"Never take your eyes off your foe," Petrus explained as he walked by Alerio. "I'll remember that the next time we meet, Legionary. Then, I'll kill you."

Men ran to the dead Etruscī, grabbed hold of his ankles, and dragged off the carcass. Another man walked the sand raking it until all traces of the fight were erased.

"Were you pleased by the sacrifice?" shouted the guardsman announcer. He was answered by wild cheering. "Gladiators forward! Bring on the next two barbarians!"

Alerio faced the other tent and saluted Daedalus.

"Legion training one, swordsman instructions zero," Alerio taunted.

Without replying, Daedalus shouted something into his tent. In response, an even bigger Etruscī warrior ducked and brushed the sides of the tent opening as he lumbered into view. The Corporal still didn't say anything. He let the leering grin on his face speak for him.

"Eolus! Give him his shield and sword and send him out," Alerio called into his tent.

Moments later the wiry Insubri emerged.

"He is a big bastardis," Eolus swore as he stopped beside Alerio. "Why me?"

"Look at how he holds his shield," explained the Legionary. "Far away from his body."

"And that helps me stay alive, how?" asked the Insubri.

"Thick arms, legs, chest, and body," Alerio observed. "Stay away from him and he'll soon need a nap."

"Nap?" Eolus commented as he strolled up the ramp and onto the sand.

The announcer glanced to his left and tilted his head back to look up at the giant Etruscī warrior. Then slowly he faced right and, in an exaggerated manner, studied the leaner Insubri. With a smirk on his face, he held out his hands as if asking a question.

The crowd laughed and people ran for the betting stands. He gave them a long time to place their coins before he put his palms together.

"Citizens of the Republic, the funeral games continue," he announced using his joined hands to point at the combatants. "I give you Insubri against Etruscī! Fight!"

After the quick engagement at the start of the first fight, he jumped back from between the two gladiators before rushing down the ramp.

***

Eolus let his shield hang off his arm and his sword point drag in the sand as he paced back and forth. The crowd didn't like it and they voiced their opinion. Ignoring the taunts, the Insubri continued his casual strolling.

The Etruscī finally grew impatient. Swinging his sword across his shield, he stepped forward. Eolus ducked and ran to the other side of the arena. The giant stalked after him but the wiry Insubri hopped to the side when the blade swung again.

Many people jumped to their feet and yelled insults at the fighters. Eolus jogged to the front edge of the arena and faced the crowd. Then he shrugged as if he didn't understand their reactions. The giant stomped across the arena.

Eolus glanced over his shoulder then back at the throng. Screams at the expected death of the Insubri arose from the spectators. Just as the giant planted his feet, the Insubri crossed his shield and sword in front of his chest. He fell backwards and rolled. Coming up beside the giant, Eolus sliced a slab of flesh from the Etruscī's back before skipping to the far side of the arena. To the delight of the crowd, fat drops of blood rained down on the sand.

Angry and in pain, the Etruscī lumbered towards Eolus. Swinging his sword hard from side to side, he charged. But, the Insubri rolled away from the blade and used his shield to deflect a blow when the giant twisted in his direction.

Eolus ran to the left side of the arena and rested his shield and sword on his knees as if exhausted. Then, he tossed back his head and yawned with a wide opened mouth. The giant, recognizing that he was being mocked, ambled towards the Insubri.

Expecting the Insubri to dodge away, especially with him jerking from side to side as if deciding which way to run, the giant held his shield out as far as his arm would extend. With one direction blocked by the shield and his sword raised as if an extension of his arms, the Etruscī shuffled forward.

Eolus was so confused, he almost didn't react. The giant had his arms out wide to keep him from bolting. It was as if the Etruscī wanted to give him a hug. After too long a wait, Eolus rushed inside the giant's arms and buried his blade. Driving upward, the tip split the man's heart and stuck. As he attempted to free the blade, the giant toppled over on him.

Two city guardsmen on the far side jumped onto the sand and ran towards the downed fighters. With daggers in hand, they fumbled with rolling the giant off the Insubri.

Alerio shouted, "Cimon! Drustanus!"

He vaulted onto the sand and sprinted towards the guardsmen. They had the dead Etruscī rolled to the side and one had a foot on Eolus's chest. The other pulled back his arm preparing to stab the Insubri.

Alerio leaped and twisted sideways in the air. His leg hit the one stepping on Eolus and his shoulder plowed into the one holding the knife. The three tumbled back tangled up in a mass of elbows, knees, fists, and headbutts.

Four city guardsmen raced from beside their tent and ran towards the melee. Then they stopped. Marching across the arena were four heavy infantrymen. Their shields parted slightly to allow for the steel blades of their gladii. With only their eyes visible between the tops of their shields and bills of their helmets, the Legionaries presented a wall of horror.

"Do not interfere," Drustanus warned the city guards from behind his shield. Then to Alerio, who was fighting with the original two, asked. "Do you require assistance?"

Alerio hammered a fist into a guardsman's chin and the man fell to the sand. After that, he grabbed the other and drove a knee into the man's solar plexus. The guardsman folded up and expelled all the air from his lungs. Gasping and coughing, the man crawled away.

Alerio pushed to his feet. "I believe I have it under control," he said as he brushed sand from his tunic and scarf.

"Euge! Euge!" shouted the crowd. "Great show. Euge!"

"They think you're the comic relief for the funeral games," suggested Cimon.

"I might be. Who saves a barbarian?" confessed Alerio before ordering. "Let's finish the show. Cimon, standby, Drustanus right pivot."

The four Legionaries stomped their left feet in the sand and as a single line swung to face the attendees. "Salute and about face and forward march."

The crowd cheered the five Legionaries as they marched down the ramp. While four smiled and basked in the applause, one blushed. Lance Corporal Sisera didn't look at Senator Maximus sitting on Consul Flaccus' platform. He feared what the look his patron's face would relay.

Alerio's day in the public eye wasn't done. There was still one more death match owed to the dead.

***

"Gladiators! Gladiators to the sand," the announcer called out.

Eutropius collected his javelin and shield and asked, "Any words of advice, weapon's instructor?"

"Stay alive," replied Alerio.

Eutropius took his position beside the announcer. They waited patiently but, not so the crowd. Groups stood blocking the betting stands waiting to see the final fighter. When he came from the tent, they couldn't make up their minds. Both barbarians were the same height and same build. As far as physical clues went, it was a toss-up.

"Citizens of the Republic, the funeral games continue with a final match," the announcer explained. "I give you, Insubri against Etruscī! Fight!"

The announcer ducked and backed away. He didn't slow down until he was at the bottom of the ramp.

The Etruscī warrior asked, "Why should we fight each other? We were brothers a couple of months ago. Basking in the defeat of the Legion."

"For one of us to go free," replied Eutropius as he slid his foot back to improve his stance. "To return to our homeland and continue to resist the Republic."

"And so, it is, one of us must die so one may live," the Etruscī said softy. He shook his head and as he lowered his eyes, he let his shield droop to the side.

Eutropius saw the opening and started to attack. Then, he glanced down at the Etruscī's feet. They were in a perfect fighter's stance and his knees were slightly bent. He might have been speaking philosophically and bowing his head, but the man was ready to pounce. To test the theory Eutropius twirled his javelin. Before he could completely step back, the sword slammed into his shield.

"What happened to brotherly love?" inquired Eutropius as he shifted to the right.

"One of us must live," the Etruscī replied. "I decided it should be me."

He began a series of blows to Eutropius' shield. Each strike in the same place and with the same intensity. Almost as if he didn't have a different tactic in his arsenal. He pounded until the Insubri fell into a defensive rhythm and began to anticipate the next hit.

'Trap', the word popped into Eutropius' mind when he pushed his shield early to deflect the anticipated strike. If a fighter wanted anything in a battle, it was to know where and when your opponent would react. Eutropius so far had been predictable, deadly predictable.

On the next blow, the Insubri angled his shield. The blade struck and slid low and wide. Eutropius swung his javelin over his shield and slammed it into the Etruscī's helmet. The man rocked back but Eutropius didn't give him time to recover. Jabbing over both shields, he stabbed four times before the Etruscī collected himself and backed away.

Eutropius knew he'd broken flesh by the roar of the spectators. When the Etruscī raised his shield to prevent an attack over his shield, the Insubri dropped to his knees and raked the javelin's point across his opponent's ankles. Blood spurted from the slices and the man collapsed to his knees.

Rolling back, Eutropius jumped to his feet and ran around behind the Etruscī. While trying to turn, his opponent fell over when his feet didn't respond to the commands. The javelin severed his spine and Eutropius left it sticking out of his back like a flag pole.

"I'll take my pony, my safe passage letter, and my life," Eutropius said to Alerio as he dropped his shield and stripped off his helmet. "You taught me well, Legionary. I'll remember the lessons."

***

Blood from the last fight must have been for the crowd as the man with the rake didn't bother to clean up the sand. Both Consuls left their platforms and started down the hill trailing their entourages. Because it was a nice afternoon, the crowd stayed. They were drinking, eating and a few were acting out combat scenes from the three matches.

Corporal Daedalus and most of the city guards had left. Only a few hung around to watch the citizens enjoy the after effects of the funeral games.

"Good job, Lance Corporal Sisera," Senator Maximus gushed. Then he scolded, "We could have done without the Legion demonstrations. Especially after my talk about Sicilia."

"Yes General. I apologize," Alerio replied. Relief flooded his stomach at the Senator's words.

"Now, I want to see my barbarians," demanded Maximus.

He brushed by Alerio as did Consul Flaccus, the five Senators, and Belen. Alerio followed them into the tent. As he entered, he heard Maximus telling his group the strengths and weaknesses of the three Insubris. Alerio relaxed when Belen handed each warrior a piece of parchment.

"I am a man of my word." Maximus boasted. "Those are your letters of safe passage. A cavalry escort will be here soon and Belen has clothing for you. I don't think Master Kellerian will let you keep his armor."

The Armorer stood at the rear of the tent next to a smoking brazier. He bowed slightly at the mention of his name.

Before Maximus or anyone else could say more, Consul Caudex's voiced carried to them from outside.

"Citizens of the Republic! The Qart Hadasht Empire is threatening our trade route through the Messina Strait," the Consul yelled.

Consul Flaccus, Senator Maximus, and the others hurried out of the tent. Alerio stuck his head out to see Appease Caudex standing in the arena with a fistful of bloody sand in each hand. Behind the Consul, Tribune Gaius Claudius, standing straight and tall, was the perfect image of a Legion officer.

"They have taken Messina and stolen the riches of the port and the surrounding lands," he continued. "By heritage, the Sons of Mars are descendants of the Republic."

The crowd stopped mingling and everyone on the slope turned to watch the new entertainment. After witnessing the blood matches, they were excited and Consul Caudex was saying the right things to arouse the public.

"We have suffered financially from recent wars. Now is the time. We must march on, we must fight for, we must own Sicilia! The island's riches wait to fill our coffers. It's there for the taking. You witnessed the precision of our Legionaries, here on this very sand today. Now is the time for the Qart Hadasht Empire to taste the steel of our Legionaries."

The crowd was yelling their approval. Consul Flaccus whispered something to Senator Maximus. They marched away from the cheering and the rest of Consul Caudex's speech.

"Tomorrow, in the Senate, I am asking for a Legion to go south and throw the Empire out of Messina and off Sicilia," Caudex bellowed. He began letting the blood-stained sand pour through his fingers. "Our Legions have beaten the Etruscī and the Insubri. Now it's time for the Empire to learn the power of the Republic. They will leave Sicilia. Or, by my hands, their blood will flow and color the sands of Messina red."

***

Alerio pulled his head back in the tent.

"Has Senator Maximus left?" asked Tomas Kellerian. When Alerio nodded yes, Tomas turned to Seventh squad, and shouted, "Now!"

The Legionaries jumped on the Insubri warriors. They held the barbarians down with their right arms stretched out.

58

"Master Kellerian, I don't understand what we're doing," protested Alerio. "These savages have been freed and given safe passage."

"You asked for my condition to train them," the Armorer replied as he walked to the brazier and lifted out an iron bar. One end glowed red-hot. "I spent my life defending the Republic against barbarians like these."

Tomas pulled a sharp pair of clippers from his belt. Kneeling on Petrus' arm, he sheared off the man's little finger and his ring finger. While the Insubri screamed, Kellerian cauterized the stumps. Next, he knelt on Eolus' arm and preformed the same brutal surgery. After cutting off Etruscan's fingers and sealing the nubs, the Armorer stood.

"My condition? That after they learned to survive the arena, they would never properly hold a sword, again" Master Kellerian explained. "In the future, no Legionary will fall from their blades. That, Lance Corporal Sisera was my condition."

Chapter – 12 Wisdom of the Clay Ear

Thomasious Harricus stood in the doorway and watched as five Legionaries marched into the courtyard of the Chronicles Humanum Inn.

"Take a load off," Alerio ordered the Legionaries as he broke formation and headed towards the Innkeeper. "Good afternoon, Master Harricus."

"Lance Corporal Sisera. I assume I'll have to feed them?" inquired Thomasious. He was pointing at the infantrymen who were stacking their shields and lifting off their helmets.

"Legionaries are always hungry," Alerio agreed. "A hot meal would be appreciated."

"I'd like to have a look at your cook's pantry," said Cimon, the squad's best cook. "Would that be possible?"

"Fine with me. Come inside Alerio and tell me about the Senators' and Consuls' reactions to the funeral games," suggested Thomasious.

"Don't you want to know who was victorious?" inquired Alerio as he mounted the steps. His pride was hurt as the Innkeeper didn't seem curious about his part in the games.

"Blood on the sand, the winner of a horse race, or a powerful thespian performance of a play, is only one aspect of any public spectacle. But not the most important," Thomasious explained as he guided the Legionary down the hallway towards the dining room. "The real contests are the financial and the political maneuvering taking place out of the public's eye."

***

60

There were a few customers in the dining room. Thomasious ushered Alerio to an isolated corner table.

"What maneuvering does a funeral game provide?" inquired Alerio as they sat.

"Senator Spurius Maximus, as the sponsor of your gladiators, gets the bragging rights if they win," explained Thomasious. "For the next week, he will be the center of attention while extolling the virtue of his fighters. He needs that since his protégé, Marcus Flaccus is the most honored man of the year. The old General doesn't like being overshadowed."

"Then what did it mean when Consul Caudex received so much attention from the crowd at the end of the funeral games?" asked Alerio.

"Gamesmanship, pure and simple. He turned defeat into victory," Thomasious replied. "Without the afterglow of winning, he took advantage of the gathering to sway the citizens to his cause. I imagine Maximus and Flaccus weren't happy."

"They walked off during Consul Caudex's speech," Alerio related. "But why did the city guard come after me? I'm not political."

"Most likely the work of a Caudex solicitor, seeking to give the Consul an advantage," Thomasious ventured. "It wouldn't take many coins to convince the city guard, especially as one of their own was training the other three gladiators. Toss in some assurances to the bet takers and no one would worry about holding you in a cell for a few days. Or, putting you in the care of a physician until you healed."

"A final question, Master Harricus. What advantage did Consul Caudex gain by riling up the crowd with talk of war in Sicilia?" asked Alerio. "He's a Consul. Shouldn't he be debating that in the Senate?"

"The citizens of our Republic are a powerful force," explained Thomasious. "Not many Senators want to go against public opinion. If Caudex has won over the public, then there will be war in Sicilia. Now, let's get you something to eat. And you can tell me about the matches."

Pleased at last to be able to talk about a subject he knew, Alerio described each fight and the fighters. Later that afternoon, Lance Corporal Alerio Sisera marched Seventh squad to the Legion camp and reported to Centurion Seneca. In the morning, he joined a cavalry patrol headed south towards the Southern Legion.

Act 2

Chapter – 13 Port of Ostia

Four Republic Triremes rested on the beach along with Legion patrol boats. Against the piers were six Greek Corbita with five more of the merchant transports lashed to their seaward side. Since the first light of dawn, Legionaries had been passing supplies and equipment up to the boats. A Legion quartermaster strutted along the rails of the rafted together transports.

"Don't overload that ship with supplies," he roared. "Leave room for the troops. It won't do anyone any good to assault Messina with a ship of supplies. Unless grain can crawl out of their sacks and swing a gladius, you want Legionaries on that boat. You over there! The Legionaries need supplies when they land. Take on more!"

He encouraged, directed and scolded as the sun rose. Soon the stacks of supplies on the docks dwindled as they were transferred to the eleven Corbita. Watching the loading were Tribune Gaius Claudius and Consul Appease Caudex.

"Take and hold Messina. I'll be along with the Legion in a few weeks," Caudex ordered. "And Tribune Claudius, don't fail me. I need Messina as a base of operations."

"Yes, General. Is it proper to call you General, yet?" asked Gaius.

Appease laughed and shrugged his shoulders.

"It's not official until the Senate votes tomorrow," Consul Caudex admitted while standing taller and pushing out his chest. "But, witnessing the advance units of my Legion about to depart, I'll claim the title starting now."

"Very good General Caudex. If you'll excuse me, I want to speak with our warship Captains," Tribune Claudius informed the Consul.

"Yes, yes of course. And I must return to the Capital to prop up my supporters," announced Appease. "Maybe make a few public speeches to remind the Senate of my popularity."

"By your leave, General?" asked Gaius.

"Dismissed, Tribune."

Gaius saluted, turned and marched off the docks. While he moved towards the beach, four hundred heavy infantrymen, one hundred sixty Velites, and about fifty support personnel formed lines. The Legionaries at the head of the lines began walking up the ramps to the transports.

***

The four Trireme Captains stood watching the boarding.

"Tribune, good morning," they said as Gaius approached.

"I want my Senior Centurion on the lead warship. My First Sergeant on the seaward flanking Trireme and me on the other," instructed the Tribune without acknowledging their salutations. "When do we row out?"

"The transports are slow. We'll let them get underway before we shove off," a Captain replied. Then he added, "We'd like infantrymen on our ships. In case…"

"I know. In case we meet any Qart Hadasht warships," Gaius interrupted the Captain. "How many?"

"Two squads on each Trireme," answered the Captain. "If…"

But the Tribune had already walked away.

***

"First Centurion, give me eight squads on the beach for the warships," Tribune Claudius ordered.

"Yes, sir. It'll slow us down as we'll need to pull them from the same Century," commented Senior Centurion Georgius.

"I said eight squads on the beach. I didn't say hold me up," Gaius said between clinched teeth. "Eight on the beach from the back of the lines. There. Problem solved."

"Yes, Tribune," Georgius replied as he marched to the lines of waiting Legionaries.

"Sir, what do you need?" asked First Sergeant Brictius as the Senior Centurion approached.

"Peel off eight squads from the end of the lines and put them on the beach," Georgius relayed the order. "And don't tell me about unit integrity. Just get them out of line and on the beach."

"Yes, Senior Centurion, right away," Brictius replied. He spun and began talking as he walked. "Which squads are here from Fourth and Fifth Centuries?"

"Eighth of the Fifth," a Lance Corporal answered. "Third of the Fourth," another reported.

"You two, pull your squads out and collect three more from your Centuries," Brictius ordered. He glanced in the Tribune's direction and noticed the Staff officer was busy speaking with the Ostia Post commander. The Senior Centurion had his head in a scroll held by the quartermaster. Turning to the squad leaders, he said softly, "Find your line mates and pull them off the boats if necessary. But do it quietly and make it quick."

"Yes, First Sergeant," they said before rushing up ramps to locate the squads.

First Sergeant Brictius had spent most of his career in the north. In battles up there, Legionaries lived and died by knowing which squads fought beside them. A Century down to four squads was still a formidable force as long as the pivots recognized the man on the adjacent squad. He wasn't about to break off squads from different Centuries because a Staff officer was in a hurry. Besides, the Centurions, Sergeants, and Corporals would trouble him no end as they searched for their missing Legionaries.

***

With shouting from the Greek Captains and loud responses from their crews, the seaward Corbita untied and pushed off from their sister transports at the pier. Rowing slowly, they cruised headed south in a staggered line. Then the five at the dock shoved off and joined the line.

Once the transports were underway, rowers and infantrymen boarded the Triremes. After being pushed off the beach, the warships stroked until they surrounded the convoy. The Republics first campaign to fight an enemy outside the Italian peninsula had gotten underway.

Chapter – 14 Port Rhégion

A week later, the convoy rowed into the Messina Strait. The Triremes delayed beaching while the first five Corbita tied up at the pier. The final six staggered in, and one by one, they tied up on the Strait side of the docked transports.

The Republic warships rowed hard against the strong tide of the Messina Strait to maintain vigilance.

"Captain, I demand you land and let me get about my business," Tribune Claudius insisted.

"Tribune. You have seven Centuries of Legionaries in slow moving tubs," the Captain replied between shouting commands to his first oar. The warship had been taken too far south by the current. It came about and headed north. "If a Qart Hadasht Trireme decided to sink one, you'd drown a lot of good men. Let the Corbita get lashed together first."

"You have three other warships," observed the Tribune. "What difference would one more make. Plus, there isn't an Empire warship in sight."

The Legion Captain raised an arm and pointed across the blue and deceptively calm looking waters of the Messina Strait. North of them, portions of low walls, a few clay roof tops and a Citadel high on a hill were observable from the middle of the Strait. Then he indicated the tower on the Rhégion side.

"There are two of them almost within ballista range," the Captain told the Tribune. "Riding on the tide at the mouth of Messina Harbor. I received the message from the signalman in the tower."

"That's two, you have four," Tribune Claudius explained the math as if talking to a small child. "Put me on the beach and you'll still have three, against their two! It's simple. Would you like me to write it down for you?"

"No, sir. The reason they didn't come out of their harbor is, we do have four," the Captain said. "If we only had two Triremes as escorts, the Republic would be buying sunken Corbita, not leasing them from the Greeks."

"On what assumptions do you base those insights?" demanded the Tribune.

"Experience, sir. The Qart Hadasht warships are better at handling and rowing," the Captain admitted. "The Empire has ruled the seas since before my grandfather was born. If we don't outnumber them, we normally row away.

But we can't row away while guarding Legionaries trapped in slow moving tubs."

The Tribune stomped away. The only path open to him was down the three-foot-wide center boards running the length of the trireme. Mumbling to himself, he didn't notice the twenty infantrymen who stepped on rower's benches to clear the way. His eyes were on the Citadel at Messina.

The last Corbita rowed in and tossed out lines. Crewmen on the other transport caught and pulled the lines. When the two ships were rail to rail, the sailors tied the ships together. Legionaries climbed over the rails and, with relief, made their way from ship to ship until they stood on solid ground.

As the Legionaries crawled over and across the transports, the four Republic warships rowed to shore. Tribune Georgius stood at the bow shuffling his boots impatiently and glaring down at the pebbles and sand of Rhégion beach.

"Tribune, please move back to midship, sir," requested a sailor.

"Do you know who I am?" Gaius asked as if everyone on the warship hadn't spent a week with him.

"Yes sir, I do. But you're standing on the ramp," the rower explained. "We can't lift it and lower it until you move back, sir."

Chapter – 15 Southern Legion Planning and Stratagies

The old man knelt, knees deep in freshly excavated soil. A root ball clutched in one hand as he patted a flat place in the bottom of the hole. Carefully, he sat the roots on the flat place and began scooping and lightly packing soil around the stem of the plant.

"Tribune. You have a visitor," Southern Legion's First Sergeant called from the doorway.

"Just a few moments, Sergeant Gerontius," Velius replied with his head bent forward.

"I want to speak with Tribune Velius," Gaius Claudius announced as he brushed by the First Sergeant. Out back of the Southern Legion's command building, he saw only a gardener on his knees digging in one of the mismatched squares of plants. Overhead a variety of vines crept around on trellises. "I demand to speak with Tribune Velius. Where in Hades is he?"

"It's not Hades. It's the Southern Legion. Of course, we have adherents of Tellus across the Strait," the old man mumbled as he tamped down the soil around the stem. "At least they should be as often as they want to bury people in the Goddess' earth. Or send them down to Neptune's realm."

"Nobody asked you old man," sneered Gaius. "Keep your opinions to yourself. Now, where is the Tribune?"

"You insist on asking questions and not listening to the answers," the old gardener commented as he pushed back to a kneeling position.

Gaius lifted a foot as if to stomp on the newly planted stem.

"I wouldn't do that, Tribune," warned Gerontius.

"You dare to threaten a staff officer, Sergeant?" Gaius shot back. "I'll have you whipped at the punishment post."

"Look down, sir," suggested the First Sergeant.

Gaius glanced down to where his foot would have landed. The gardener held up a trident styled gardening tool. Each prong was needle sharp and pointed at the Tribune's hovering foot.

"It's the southern soil, you see," the gardener explained as he pushed on his knees to stand. "Rocks and clumps of hard clay. Terrible for the plants."

The old man walked to the doorway and dropped the tool into a bucket beside the entrance.

"First Sergeant. Bring our guest in," the gardener said as he disappeared through the doorway.

"Yes, Tribune Velius," Gerontius replied before turning to Gaius. "Sir, you'll find the Tribune in his office."

Gaius Claudius stomped through the door and didn't see First Sergeant Gerontius' salute.

"I'm here to clear the Qart Hadasht out of Messina," announced Gaius Claudius. He paused by the large table occupying the center of the room. "I don't have time for games."

"What do you have time for?" inquired Velius.

"What? Look here Velius, I'm marching my Centuries into Messina tomorrow morning," Gaius exclaimed. "Any information would be appreciated."

First Sergeant Gerontius crossed the room. He almost reached the interior door when the old Tribune called to him.

"First Sergeant. Would you locate my favorite spy and have him report here immediately?" instructed Velius. "I don't require parade ground spiffy, just his body here as soon as possible."

"You might him to...," began the First Optio.

Velius shook his head and waved off the suggestion.

"Right away, Tribune," Gerontius promised as he vanished through the doorway and down the hall.

"Let me show you a few things," Velius offered as he rolled the cover off the map table.

"Good map," exclaimed Gaius Claudius. The Tribune walked around it before placing a finger on the harbor of Messina. "We'll row into the harbor, secure the port. Then attack up the main road and take the Citadel. What kind of opposition, am I facing?"

"Excellent, a definitive question. I have hopes for you yet," Velius mumbled under his breath. Then in his speaking voice replied, "Three hundred infantry, four hundred irregulars, and seven hundred rowers depending on how many Empire warships are in port."

"I brought four hundred heavy infantrymen and one hundred sixty Velites," boasted Claudius. "It should be more than enough to oust the Empire's mercenaries."

"Have you ever taken the field against Qart Hadasht forces?" inquired Velius.

"Not them specifically. But in the eastern region, I was on the General's staff and we planned counterattacks against the rebels," Claudius stated. "Close up in a defined area like Messina, it'll be easier to bring them to the fight. Much better than chasing evasive rebel forces."

Tribune Velius turned his head away and rolled his eyes. In his years with the Legion, he'd met a number of staff officers who assumed field commands. Some listened, learned and became fine commanders. Others got stuck in the glory of working on a General's staff. They believed their experience in the rear with maps and symbols, representing Legion and enemy forces, gave them battlefield expertise.

Before Velius could begin questioning and picking apart Gaius Claudius' plan, there was a rapping at the backdoor.

"Sir, Lance Corporal Alerio Sisera, reporting as ordered," a Legionary, covered with pitch and bits of fiber, stood on the threshold.

"Come in Lance Corporal," Velius invited. "They have you caulking patrol boats, do they?"

"Yes sir," Alerio answered as he saluted the two Tribunes.

"Hold on! I recognize you," Claudius said with a sneer. "You're the weapon's instructor who trained the barbarians. And strutted around the arena like a prized cock. What is he doing here?"

"Lance Corporal Sisera is my expert on the Sons of Mars and the Empire troops in Messina," explained Velius. "He has…"

"I don't care what he has, or hasn't," growled Claudius. "I'll not take advice from a barbarian lover."

Alerio bristled at the comment but held his tongue. Arguing with a staff officer would only get him a session on the discipline post. Thankfully, Tribune Velius came to his defense.

"Tribune Claudius. I am attempting to aid you in your attack on Messina," Velius explained in a soft voice. Both Alerio and Gaius Claudius had to lean towards the old spy master to hear his words. "Lance Corporal Sisera has met Admiral Hanno. Plus, he has contacts in the Sons of Mars. Maybe we can use his knowledge."

"Now you've informed a possible traitor of my plans," Claudius exploded. "I want that man held under guard until after I launch my operation. For the security of my plan, I demand it."

Velius smiled letting the expression crease his thin, wrinkled face.

"Lance Corporal Sisera. Report to First Sergeant Gerontius and inform him that you are under arrest," Tribune Velius instructed. "No charges will be forthcoming. However, you are to be under guard until Tribune Claudius' operation is underway."

"Yes sir," responded Alerio with a salute.

As the Lance Corporal disappeared from sight through the interior door, Claudius glared across the map table at Velius.

"I've heard about the relaxed attitude of the Southern Legion," he challenged. "Here at the end of the Republic, you've lost your military bearing. In the Legions I've served with, a Lance Corporal like Sisera would have been taken away and locked up."

Velius half closed his eyes as if trying to bring the other Tribune into focus. Then he inquired, "How many Legions have you served with?"

"I was on the General's staff in the Eastern Legion. And was promoted to Military Attaché to the Senate for the Central Legion," Claudius said with pride. "Now, I'm a commander for Caudex Legion."

"I've served with six Legions in my career," Velius informed him. "The Southern Legion is my first experience with a garrison command. I don't have much to compare it to. You are quite possibly correct. Let's get back to your operation."

Later in the afternoon, Tribune Claudius left without much new information. The plan he and Consul Caudex had formulated was solid. Hit Messina rapidly after arriving before the Empire knew what they planned. This meeting with Velius had been a waste of time, thought Gaius Claudius as he strolled through the Legion Post.

In the Planning and Stratagies room, Gerontius stuck his head through the interior doorway.

"Anything I can do for you, or the assault force, sir?" he asked.

"First Sergeant, let's gather the Southern Legion and hold a sunset parade and inspection," suggested Velius without looking up from his relief map.

"Sir, you know the Legion is spread out along the coast for over a hundred miles," replied Gerontius. "I could form up the Post garrison and the boat handlers for an inspection if you want."

"No. That won't be necessary," Velius said as he rested two fingers on the map. They barely covered the harbor at Messina. "But you might want to alert the Medics and the patrol boat crews. Tomorrow could be a busy day for them."

"Yes, Tribune, I'll put them on standby."

"Dismissed, First Sergeant," Velius whispered. He ran his fingers the short distance from Messina, down the Strait to where he let them rest on the port of Rhégion.

***

Tribune Gaius Claudius strutted out of the Post gate, heading towards where his Centuries were camped. As he passed between rows of upside down patrol boats sitting on support frames, he noted Lance Corporal Sisera. Rather than being detained, Sisera was holding a hammer and a broad headed spike. Hot, wet pitch and fibers dripped from the end of the spike.

"Sergeant. Why isn't that man locked up?" demanded Claudius of a scarred NCO who seemed to be in charge.

"We don't lock people up in the Southern Legion, Tribune," Martius, the Chief of Boats, explained. "The Legion is shorthanded. Instead of locking them in a cell which requires guards, we give them the worst job possible."

"But he was performing that tasked before his arrest," noted Claudius as the Lance Corporal pounded the pitch and fiber between boards on a boat. "Was he under arrest then?"

"No, sir. He was taking an advanced class in boat handling," Martius replied. "If you're going to be a coxswain of a patrol boat, you've got to know how to maintain your boat."

Tribune Gaius Claudius stormed off, resuming his trek towards his camp. Halfway there, he glanced back still fuming at the nonchalant attitude of the Southern Legion. A group of Legionaries rushed through the gate and snatched up hammers and broad headed spikes. He didn't understand the commotion so he continued to his unit.

"Senior Centurion Georgius. Command meeting in my tent," Claudius ordered as he walked between the Legion tents. "Have all the boat Captains attend."

"Even the Greek Captains?" inquired his Senior Centurion.

"I said all. Was I not clear?" Claudius challenged.

"Yes, Tribune. You were. I'll round them up," Georgius agreed as he marched away.

In his tent, the Tribune poured a mug of wine and sipped it while he waited.

Chapter - 16 Dawn Attack

"Lance Corporal Sisera, get your cūlus out of bed and join me," Gerontius called across the barracks.

"On the way, First Sergeant," Alerio replied as he swung his legs off the bed and reached for a tunic and his hobnailed boots.

"Follow me," Gerontius ordered when the Lance Corporal materialized from the dark.

"What's up?" Alerio asked while rubbing the sleep from his eyes.

Outside it was dark although the mountains to the east displayed a crown of illumination. They crossed the Legion parade ground and bypassed the Command Building. At the narrow west gate, Gerontius pushed through and they crossed a gravel area arriving at the base of Rhégion tower.

"We're going to watch the Legion's assault on Messina," the Senior NCO advised as they climbed the ladder.

"I'd rather be in a shield wall," Alerio admitted as he climbed. "No offense First Sergeant but, facing Empire troops is preferable to spending the morning with you."

"What? You don't like me?" teased the NCO.

"It's not that, First Sergeant," Alerio informed him. "It's standing on formalities the whole time."

"If that's your problem, Lance Corporal, you're going to hate today," Gerontius said as he climbed through the floor of the observation level and stepped away from the ladder.

"What do you mean?" inquired Alerio as his head poked above the platform.

"Because the pleasure of your presence was requested by Tribune Velius and Senior Centurion Patroclus," announced Gerontius before he paused and said. "Good morning, sirs."

"Sisera, get up here and give us an idea of what Tribune Claudius faces in Messina," Velius requested.

Alerio leaned over the short wall and down at the docks of Rhégion harbor. Although still dark, lanterns and torches on the eleven Corbita transports showed crewman

79

stirring on the ship's decks. A glance to his left showed only the dark beach with faint shapes of the four Triremes.

"Over there, lookouts will be posted at the top of the Citadel," Alerio stated as he stood straight and pointed. Realizing no one could see his outstretched arms, he added. "On the hill of Messina, waiting for light to report on any ship movements."

"Our signalmen do the same from this tower," broke in Senior Centurion Patroclus. "Tell us about their defenses."

"When they see our ships launch, they'll alert the garrison and their warship rowers," Alerio reported. "Our convoy will head north and out of the Strait. Once clear of the current, they'll come about and row for Messina harbor. By then, the docks will be guarded by soldiers and the harbor patrolled by their ships. When our convoy reaches the port, they'll have to stop and untie the merchant ships strung across the mouth of the harbor, blocking access."

"What about our warships?" inquired Velius.

"When the merchant ships blockading the harbor swing free, the Empire warships will come out and bypass our Triremes. They'll concentrate on ramming and sinking the troop transports before battling our warships. The few transports that make it through will have to use the docks because of their deep draft. Legionaries making it off the transports will face lines of Empire infantry on the pier. If they drive them back, the Legionaries can form a shield wall. Then, it's a battle of attrition."

"Your description sounds bleak," ventured Senior Centurion Patroclus.

"It is, sir. Messina's strongest defenses are along the harbor," Alerio replied.

"Can we expect any help from the Sons of Mars?" asked First Sergeant Gerontius.

"No, Sergeant. Admiral Hanno had them disarmed when he arrived," Alerio reported. "Maybe once the Republic has a foothold they'll supply food and fresh water. But, they'll be no help during the initial assault."

Below them and to the left, the voices of NCOs and Centurions called out as they mustered the Centuries. Soon, lines of armored Legionaries appeared on the docks below. The troops began to file onto the transports.

"Remember this day," advised Tribune Velius. "It's the first time forces of the Republic have crossed over a body of water to engage an enemy."

"The Legion has rowed across rivers," Senior Centurion Patroclus reminded the Tribune.

"Would you equate the Messina Strait with a river?" inquired Velius.

"There are no rivers that deep or, with currents running that strongly. Unless you include mountain streams," listed the Senior Centurion. "For clarity, let's say crossing a major body of water."

"Fair enough. This is the first time, Legion elements have crossed over a major body of water to engage an enemy," Tribune Velius stated correctly. "I'm not sure if it means the end of the Republic. Or the start of something grander. We'll have to let history decide."

***

"Georgius. I want them loaded before sunrise," Gaius Claudius reminded his Senior Centurion for the fifth time. "Where is First Sergeant Brictius?"

"He's on the dock, facilitating the boarding, sir," Georgius replied.

"Excellent. Today, we shall lunch at the Messina Citadel, First Centurion," Claudius exclaimed. "I want Brictius on the first transport. Let him form an advanced line. You'll come in on the third transport to take command of our spearhead attack."

"And where will you be, sir?" asked Georgius

"I'll come in on the first Triremes and secure the beach," Gaius Claudius said with pride. "My elements will fight their way to where you've set up my command post. Then we'll push the Empire out of Messina. Now go see about the loading while I coordinate with the Triremes' Captains."

Senior Centurion Georgius had seen maps of the harbor. The beach was far from the dock and the path to the city ran through the dock. There was nothing between the two landmarks to protect. The fight for Messina would begin at the dock. The Senior Centurion kept his opinion to himself, saluted, and walked away.

"What do you mean, we shouldn't row out?" asked the angry Tribune. "If you have reservations about this operation, you should have voiced them at the command meeting last night."

"I did, Tribune. You said you'd consider them in the morning," the warship Captain replied.

"Apparently, I have and decided to go ahead with the attack on Messina," Claudius announced. "As soon as we have sunlight, I want to be on the way. Is that clear?"

"Yes, Tribune," the four Legion Captains replied.

Alerio watched as the first line of transports pushed off and were caught in the north bound current of the Strait. The crews backed their oars down attempting to slow their progress. But the Corbita transports were under powered and soon, the first six were strung out while the last five were just untying from Rhégion pier.

Two Triremes launched from the beach and rowed frantically to get ahead of the lead transport. They had almost reached them when Qart Hadasht warships emerged from the Messina harbor.

First Sergeant Brictius shouted at the Greek Captain of the transport as the harbor of Messina slid by.

"Turn the ship, you gutless sack of merda," he bellowed.

"Current has us," the Greek replied while pointing at the harbor entrance. "Blocked, it's blocked."

Brictius hoisted himself up on the pilot deck, glared at the Captain before turning to study the harbor. Sure enough, merchant ships were tied bow to stern across the mouth of the harbor.

"We need to board those ships," he declared. "When can we turn?"

The Captain indicated ahead where the land narrowed and the waters of the Strait seemed to boil against the shorelines.

"When can we come about?" asked the First Sergeant.

"Out past the Strait's current in the open water," the Greek reported. Then he called attention to the ships behind them. "Better here than back there."

First Sergeant Brictius spun around and he ground his teeth in frustration.

***

Senior Centurion Georgius' transport started to turn towards the harbor. The current gripped the deep draft of the Corbita, causing it to sail sideways as the four crewmen strained to row across the Strait. He judged they wouldn't make it based on how swiftly the shoreline fell behind them.

"What's our alternative course?" he asked the Greek Captain.

"Make it to open water and turn around," the Captain related. "But we may not make it."

"What do you mean?" demanded Georgius.

The Captain lifted a hand from the rear steering oars and pointed at the hook of land that protected Messina harbor. Waves rolled back from an Empire warship's ram and swiftly, the ship itself rowed fully into the Strait. The ram, riding just below water level, tossed back white foam and blue water. Before Senior Centurion Georgius could shout a warning to the fifty-five armored Legionaries huddled in the cargo hold, the ram slammed into the transport's side.

The ram punctured the hull and the Qart Hadasht rowers on the port side shipped their oars. With the Starboard oars doing power rows, the Empire warship turned further off its attack angle. As the warship arched away, the ram splintered and shattered a gash half the length of the transport.

On the pilot deck, Georgius actually looked down on the deck and the rowers of the Empire warship. Below the waterline, the ram killed two Legionaries on the initial punch through the hull. No one else died as the brass head and shaft moved down the hull as unstoppable as a boulder tumbling down a mountain. Some managed to remove their helmets before the cold waters of the Strait slammed into the fifty-five Legionaries. And as if fingers, the water pulled the transport over, trapping them in the overturning ship. Their

85

screams became muted gurgles as the Corbita was sucked down into the depths of the Messina Strait.

***

First Sergeant Brictius screamed his anger as the Empire warships rammed three transports. The ships flipped over and his heart broke as one hundred and sixty-five of his Legionaries died without a chance to fight back. Then the first two Legion Triremes rowed at the Empire warships.

At first, they gave him hope of revenge. But the Empire ships easily avoided the rams of the Republic ships. Looking far to the south, he sought the other two Triremes. They weren't in the water. Both rested on Rhégion beach, near where they were when the convoy launched.

At the pier, five transports had made it back to the dock. A quick count and he realized only two others were underway. They, as well, were caught in the current being propelled north. Thankfully, the Empire warships were busy with the Republic's Triremes. The transports slipped by the battling warships.

Just before his transport rounded a finger of land and he lost sight of that part of the Strait, an Empire warship rolled and turned. Its starboard side oars momentarily out of the water jutting towards the sky. Then the warship righted itself and the ram angled down the side of a Republic's Trireme.

***

Alerio gasped at the quickness of the Empire warships. He understood the sluggish nature of the transports, but he was embarrassed by the poor performance of the Republic's Triremes.

With the three transports at the mouth of the Strait and his sister Trireme floundering, the last Republic warship rowed for the safety of Rhégion beach. As if vipers returning to their snake pit, the warships of the Qart Hadasht Empire slithered back into Messina harbor.

"Lance Corporal Sisera. My eyes aren't as good as they once were," admitted Tribune Velius. "Are those storm clouds to the north?"

Alerio, the Southern Legion's Senior Centurion, and the First Sergeant cupped their hands over their eyes to study the distant sky.

"Storm clouds and moving fast, Tribune," answered the signalman. He stood behind the group holding a tube of rolled leather up to his eye. As if a lopsided unicorn, he moved the tube searching the sky to the north. "It's a bad one. There is one positive note."

"What's positive about any of this?" growled Gerontius.

"The Strait is turning, First Sergeant," replied the signalman. "The transports can make a run back to Rhégion on the southbound current. If they hurry."

Everyone in the tower gazed northward straining their eyes searching for the three transports. Then, rain in the distance fell slanting to the west. Before the transports appeared at the mouth of the Strait, visibility dropped to nothing as rain and gusting winds reached the tower.

Chapter – 17 Dangerous Strait

"Have the men remove their armor and drop their gladii," shouted First Sergeant Brictius at one transport then he repeated the order to the ship on the other side. "Drop armor and gladii."

The three transports circled around and rowed side by side headed back in the general direction of the Messina Strait. Brictius' wasn't the only voice yelling. The three Greek Captains alternated between pointing at the darkening sky to the north and the entrance to the Strait ahead.

"What's the problem?" Brictius asked the Captain of his transport.

"One wants to head east and find a safe harbor," the Greek replied. "The other is 'ita ut' about the direction. He'll go along with whatever we decide."

"Let me settle this for you," the First Sergeant advised the transport's Captain. "You will take my Legionaries back to Rhégion. Is that clear?"

The Captain had watched the loading of the troops and remembered the First Sergeant slapping men who were physically bigger. None of the slackers had even protested the slaps or challenged him. He didn't know much about combat NCOs but he recognized a dangerous man when he saw one.

"We go to Rhégion," the Captain called to the other transports. Then to his crew ordered, "Stroke, stroke. Hurry men, we've got to out run the storm front. Stroke, stroke…"

The three transports fell in line and rowed to the mouth of the strait. The storm began with a sprinkling of rain and a steady breeze from the east. By the time the third Corbita entered the narrow waterway, a heavy downpour soaked the crews and the Legionaries. Fighting to maintain their heading in the center of the channel, the Captains and rowers watched the rocky shorelines. Even a slight variance off course and their transports would be dashed against the rocks, their keels broken, and they would be smashed against the breakers and drowned in the storm surge.

The storm hit full force. Visibility dropped until the Captains could barely see the ship's rails through the driving rain. Having no options, the crews rowed on blindly down the Messina Strait. Then, as if a giant hand swatted the three ships, a gust of wind drove the transports towards the west bank.

***

The wind skimmed the top of the water sending waves into Messina harbor. Once the tides crashed on the beach, the water retreated rapidly past the hook of land. The surge collided with the southern current creating, momentarily, an underwater wall of east flowing water. The wall pushed its way into the current of the Strait.

The water wall lasted just long enough to nudge the deep draft Corbita transports away from the rocks. Then the wall of water merged with the southern flowing current and dissipated.

Wind regained control of the transports and the crews of the three ships and their Legionary cargo were tossed against the hardwood of the transports. As the ships keeled over, the bows swung westward. In the blinding rain and howling wind, the three transports crashed into the shoreline.

***

The transport's Captain laid shaken and mystified. His ship should be breaking up against the rocks. His body should be in the water being torn and broken on those rocks. Instead, he was face down on the boards leaning against the rails of his ship. Peering through the sheets of rain, he saw land.

"Off the ship," he cried out as he attempted to stand on the slanted deck. "Get off the ship."

First Sergeant Brictius heard the order and crawled up and across the slanted deck to the cargo hole. In the bottom, Legionaries moaned or screamed out in pain. They were tangled up in arms, legs, loose armor, javelins, and gladius belts and sheathes. Reaching a hand down, he grabbed a Legionary and pulled him from the labyrinth. That Legionary flipped onto his belly and hoisted another from the jumble of bodies. When there was a line of Legionaries flowing off the transport, Brictius jumped over the rocking rail and landed on a rock and clay beach.

As he raced to the next transport to see if they were unloading, he saw the state of the three ships. His transport lay on its side, half in and half out of the water. The stern of the next ship faced him, meaning the Corbita had spun around before washing ashore on the beach. The last ship rested almost upright. At first, it pleased the First Sergeant and gave him hope. Then, he realized a boulder had caved in the side of the transport. It was the rock imbedded in the hull that held the ship upright. More troubling for him, no Legionaries were coming over the rail.

"Give me two squads," he shouted as he ran towards the third ship. "Get it together people. Two squads, on me!"

His orders were just what the shaken Legionaries needed. If Brictius had requested help in a general manner, no one would be sure who should go with their NCO. But, he'd called specifically for two squads. Legionaries were trained to respond as units in times of crisis. Two squad leaders hearing his order counted heads and slapped backs as they sent their men running after the NCO. Then, they followed repeating the cry, "On the way First Sergeant. On the way First Sergeant."

Suddenly, the tossed and battered Legionaries and their Centurion awoke from the confusion of being shipwrecked. They began organizing medical staging areas and a few brave men climbed back in the rolling and bobbing ships to toss armor, shields, and weapons onto the beach.

For the rest of the afternoon, the rain fell, the wind blew, and the Legionaries and surviving crewmen moved wounded and equipment off the rocks. Further up the bank and away from the edge of the water, they dropped their loads and sat miserably waiting for the storm to end.

***

The rain slowed, although the low hanging clouds threatened more showers. One of the transport Captains grew curious. He climbed to the top of the bank to check their location.

He stopped abruptly and his mouth fell open. With a sword point pressed against his chest, he gazed at the harbor of Messina. Somehow, the ships had crashed on the back side of the harbor's hook. A shield was shoved in his face forcing him back down the embankment. As he retreated down the slope, more shields appeared until the entire crest was lined with soldiers.

"Where are we?" inquired another of the Greek Captains.

"Messina harbor," he replied with chattering teeth. "Just over the hill on the other side of the infantry."

"Infantry?" asked First Sergeant Brictius. "Where?"

The Greek Captain pointed up into the haze and explained, "Qart Hadasht infantry, up there."

"Legionaries! Arm up and form squads," he shouted.

Then a deep voice called from the fog, "I am Admiral Hanno of the Qart Hadasht Empire. If you raise a sword, you will die. If you challenge me, you will die. If the wind shifts and I change my mind, you will die."

92

"What if I fart?" a Legionary standing off to the side of the First Sergeant asked.

"You heard the Admiral," another Legionary answered. "You will die."

The one uninjured Centurion was young and inexperienced. The other was broken and laid with the injured. First Sergeant Brictius hadn't had an opportunity to speak with the young Centurion, or the two Sergeants and Corporals. Or even check to see which was healthy. Now, he passed the word to have the NCOs and the young officer converge at his location.

***

"We have a decision to make," Brictius explained. "We have two broken Centuries. Maybe two-thirds of our men are fit. Do we surrender? Or do we go down fighting?"

"What do you think, First Sergeant?" asked the Centurion.

"I believe sir, that we rely on the mercy of Admiral Hanno," Brictius replied. "If he wanted us dead, his troops would have come off the hill and slaughtered us without the pretty speech."

"Then, First Sergeant, let's ask what terms he'll accept," the young officer suggested.

"A fine idea, sir," Brictius said. "Shall we go and talk with the Admiral?"

They straightened their shoulders and both marched up the hill and into the fog.

Chapter – 18 Blame Rests with the Commander

"Sir, Lance Corporal Sisera reporting as ordered," Alerio announced as he stood in the doorway of the office.

He was hesitant and worried as Tribune Gaius Claudius sat across the desk from his Senior Centurion Patroclus. Tribune Velius' smile, however, let him know it wasn't going to be a trial. Or so he hoped.

"Come in Lance Corporal," Patroclus urged with a wave of his hand. "As you know, the advance units for the taking of Messina have been cut in half. What we want to know is how would we get the remaining force, plus Centuries from the Southern Legion into Messina?"

"It has to be done from inside Messina," explained Alerio. "The barricade has to be cut open just before our ships bring in the troops. If it's done too soon, the Qart Hadasht will flood the docks with troops and send out their warships to sink our transports. Just like yesterday."

Tribune Gaius Claudius shifted uncomfortably at the mention of the loss of six of his eleven transports and a Legion Trireme. Pointing a finger at Alerio, the Tribune opened his mouth and started to say something. Patroclus cut him off.

"Tribune Claudius. You tried your preconceived plan. It failed miserably, I might remind you," Southern Legion's Senior Centurion said harshly. "Let's hear what my Lance

Corporal has to say. Or, you can head back to the Capital and make your excuses to General Caudex."

Anger flashed across Claudius' face and Alerio expected him to challenge Patroclus' wording. But he didn't. Instead, he grumbled, "All right, I'll listen."

"It'll be the first time in your life," mouthed Velius with his lips.

"Do you have something to add, Tribune Velius?" asked Patroclus.

"No Senior Centurion," begged off the old Tribune with a tight smile.

"Continue, Lance Corporal Sisera," the Senior Centurion instructed.

"We'll need help from the Sons of Mars," Alerio said.

"You're going to trust a pack of pirates with our plans?" demanded Tribune Claudius.

Patroclus jumped to his feet with his fingers curled into fists.

"Sisera. Tribune Velius. Please wait in the Planning and Stratagies office," he growled.

Alerio walked into the hallway and Velius closed the door behind them. From inside the office, they could hear Patroclus yelling.

"Over three hundred Legionaries under your command died," he bellowed. "You killed half your command and now you question me and my staff. If Sisera says we need the Sons, then by Mars, we need the Sons. That young Lance Corporal has survived combat against Hoplite Phalanxes and Syracuse cavalry. And he brought back intelligence that you and Consul Caudex used to plan this operation..."

The voice faded, although the walls rattled, as they passed into Velius' office and work area.

***

Chief of Boats Martius had just finished inspecting the repairs on the patrol boats. Fifteen were seaworthy but two needed additional caulking. He watched as his work detail for the day meandered through the Post gate in the early morning light.

On the beach, the fog from yesterday's storm lingered. It would soon burn off and several of the patrol boats and the Triremes would launch and patrol the Strait looking for survivors. He didn't hold out much hope.

"Empire warship," the signalman in the tower called out. "Southbound."

Every Legionary in the Southern Legion knew what was expected of him. Where the dark beach had been empty, it was soon lined with ranks of men holding up their gladii. Most of them were doing mundane tasks and lacked helmets, armor, and shields. It didn't matter, the display of defiance was obvious to everyone on the approaching Empire warship.

The oarsmen ceased rowing and an archer appeared on the warship's deck. He drew back and an oversized arrow arched through the sky. It impacted near one of the upside-down patrol boats. Martius limped to it and plucked the arrow from the clay and sandy soil.

A piece of parchment was fashioned to the shaft. He untied it. A moment after reading the message, he smiled and limped, as fast as his bad leg would allow, towards the Headquarters' building.

***

There was a pounding on the door to his office and Patroclus, already irritated, asked gruffly, "Who is at my door? Why are your disturbing me? And what in the Hades is so important?"

The door opened and his First Sergeant leaned in with a big grin on his face.

"Sirs, a message from Admiral Hanno," Gerontius explained. "I thought it best to bring it to you right away."

Patroclus held out his arm and made a give-it-to-me motion with his fingers. After grabbing the parchment from his First Optio, the Senior Centurion read it. With a smile, he handed the note across his desk to Tribune Claudius. While the Tribune was reading, Gerontius cleared his throat.

"Should we prepare to launch patrol boats, sir?" he asked.

"Get them crewed and on the beach," Patroclus instructed. "Wait for my orders to launch."

"Yes, Centurion," the First Sergeant replied as he backed out of the room.

"There is your pardon, Tribune," Patroclus announced pointing at the note. "And maybe a second chance. Are you ready to listen?"

Gaius Claudius glanced up from the parchment. His face showed a mixture of agony and hopefulness. "Let's hear what Lance Corporal Sisera is proposing."

The note passed to Velius after the old Tribune and Alerio were brought back into the room. Alerio received the message last. While reading it, he wondered, 'what type of man wrote this.'

'To the Commander of the Republic's rubble hoard. I have plucked one hundred and sixty-five of your farmers from my ocean. I warn you against crossing salt water without my permission. The next time I catch your vermin swimming in my water, I'll drown them and send their bloated bodies floating to you on the southern current. You stay on your side of the Messina Strait and I'll stay on mine. Until such time as I deem to cross it. You are warned.

Send nothing larger than patrol boats and take your herd off my land.

It was signed, *Admiral Hanno of the Qart Hadasht Empire*

"Can he be trusted?" inquired Senior Centurion Patroclus. "His two warships are more than a match for a fleet of our patrol boats."

"Unfortunately, we won't know until we cross," Tribune Velius noted, "And pick up our Legionaries."

Chapter – 19 Gifts from the Empire

Fifteen undermanned patrol boats launched from Rhégion beach. Even the coxswain and Medics rowed to save space for the return trip. As they approached the backside of the hook of land, they could see shields and armored soldiers on the crest. Further down the bank, men sprawled on the slope.

"Are they alive?" asked a rower.

"I'm not sure," Alerio replied as he stroked.

Then someone on the bank stood and waved. Other's followed. By the time the first patrol boat landed, the able bodied were carrying the injured Legionaries to the boats.

Only Legionaries were on the shoreline. As Alerio learned, Admiral Hanno, not wanting to start a war with the Greeks, towed their ships into Messina harbor for repairs.

While most of the Legionaries being rescued joked and relaxed waiting for their turn to board a patrol boat, one paced along the water's edge. When he wasn't directing the loading, his face sank into a scowl and he resumed pacing.

"Who is that?" Alerio asked as his full boat drifted free from the shoreline.

"Our First Sergeant Brictius," a half-naked Legionary replied as he gripped an oar.

"He doesn't look happy," Alerio said as he watched the rescued men take their oars.

"He isn't. I fear for the Tribune's life when he gets back."

"All together. Stroke. Use the man in front of you as a guide," Alerio instructed his inexperienced rowers. "Stroke. Better. Again, stroke."

He wished he had a boat full of trained Southern Legion oarsmen. As it was, it took a long time to cross the Strait. Fortunately, the patrol boat with Brictius was just as slow and further behind him.

***

"Oars up," Alerio instructed. "Lift them out of the water and let the boat drift to shore."

As soon as the bow touched Rhégion beach, Alerio leaped from the patrol boat.

"Pull her up on the beach and stow the oars in the racks," he ordered before sprinting up the beach.

He didn't slow down until he reached the Headquarters' building. Inside, he raced by a surprised clerk and Senior Centurion Patroclus' office. He didn't break stride until he reached First Sergeant Gerontius' office.

"First Sergeant. You're needed on the beach, immediately," Alerio gasped between hard breaths.

"Have the Qart Hadasht attacked our patrol boats?" guessed Gerontius jumping to his feet and strapping on his gladius.

"No, it's more personal," Alerio said. "Let me tell you on the way to the beach. But you've got to hurry."

As they passed Patroclus' office, the Senior Centurion called out, "First Sergeant. Is everything all right with the ferrying operation."

Gerontius stopped and they backtracked to the Senior Centurion's office. Alerio could see Tribune Claudius sitting in a chair.

"Lance Corporal Sisera reports a problem on the beach," the First Sergeant responded.

"Everything is fine, sirs," Alerio replied. "It's just a little issue with some Sergeants."

"Any of my people?" demanded the Tribune.

"No sir," Alerio lied. "We just need First Sergeant Gerontius to get involved."

"Very well, carry on," directed the Senior Centurion.

Outside, as they quick walked across the parade ground, Gerontius turned his head and addressed Alerio.

"It is about the Tribune's Sergeants?" he guessed.

"Only one, First Sergeant," Alerio replied. "He's about to commit Legion suicide."

"Who and how is he going to do that?" demanded Gerontius.

"First Sergeant Brictius is going to kill Tribune Claudius," Alerio informed him.

Then, Alerio was left strolling alone as Gerontius sprinted through the gate heading for the beach and the arriving patrol boats. By the time Alerio reached the beach, First Sergeants Gerontius and Brictius were walking away and yelling at each other. But they took the path towards the NCO barracks, not the Headquarters' building.

Alerio sank down beside a patrol boat. His head drooped from relief and exhaustion and he leaned his back against the boat.

"What are you doing, Lance Corporal Sisera?" inquired Sergeant Martius.

"Resting, Chief of Boats," Alerio replied. "Before you row me out tonight."

"And, where am I rowing you?" Martius asked with a puzzled look on his face.

Raising an arm, Alerio pointed across the Strait to the northwest. "To Messina, Sergeant Martius. You're rowing me to Messina."

Act 3

Chapter – 20 Night Ride to a Decision

The patrol boat never touched the shoreline. Slipping over the side, the Lance Corporal held his pack and bedroll above his head as he waded through the waist deep water. Sergeant Martius used a paddle to silently ease the patrol boat back into deeper water. His oarsmen knew to wait until they were far away from the drop off point before dipping their oars. With the delivery made, they drifted into the current of the Strait and away from the hook of land that created Messina harbor.

Alerio moved his feet slowly to avoid splashing as he came out of the water. From his pack, he removed a pair of heavy civilian sandals, workmen's woolen pants, a long-sleeved shirt and a felt Petasos. Once dressed, he climbed the rocky embankment. At the top, he caught a view of Messina harbor. It lay flat and black on this moonless night. The light from three lanterns on the dock reflected off the calm surface. Surprisingly, he heard only one patrol and they were farther down the bent finger of land.

Alerio followed the spit of land dividing the Strait on one side from the harbor of Messina on the other. Once it joined the mainland, he turned towards the lanterns and the dock.

On the beach below the slope, the two Empire warships rested high on the sand. On either side, ships belonging to the Sons of Mars occupied the rest of the soft, sandy beach. Far out at the mouth of the port, he attempted to see the merchant ships that barricaded the harbor. But, the night was dark and he couldn't make out their shapes.

The merchant ships at the dock were visible in the lantern light. He stepped down from the dirt path and onto the rough planking. Five steps later, he was challenged.

"What are you doing on the dock," an Empire soldier with a spear, a shield and armor demanded. "What are you doing this early in the morning? Where did you come from?"

"Hold on friend. I just woke up and you are drumming on me with questions?" Alerio said sounding confused. "I was sleeping by my ship. Woke up and decided to head home."

"The dock is closed after sundown," the soldier reported.

"Oh, I forgot," pleaded Alerio. "Should I go back to my ship?"

The soldier started to say something then just stared at Alerio. Finally, he came to a conclusion.

"Move along. The dock is closed," he ordered dipping his spear in the direction of the town.

Alerio stepped around the soldier. He walked along the dock, turned at a warehouse alleyway and, on the other side, strolled into Messina.

***

The warehouses, he passed between, were dark and deserted. Not as large as the storage and transfer buildings in the Capital, they certainly had the capacity to hold ship loads of pirated and even legal cargo. Messina welcomed both or at least the Sons of Mars did before the arrival of the Empire.

Alerio avoided the main road running through town and up to the Citadel. Taking a left, he walked by three narrow streets before finally entering one. Five blocks up, he turned off the street and entered a narrow alley between two-story residential homes. In the back of one, he climbed the wall and dropped into the home's courtyard. At a shed, he eased the door open. After unstrapping his bedroll, the Legionary fluffed out the blanket and the waterproof cover. He climbed under the cover, rested his head on the sheathes sewn into one end of the blanket and went to sleep.

Dawn broke and light streaming into the shed woke him. Alerio stretched and sat up listening for activity from the house. When a man yawned loudly as if to alert the world of his presence, the Legionary rolled up his bedding and fastened the buckles. Opening the shed door, Alerio stepped out and onto the courtyard's brick pavers.

"Good morning, Crius Nereus. Are you still the Empire's Magistrate of Messina?" Alerio asked the man sitting on the patio.

The man jerked and pointed the knife he was using to cut his breakfast sausage in the direction of the voice. Instead of being angry at the sudden intrusion into his morning, he twisted his mouth into a cruel smile.

"I am and always will be the Captain of Messina, Lieutenant Sisera," Nereus replied using a title from a previous action. "No matter what the dēfutūta Qart Hadasht cūlus calls me."

"What would you say to replacing the Empire with the Republic as your protector," inquired Alerio as he walked to the patio. Sitting in the chair on the other side of the table, he picked up the sausage. "Can I use your knife? I don't seem to have anything shorter than a couple of man slayers on me."

Crius Nereus ran his eyes over the Legionary searching for the swords. Alerio helped him understand by patting his bedroll.

"That's more than my Sons have since the Empire confiscated our swords, shields, and armor," complained Nereus. "If the Republic will let us go about our trade and let us keep our tools, the Sons of Mars will welcome the Republic."

"Regrettably, it'll take more than welcoming us in," explained Alerio as he sliced off a healthy chunk of sausage. "I'll need your help with opening the door."

Nereus reached across the table and took the knife from Alerio.

"Ah, I see. The harbor is a formidable defense," the Captain of Messina commented as he jabbed the air with the short blade. "We'll need to cut an opening in the flesh to allow the hot poker in to burn out the green rot."

106

"That's a bit graphic for breakfast," Alerio replied. "But yes, I need to open the harbor so the Legionaries can come in and remove the Empire troops."

"And that full of merda Admiral Hanno," added Nereus. "Every time I go to him about trouble between my citizens and his soldiers, he reminds me. His troops are the only thing keeping the Syracuse army from marching into Messina and putting all the Sons up on the wood."

"Any idea what Hiero the Second plans," Alerio inquired.

"According to Admiral Hanno, the King of Syracuse is petitioning the Empire to leave Messina. Hanno finds it hilarious," Nereus said with a laugh. Then in a deep voice resembling the Admiral's, he related, "The Empire does not surrender territory. We take it and rule it, forever."

"I'd like to make Messina an exception to that rule," Alerio stated. "With help from the Sons of Mars."

"I'll speak with my ship Captains," Nereus assured him. "However, before I do, there is something I need you to do for me."

"What's that?" Alerio asked.

"I need you to kill two of my Captains first," Nereus explained. "They've become overly close to the Qart Hadasht soldiers and Admiral Hanno. I can't prove it, but we've attempted several subversive activities. Each time, the Empire has been there to stop us. I believe, those two Captains are selling out the Sons."

"Crius Nereus, I'm not an assassin," protested Alerio. "I'm a simple Legionary."

"I understand it may sound like work for a stab them in the back killer. But it's not. I need them to die in public with witnesses," Nereus stated. "Think of it this way. If we plan to help the Republic and they pass on our plans to Hanno, Qart Hadasht soldiers will be waiting for your men. Make them dead or risk failing to open Messina. It's your decision."

Alerio placed the sliced length of sausage on the table and leaned his head back. While gazing at the blue sky, he inquired softly, "What are their names?"

Chapter - 21 Pirate's Den

Alerio kept to the shadows on the way across Messina. Roving patrols of Qart Hadasht soldiers appeared and when he saw one, he ducked over to the next street to avoid them. According to Nereus, the Empire troops occasionally took sailors off the streets for questioning. With the mission for the Sons of Mars' leader on his mind and no crew to claim, he'd prefer to reach his destination unseen.

The mission bothered him. It was one thing to kill during a battle or even when attacked on the streets. But murdering a man, or two in this case, by seeking them out with the only intent being murder, didn't sit right with the Legionary. On the other hand, if removing two collaborators allowed the Legionaries to reach Messina unchallenged, he would do it.

'I guess this is my initiation into the dark arts of being a spy,' Alerio thought as he leaned on a wall. Across the street, a Sons of Mars pub seemed lively.

Candlelight from the windows reflected on the pavers of the street and voices carried from inside whenever someone opened the door. And the door opened a lot. A steady flow of customers staggered out and groups of customers happily went into the Pirate's Pride.

Alerio adjusted his Petasos, as any good spy would do, to hide his face. With the brim almost to the bridge of his nose, he crossed to the entrance.

***

It wasn't hard to identify the three Sons of Mar's Captains in the establishment. Solicitous crewmen identified the Captains by occupying chairs around his table while others formed a ring around their leader. The other tables in the Pirate's Pride had patrons sitting, talking and being mostly ignored by the individual crews.

"Vino, honey wine, or fresh goat's milk?" the proprietor asked from behind a plank counter top. The rough weathered boards, obviously from an old ship, rested on barrels.

"Goat's milk?" inquired Alerio.

"This is your first time here, isn't it?" remarked the proprietor. "Goat's milk, hot and fresh from the she goat's teats. Good for what ails you."

"I'll pass on the goat's milk. Let me have the biggest mug of vino you have," ordered Alerio. "It's been a long day."

He took the mug and moved to the far end of the counter. Sipping, he listened to conversations from the Captains' tables. If both targets weren't in here, there was a courtyard in the back to check.

Nereus had described Captain Ferox Creon and Captain Gallus Silenus. It proved to be unnecessary. A rower reared back and bursts out laughing.

"I never did that," pleaded the laughing sailor. "tell them, Captain Silenus. Never once did I eat a living squid."

An older man shook his head and shrugged his shoulders in a noncommittal manner leaving the sailor without support.

"You've eaten almost everything else," teased another rower.

Alerio, having marked Silenus, turned his attention to the other Captain's table. Soon, he confirmed it wasn't Ferox Creon. Moments later, at the table closest to the end of the counter, the Legionary heard someone address Captain Creon.

With his targets identified, Alerio pondered his tactics. Both were surrounded by loyal crewmen. They sat on opposite sides of the great room divided by distance and a third crew. Silenus near the entrance and Creon closer to the courtyard doorway. Unless there was a distraction, Alerio couldn't simply stroll over and slit Silenus' throat. Then cross through the third ship's crew, push into Creon's crew, cut their Captain's neck and walk out of the Pirate's Pride. As he was thinking about starting a fire to create a distraction, an oarsman climbed onto a table and whistled for everyone's attention.

"And it's, stroke lads, stroke!" he announced when it quieted down.

"Did you say? And it's, stroke lads, stroke!" challenged a sailor from across the room.

"Yes, I did. You untalented carp," the rower on the table replied.

The sailor climbed onto his table and stated, "A pelican carries a better tune than you."

Then the rower in a basso voice called out, "And it's, stroke lads, stroke!"

Everyone in the Pirate's Pride joined in the singing:

Rowing our ram down their throat
They don't know the life we lead
Never perceive our daring deeds
Taking spoils wherever we please
Honoring our fathers' oath

Messina where the harbor waits
Safe from toils, safe to sell our spoils

Our strut is wide with pirate pride
Until next we ride the tide
Row out to sea with pirate pride

And it's, stroke lads, stroke!
Rowing our rail under their sail
They fear and quake at our desire
Never sure if our heart's afire
Give it up afore facing our ire
Of the Sons of Mars, we hail

Messina where the harbor waits
Safe from toils, safe to sell our spoils
Our strut is wide with pirate pride
Until next we ride the tide
Row out to sea with pirate pride

And it's, stroke lads, stroke!
Rowing our ship from their warship
Apologies to the merchant troubled
Their sails we barely ruffled
Their sides we only snuggled
We are but sailors
Not sea thieves, not brigands, or pirates

Then it's home to Messina
Messina where the harbor waits
Safe from toils, safe to sell our spoils
Our strut is wide with pirate pride
Until next we ride the tide
Row out to sea with pirate pride

With every crew in the pub tilting their heads back
trying to out sing the other crews, Alerio reached back and
placed his left hand around the hilt of the Ally of the Golden
Valley dagger. It was fitting that a gift from assassins would
be used to perform assassinations. He held the large mug
tight in his right hand and swung the vessel in time with the
singing. As if simply wandering the room, he made his way
towards the front door. Then, he turned his back on Captain
Silenus. As innocently as possible, he backed between
Silenus' crew.

> *And it's, stroke lads, stroke!*
> *Rowing our rail under their sail*
> *They fear and quake at our desire*
> *Never sure if our heart's afire*
> *Give it up afore facing our ire*
> *Of the Sons of Mars, we hail*

Alerio's leg touched a chair and he drifted further back.
A glance over his shoulder identified the Captain's location.
The Legionary adjusted as the singing continued.

> *Messina where the harbor waits*
> *Safe from toils, safe to sell our spoils*
> *Our strut is wide with pirate pride*
> *Until next we ride the tide*
> *Row out to sea with pirate pride*

Captain Gallus Silenus stood an arm's length away.
With his head thrown back as he sang, his neck provided an
excellent target. Alerio tightened his grip on the curved
dagger and dropped the mug alongside his leg. It would be

113

a good bludgeon to clear a path once the Captain was down. He waited for the lusty opening line.

And it's, stroke lads, stroke!

Then, Alerio pulled the dagger…

A thick pair of arms encircled his body, trapping his arms at his sides.

"Lieutenant Sisera. What are you doing in Messina?" asked a sailor as he hoisted the Legionary off his feet. Grinning happily up at his shocked and trapped captive, the sailor spun him around. "Lieutenant Sisera. Look, everyone, it's Lieutenant Sisera come to drink with us."

"Do I know you?" Alerio choked out as his ribs contracted from the squeezing.

"You made me a Lieutenant," the sailor gushed.

"I made you a Lieutenant?" breathed out Alerio as the sailor gave him a last hard hug before setting the Legionary back on his feet.

"Sure, when you took my armor and went to kick the merda out of those two Hoplite cūlus," explained the sailor. "We switched armor and weapons and you called me Lieutenant. Then ordered me to mount your horse and ride to Captain Nereus. The mentula!"

The singing had stopped and everyone in the pub had their eyes on the odd reunion.

'Something feels off,' thought Alerio as he guided the dagger back into the sheath. Then out loud, he asked, "Why did you call Captain Nereus a mentula?"

"Take your pick," the sailor spit out. "He and Admiral Hanno must be dēfutūta from all the time they spend together. Or maybe it's the men locked away under guard from questioning Hanno's orders. All while our useless Captain makes excuses for the Qart Hadasht peacock."

Alerio scanned the rowers within earshot. To a man, they nodded agreement at the sailor's description. Turning to Gallus Silenus, he questioned.

"Captain, why does Crius Nereus want you dead?" Alerio inquired.

Before Silenus could reply, the front door banged open. Captain Milon Frigian jumped over the threshold and slammed the door behind him.

"Creon! Get out of here," Frigian shouted. "There are twenty Qart Hadasht soldiers heading this way."

Captain Frigian noticed Silenus and Alerio.

"Lieutenant Sisera? What are you doing here?" then, Frigian shifted to Silenus and suggested. "Gallus, if I were you, I'd make a hasty retreat as well."

"Captain Frigian. I really need to speak with you," Alerio said. "But here is not the place. For reasons I don't have time to explain, I also need to get out of here before the soldiers arrive."

Frigian looked at Silenus and cocked his head to the side.

"Bring Lieutenant Sisera," Silenus ordered the sailor who had hugged the Legionary.

"Drop him at Adiona's Temple," Frigian instructed. "I'll catch up after suffering the indignity of bowing to the Empire."

The sailor shoved Alerio past a line of rowers. They moved to the doorway leading to the courtyard. Three oarsmen stood on the shoulders of six more who had linked arms to create a stable base.

"Raise your arms Lieutenant," the sailor said as he gripped Alerio's elbows and lifted them to the Legionary's ears. "Up you go."

Alerio's wrists were grabbed and he was lifted from the floor. When his head came level with the roof top, the center man clutched his chest and Alerio was vaulted over the man's head. He landed hard on the clay roof tiles.

"This way," ordered Gallus Silenus. "And watch your step."

Alerio followed the shadows of Ferox Creon and Gallus Silenus over the roof and across to the neighboring building. It was the perfect time to kill them. Except, they weren't the ones, who needed killing.

Chapter – 22 Temple of Adiona

Ferox Creon and Gallus Silenus paused on the edge of the roof. From the street below, the scuffs of boots marching by carried to Alerio.

"Drop down. At the end of the buildings, head towards the harbor," Silenus instructed. "Before you reach the warehouses turn left and climb the hill. Stay on the port side of the hill so the soldiers guarding the docks don't see you. Go to the other side of the temple and wait."

Leaving him with those directions, the Captains crawled to the edge, swung their legs around and rolled their lower bodies off the tiles. Using their fingers, they hung momentarily before dropping to the street. Then they ran into a dark alleyway and vanished.

Alerio mimicked their movements and hit the street with bent knees. At the last building, he turned right and followed the line of buildings. On his left, Messina's defensive wall was barely visible in the starlight. Still, he could make out where it rose and fell, following the low rolling hills on the north side of the town.

A couple of blocks ahead was the wide avenue dividing the shops at the edge of Messina from the warehouses. Sprinting away from the building, Alerio reached a tree lined path that climbed a steep hill. As instructed, he stayed to the left of the trees and, instead of using the smooth path and stairs, he scrambled over rocks and through depressions to reach the top. Between the trees, he could see the harbor but couldn't tell where the water ended and the dark land began.

117

On a flat, cleared area at the top of the hill, Alerio faced a long, tall clay brick structure. Easing along the side, he worked his way to the side facing the harbor.

No wall blocked access to the interior of the building. Peering around the brick sidewall, he saw a large brazier deep inside. Far enough from the open end so rain couldn't reach the fire burning in a shallow bronze pan. Visible in the flicker of the flames, stacks of wood and charcoal mounds occupied the back wall of the building. As a Temple, it wasn't impressive. Edging back along the side wall, Alerio moved around to the back of the Temple and walked to the other side. In the starry night, the defensive wall appeared as a pale line passing a few paces from the toe of the hill and running to the harbor.

Alerio sat down and rested his back against the rough brick wall. So far, his mission as a spy sent to find confederates to open the harbor for the Legionaries had been a failure.

***

"Adiona is the Goddess of safe returns from voyages," explained Milon Frigian as he walked around the Temple and sat next to the Legionary. "Adherents keep the fire burning day and night. It's the first thing we see when we row into Messina."

"It's not visible from Rhégion tower," commented Alerio. "And no offense, but it's pretty rough and plain for a Temple."

"Because the Temple is facing the mouth of the harbor," Frigian informed Alerio. "If it faced east, we'd row into the hook and not the harbor. Not a pleasant ending to a trip. As for the Temple, it's the fire that honors the Goddess, not the building."

They sat quietly gazing at the night sky. Finally, Frigian spoke.

"Why are you in Messina, Alerio Sisera?" he asked. "I thought you were done with the Sons."

"I'll tell you. But first explain why Crius Nereus wants Ferox Creon and Gallus Silenus killed," Alerio inquired. "Not just dead, but publicly murdered."

"So that's why you were in the Pirate's Pride. To kill two of the Sons of Mars' Captains," Frigian ventured. "Creon is challenging Nereus for the leadership of the Sons and Silenus is backing him. The reason Nereus needs them murdered in public is so the killer can be caught. Of course, he'll get a knife in the back trying to escape before he can be questioned."

"Couldn't Nereus have them killed in their beds?" asked Alerio. "Or in an alley?"

"If we thought Nereus or the Qart Hadasht troops had anything to do with killing a Sons' Captain, the rest of us would row out and never come back," Frigian explained. "No, it had to be public and the culprit captured and identified. You, Lieutenant Sisera, were a gift from the Gods to Captain Nereus."

"A sacrificial lamb it seems," complained Alerio. "I need the Sons to help to open the harbor and let Legionaries into Messina."

"We begged for the Republic or the Empire to come in before the Syracuse army annihilated us," stated Frigian. "The Empire responded. Now, the Republic wants to sneak in and battle house to house in brutal street fighting to remove the Qart Hadasht. Your Republic practices an odd form of diplomacy."

"That's politics. I'm only a Lance Corporal with a mission," declared Alerio. "Will the Sons of Mars help me or not?"

"It's actually humorous. For Lance Corporal Alerio Sisera of the Republic's Legion, we wouldn't do merda," Frigian informed him. "However, Lieutenant Alerio Sisera of the Messina Militia is a different story. For the weapon's instructor who trained our infantry and the hero of our battles against Syracuse forces, the Sons will assault the Citadel. For our Lieutenant, we'll battle Qart Hadasht infantry and die on the slopes. Which man am I speaking with?"

"I'm only one man, Captain Frigian. But I can promise you this," Alerio said. "If you help me bring in the Republic forces, it won't be the Messina Militia attacking the Citadel. It'll be the heavy infantry of the Legion. And they will turn the slopes red with Empire blood."

"Then we need a plan, Lieutenant Sisera," Frigian exclaimed. "Because I was only kidding about dying on the slopes."

"Speaking of kidding, what is with the Pirate's Den?" inquired Alerio. "Fresh goat's milk?"

"That's not a joke," explained Frigian. "We are pirates and when we board a merchant ship, we don't know what we'll face. Between the fear, the bad water, and the rough seas, some men develop pain in their guts. It gets worse when they think about rowing out. For those men, the pub serves goat's milk. It signifies, without them admitting it, that they are unfit for a voyage."

"I'm glad I didn't order the goat's milk," Alerio teased.

"You might need it after I tell you my plan," suggested Frigian.

***

Crius Nereus relaxed on his patio. The night sky displayed thousands of stars. He missed the days when he captained a ship and took spoils from unsuspecting merchant vessels. Now it was cutthroat politics and defending his position as leader of the Sons of Mars from his own Captains and Admiral Hanno.

In the morning, when he was called upon to identify Sisera's body, he'd express shock and confusion at why the Legionary would murder two of his captains. As a sort of homage to the young man, Nereus rested a hand on one of the swords he found in Alerio's bedroll.

In all probability, the dead Captains' crews would slay the Legionary. The coins he gave the Empire's night watch Sergeant insured Sisera's death. It was a small investment to secure Nereus' future as Captain of Messina.

A scraping at the wall of his compound drew his attention. Then, a body appeared on top of the wall before it dropped into his courtyard.

"Good morning, Captain," Alerio said from the dark.

"Alerio Sisera. Did you complete the first part of your mission?" Nereus inquired. Something in the young lad's voice made him move his hand from the pommel of the sword to the hilt. "Now we can plan the second part. Are you injured?"

"Just my feelings and sense of honor," replied Alerio. "I just came from the Temple of Adiona where I had an interesting conversation with Milon Frigian."

"I take it Ferox Creon lives and you've thrown in with his rebellion," accused Nereus. Then he asked, "So, what is next for us, Lieutenant Sisera?"

"You have my pack and bedroll," Alerio informed him. "Of course, there is the problem of your fondness for Admiral Hanno. Does it go deep enough for you to tell him about my mission?"

"No! Never would I divulge or turn you over to the Qart Hadasht soldiers," Nereus avowed. "Come sit and enjoy the stars with me."

Alerio took two slow steps then a sword blade slashed from the dark. Jumping back, he drew the dagger.

"You just answered your own question," Alerio said as he countered a second slash from the sword. The short blade parried the sword and Alerio stepped forward.

122

Nereus realizing he missed with the surprise attacks, leaped off the patio. Figuring he needed room to chop and stab, he moved to the center of the courtyard.

"I won't turn you over to them," Nereus assured him. "Because once I kill you with your own sword, I'll feed your body to the pigs. Then, I'll find another way to dispose of Captain Creon."

No sensible fighter liked night combat. Unless you were in physical contact, and even that was iffy, there was too much left to luck. Alerio circled to his left, picked up a clay planter, and talked as he moved.

"The Legion will come here," Alerio said slowly so Nereus could follow the voice. "When they take Messina, you could still be Captain of the City."

"How do you figure that?" demanded Nereus. "Come on Legionary, tell me about surviving. Or better yet, let me tell you about surviving."

The clay planter smashed into the patio. Nereus turned to his left in the direction of the disturbance. Alerio rushed in but the Sons' Captain was an experienced street fighter.

Nereus, his body towards the breaking planter, twisted back to swing the sword. The long blade swiped to the right cutting the air at belly height. But Alerio was already under the arc and locking his arms around Nereus' legs. Alerio drove with his legs, lifted the pirate leader, and slammed him to the courtyard floor.

The pommel of the sword smashed into the back of Alerio's left shoulder. Even with the breath knocked out of

123

him, Nereus fought. His knees churning and the butt end of the sword striking again and again.

Alerio had enough. He slammed his left fist into Nereus' chin and drove the blade of his dagger between the Captain's ribs.

"What's next for us, Captain Nereus?" Alerio asked as he twisted the blade. "You die and I complete my mission."

Chapter 23 – Communicating a Simple Plan

The Sons of Mars' bireme rounded the hook and headed south down the strait. All one hundred and twenty oars splashing in rhythm.

"Sons of Mars," shouted the signalman from the Rhégion Tower. "Warship!"

Unlike the greeting for the Empire warship, most of the Legionaries working on the beach simply waved. No one worried the ship would land and start a battle. It was strange when the bow angled for the beach and the two tiers of rowers backed down their oars. For a moment the long ship idled in the current. Then, a package was tossed towards the shoreline and the oars stroked and the ship angled back to the center of the channel.

A Legionary splashed into the Strait, snatched the package from the water and waded back to shore.

"Sergeant Martius. Your name is on the package," the Legionary exclaimed as he marched to the Chief of Boats. "Do you have relatives in Messina?"

"Not that I know of," the scarred veteran admitted. "Give that to me."

He pulled the waxed ends of the package and unfolded the oiled goatskin. The open flap exposed a piece of parchment.

Chief of Boats, this message is for Tribune Velius. To authenticate, A weapon's instructor doesn't need a saltwater soaked rag on his left hand, it's better for cooling the head.

Sergeant Martius remember the first day of combat rowing class and Lance Corporal Sisera sitting with the rag on his head rather than soothing the blisters on his left hand. Seems, he already had hard skin on that hand from weapon's drills. The Sergeant headed for the Headquarters' building.

***

"But how do we know it's Sisera and not a trap," demanded Gaius Claudius. "And suppose he's held captive and was forced to write the missive?"

"Then let's all retreat to the Capital and we'll let the Senate debate the issue," suggested Tribune Velius. "Politicians are excellent at talking. Hold on. Something just occurred to me. That's right, we are the Legion and we are bad at talking. Whatever are we going to do?"

Gaius Claudius looked confused but the Senior Centurion wasn't. He twisted his mouth into a sneer.

"The Tribune is saying, Legionaries act on available information," Patroclus declared. "Tomorrow night Lance Corporal Sisera and crews from the Sons of Mars will open the barricade vessels. There's only one question we have to answer. Are we rowing over when he gives the signal?"

First Sergeants Gerontius and Brictius reached out together and smoothed the map flat. Sisera's rough drawing showed the tip of the hook, the dock, and the warehouses. From the drawing, it appeared he could assure the dock and storage buildings would be cleared of Empire soldiers. Yet, it was only a foothold in Messina.

"We can hold the areas between the warehouses with eighty infantrymen," Brictius announced. "Fighting our way from there will be bloody and hard work for the lads."

"Straight up the main road to the Citadel?" asked Gerontius.

"Not a good strategy," Tribune Velius said jumping into the discussion. "Too many side streets. You'll have Empire troops coming from the sides and getting in behind your advancing units."

Senior Centurion Patroclus placed the heel of his hand along the dock. As he swept it forward covering more of the town, he explained, "You'll need to take Messina street by street maintaining a unified front. You'll push the Qart Hadasht back to the Citadel and crush them on the slope."

The four men turned to stare at Tribune Gaius Claudius. Ignoring them, he walked to the map. Placing a finger on the lines representing the dock, he stated, "I'll be on the first boat."

First Sergeant Brictius' mouth fell open but he recovered and put on a blank face.

"Very admirable, Tribune," offered the Senior Centurion. "But unless you're trained to stand in a shield wall, our first units must be infantrymen."

"But who will go in on the first wave?" inquired Claudius. "Who will command the infantry?"

"That's my job, sir," Brictius assured him. "I'll be on the first boat. The Century's Centurion will be on boat three."

"And I'll be on the second boat," announced First Sergeant Gerontius.

"We have lots to do before tomorrow night," Senior Centurion Patroclus suggested. "I want reports of units from the Southern Legion and equipment we're sending with Tribune Claudius."

"First Sergeant Brictius and I have a lot to accomplish before we launch as well," Claudius stated with a nod to his First Sergeant.

Act 4

Chapter – 24 Armor, Shields and Swords

Alerio sat in a house a block from the warehouses. Lounging around him were twenty-five Sons' of Mars and Milon Frigian.

"And you're sure the Legionaries will come?" asked Frigian. "Because once we set this in motion, there's no turning back."

"I'm more worried about the first phase," Alerio commented. The crewmen were leaning in and listening. "We've got to move fast and, once in position, hold until the infantry arrives."

"We'll hold," Frigian assured him. Then looking around the room, he asked, "Won't we?"

The response of "Yes, Captain" echoed around the small space.

Three raps on the door announced a visitor. Before anyone could answer, the door opened and closed quickly.

"The Sergeant of the Guard has finished his rounds," the newly arrived sailor reported. "He's working his way back through the western guard stations."

"And the roving patrols?" asked Alerio.

"They're moving counter to the Sergeant," the sailor replied. "If they hold true to the pattern, they'll reach the base of the Citadel before starting back down. The patrol on the hook is moving towards the point."

"Captain Frigian, are you ready for some larceny?" inquired Alerio.

"Go inform the other houses, we are moving," Frigian ordered four of his oarsmen. Then to Alerio, he said, "Larceny is my middle name, Lieutenant Sisera."

Twenty-one of the oarsmen began winding ropes around one hand. The four singled out by Frigian moved to the doorway and left. They were assigned to contacting the houses were the rest of the crew members were staged. Then Alerio and Milon Frigian snuck out followed by the twenty-one rowers.

One block down and across from the warehouses, Frigian selected pairs of men and sent them across the avenue. Each pair vanished down alleyways and streets between the warehouses. Ten teams had been swallowed up by the dark with no cries of alarm arising from the guards on the dock. With one rower still waiting, Frigian whispered to Alerio.

"Not too late to withdraw," Frigian commented.

"Need a mug of fresh goat's milk, do you?" inquired Alerio.

The sailors who had checked on the rest of the crew crowded up behind them.

"That's the alleyway. You're going to the third door on that building," Frigian whispered indicating a single warehouse. "Go!"

As the five sailors raced for the street and towards the door, Frigian said, "I guess we're committed now, Lieutenant Sisera."

Alerio didn't reply. He stepped around the Sons of Mars' Captain and jogged after the entry team.

***

The door was open by the time Alerio arrived. After stepping over the threshold, he closed the door and one of the oarsmen sparked flint and a candle came to life. Its light brightened a corner of the warehouse. Soon, four more candles bent to the flame and as the wicks blazed, the lit candles moved to locations around the small section of the warehouse.

Without words, Alerio and the five oarsmen began quietly and slowly untangling armor, shields, helmets, and swords from a pile. As each piece came free, they carried them to an area with equipment in each category. After they had enough to arm twenty-six men, Alerio tapped one of the oarsmen on the shoulder. The rower moved to the doorway and slipped out.

Those left continued to pull and sort the tools of war. They had enough for another twenty-five when six men eased through the door. Without being instructed, the new men dressed in armor, helmets, and selected shields and swords. All the equipment originated from different cultures and city states. Alerio set aside Legion armor, a helmet, a gladius, and six Legion infantry shields.

Eight more men entered. They headed for the equipment while the armed ones positioned themselves on either side of the door. Alerio tapped another of the oarsmen on the shoulder and he left to collect his house of crewmen.

No matter how carefully you handled armor, shields, helmets, and swords, there were bound to be dropped swords, shields, and, the worst, helmets. Unlike heavy swords which clunked, helmets rang like a bell. The occasional clang and ring increased when the number of oarsmen dressing in the warehouse reached sixty. To Alerio it sounded similar to a street festival full of vendors and a crowd of rowdy citizens.

With his nerves on edge from the noise, Alerio left and headed back across the avenue.

"It sounds like a choir tuning up," he whispered to Frigian. "I'm not sure how much longer before we're discovered."

"Lucky for us, the guard near you walked down to speak with another guard," the Captain informed him. Behind Frigian, more oarsmen huddled against the house's wall waiting to be sent forward. "But you're correct. It's time to make ourselves known."

"Give me a count of sixty," Alerio requested before he ran back to the warehouse.

By the time Alerio passed through the doorway, Milon Frigian's count reached nine. Alerio had his shoulder armor buckled when Frigian counted thirty-one, thirty-two. At fifty-one, fifty-two, Alerio's armored skirt and gladius belt were fashioned. At fifty-nine, Alerio placed the helmet over his head. On the street, Captain Frigian counted sixty and whistled one sharp note.

Alerio barely heard the note through the thick boards of the warehouse. But he wasn't the target of the whistle. The ten men hiding in the shadows of the alleyways and streets between the warehouses heard their Captain's signal loud and clear.

***

A pair of Qart Hadasht soldiers standing and talking on the dock, heard the whistled note. But sailors were constantly communicating by sounds. On a ship under oars, words got lost in the grunts and hard breathing. Due to the frequent use of whistles and yelps by oarsmen, the soldiers ignored Frigian's note.

When two naked men staggered from an alleyway and into the pool of a lantern's light, the guards chuckled. Then they strolled over to the obviously drunk rowers.

"The dock is closed," one informed the inebriated men. "Back to town with you!"

The naked men hesitated, as if confused, before looking up at the guards in surprise. In a reflex of modesty, the rowers dropped their hands to their crotches. Their sudden shyness further amused the guards. They laughed softly looking down.

Then rope wrapped hands reached around their helmets. Both guards gagged as rope and fingers were jammed into their mouths. As the soldiers began to struggle, the naked men lowered their shoulders and charged the guards.

Unable to cry out or bring their spears down to defend themselves, the guards were carried off the end of the dock. In helmets, armor and carrying shields and spears, the soldiers plunged into the harbor. Their first instinct was to drop their shields and remove their helmets. Instead of removing their heavy equipment, they found themselves fighting oarsmen who followed them into the depths of the black water. Down they went, struggling to hold their breath while fending off arms that propelled them deeper and deeper. Saltwater burned the insides of their noses and filled their mouths, throats, and lungs. Choking as they sank, they thrashed and kicked.

It wasn't until the soldiers ceased moving that the four oarsmen released the guards, flipped over and kicked for the surface.

In the water below the dock, five pairs of swimmers broke the surface. With no guards left, the ten oarsmen took their time climbing the ladders to the rough wooden planks. Then they headed for the warehouse where the Empire had stored the Sons of Mars confiscated weapons and armor.

***

Captain Frigian crossed the warehouse and began dressing in the gaudy armor of a Greek commander.

"Pretty armor," commented Alerio as he walked over to Frigian. "What about the guards?"

"I haven't heard any of them call out," replied the Sons of Mars' Captain. Then to a broad-shouldered rower, Frigian ordered, "First Oar, take forty men back to the house. But don't fall asleep, I'll need you soon."

"Yes Captain," replied the lead oarsman of Frigian's crew.

"Lieutenant Sisera, off you go," the Captain instructed. "I've sent men to collect another crew. If you can get the Legionaries here before the entire Qart Hadasht garrison falls on us, we might pull this off."

"You hold them and try not to get killed," replied Alerio as he handed the five extra Legion shields to unarmed men. "I'll see you before sunrise."

Chapter – 25 Death on the Hook

Alerio led thirty armored oarsmen and the five carrying only Legion shields down the dock. At the end, he stepped up on the grass and the rowers followed single file. Past the beach where the Sons' ships and the Qart Hadasht Triremes rested, they marched in line. Once the column neared the banks of the Strait, Alerio assembled them in two ranks with the five toting the shields positioned at the rear.

"Move fast," he whispered. "When we locate the patrol don't yell and don't hesitate. Plow into them and put them down."

"Yes, sir," a few replied.

When Alerio stepped in front of the loose formation, one leaned forward and asked, "Wouldn't you be safer behind us, Lieutenant Sisera?"

"What? And let the Sons of Mars have all the fun?" replied Alerio. "Forward!"

On the hook of land, some of the oarsmen moved along the banks of the harbor side, others walked along the flat, dodging between trees and others stumbled over the rocks on the slope leading to the waters of Messina Strait.

The lines of oarsmen were a third of the way along the hook when they encountered the Qart Hadasht patrol.

***

It took the oarsmen behind him a few heartbeats before they realized the Legionary was moving. Alerio saw the shadowy figure appear in front of him. With a surge, he leaped forward, set his feet and powered the massive Legion shield into the first soldier. Driving with his legs, he shoved the first into the second Qart Hadasht soldier, and the two rolled back into the legs of the third. The three were down and Alerio hacked at anything on the ground while keeping the big shield to his front.

The realization that they were in contact hit the rest of the soldiers and the oarsmen at the same time. The oarsmen directly behind Alerio charged forward. On their flanks, the rowers on the banks felt the adjacent shields advance upward. Like a whip flexing before the head snapped, the lines of shields bent in a ripple as the flankers climbed to the hook's banks to keep up with their brethren. By the time the men nearest the waters reached the top, the Sons of Mars had the Qart Hadasht soldiers sandwiched between their shields.

In a face to face fight or with time to form up, the trained soldiers would have stood a chance. But they were in single file, trapped between shields and slashing swords. Despite their disadvantage, they managed to wound several oarsmen.

Just as Alerio had done, the oarsmen chopped blindly down at everything laying on the ground. Then when none of those bleeding on the soil put up a fight, oarsmen reached down and ran their blades across all the throats they could locate by feel. Unfortunately, some of those murdered in the dark were Sons of Mars rowers. Friendly casualties were one of the reasons few warriors chose to fight in the dark.

***

Alerio snatched up four Qart Hadasht shields and distributed them to four oarsmen.

"Follow me," he whispered.

The five carefully picked their way down the bank leading to the Strait. At a spot Alerio estimated was below the line of sight from the far off but elevated Citadel, he took the shields and stacked them in the shape of a box.

"The box faces Rhégion tower," he explained. "Gather driftwood and build a fire in the box. Move the shield back and forth in front of the flames. That's the signal to the Legion. Keep the fire alive and the shield moving. All of our lives depend on it."

"Until dawn or we're dead," a rower vowed. "We'll continue to signal."

Alerio stumbled over rocks as he climbed back to the crest where the remaining oarsmen waited. Once there, he took the lead and they swept the banks of the hook. They encountered no additional soldiers.

Where the land narrowed and bent like a hook, the tip formed the east side of the mouth of Messina harbor. Across the watery opening, a rocky beach jutted out from the shoreline marking the other side. Between the points of land, five Corbita transports were loosely tied bow to stern, creating a blockade.

A lit candle rose from the deck of one transport. The small flame arched back and forth and Alerio's gut tightened. Some of the noise from the fight on the hook had reached the Qart Hadasht arches on the transports. The only positive was the signal consisted of a single candle.

Chapter – 26 Contact on the Dock

Alerio and his force on the hook weren't the only ones to see the candle. On the dock, Milon Frigian also saw the waving flame. Plus, one more person witnessed the signal.

"Get ready, lads," he said to a line of oarsmen. "It's about to get interesting."

"You say that like it's a good thing, Captain," one of his men stated.

"That depends on the Qart Hadasht's response. Just prepare to defend the dock," Frigian advised as he walked away from that group. He repeated the message to a cluster of armed oarsmen standing at an alleyway, "Get ready, lads. It's about to get interesting."

"I believe I could use a mug of fresh goat's milk, right about now" one rower exclaimed.

"If we had any, I'd join you in a mug," Frigian replied. "But we don't, so we'll make do with the blood of Empire soldiers. Prepare to defend the dock."

While Captain Frigian moved down the dock giving the same warning to his men at the alleyways and streets cutting between the warehouses, the third witness to the signal flame reacted.

***

From the second floor of the citadel, the duty guard stepped away from the portal. In the back of the room, he shook his Sergeant awake.

"Signal flame from the blockade," he whispered.

"Only one?" asked the NCO.

"One candle waving," the guard replied. "Want me to go down and tell the duty officer?"

"I'll go. Get back to your post," the Sergeant ordered as he tossed back the blanket and swung his legs out of bed. "Shout out if they add more flames."

Moments later, the Sergeant was downstairs in front of a Qart Hadasht Lieutenant.

"We have a single candle flame from the blockade," the Sergeant reported.

"Doesn't sound urgent," the officer advised. "I'll send a runner and have the Sergeant of the Guard check on the dock. Our patrol on the hook will handle any problems."

"Very well, sir," the Sergeant said as he saluted and walked back to the stairs.

***

The S.O.G. was a veteran of the army with years of experience fighting against enemies of the Empire. When the runner informed him about the one candle signal, he didn't rush. However, he did send the runner to the other side of Messina with instructions to have the eight soldiers of the roving patrol meet him at the warehouses. Then he turned to his four soldiers

"Probably nothing but stay alert. Big trouble always starts small," he informed his escort unit. "Especially in the depths of the night."

They marched down the street towards the warehouses. On the south side of Messina, the eight men of the roving patrol jogged. They didn't want to face the Sergeant's ire if he arrived before them.

***

Other than a few lanterns casting spots of light on the pavers, the streets were dark. It was difficult to separate the patrol from the shadows until the Qart Hadasht soldiers were just three blocks away.

'This isn't good,' Frigian thought as he tried to count the number of soldiers in the response unit. 'They're in a hurry.' Then out loud, he announced, "Stoop down behind your shields."

It was dark beside the warehouse and the eight soldiers slowed. There seemed to be a solid shadow across the road between them and the dock. As they approached, the shadow rose up and became a wall of shields.

"Attack! Attack," Frigian shouted.

The Qart Hadasht spears stabbed and slashed the first rank of oarsmen. Those not bloodied were knocked to the side by the experienced soldiers. But the second rank and third filled in and once the surviving Sons were between the

140

spearheads and the shields, the fight became more evenly matched.

Spears clattered to the pavers and swords leaped into Qart Hadasht hands. Under the press of bodies from the oarsmen, unit integrity dissolved and the soldiers fought as individuals. Outnumbered and with three of their patrol down and bleeding on the street, the five remaining soldiers stepped back as they fought.

"To me! To me!" the Sergeant of the Guard bellowed as he ran down the avenue from the north. "Rally to me."

The five soldiers adjusted and rotated so they were stepping back towards their Sergeant. The movement surprised the oarsmen. As with any undisciplined hoard, the Sons shoved straight ahead with no regard for tactics. By the time the soldiers pivoted and were backing northward in the direction of the Sergeant, many of the oarsmen had run straight ahead meeting no resistance. More oarsmen followed them across the avenue, figuring the ones charging forward knew where to find the enemy.

An experienced combat NCO knows how to regain control and rally men in a crisis. He positioned his escorts a shield's width apart. The four men barely covered the width of the avenue but they did present a line of shields and spearheads.

"Hurry up, you mangy goat herders," the Sergeant yelled the insult. Whether at his troops or as an enticement to the Sons to come against his spears, didn't matter. To the five Empire troops in the fighting retreat, it was motivational to hear an NCO's voice doling out verbal abuse. As if this street fight was nothing more than an exercise, the Sergeant added, "Fall back into ranks. Don't you dare be the last man in my line."

From behind their shields and with slashes of their swords, the five soldiers left a trail of dead oarsmen as they rapidly retreated towards the Sergeant's shield wall. None wanted to be the last to join the ranks and suffer the Sergeant's wrath.

The five Empire soldiers took a last step back and snapped their shields into place forming a solid wall of steel and bronze. The attacking oarsmen stopped and glared. Behind them, the Sergeant began issuing orders to extract the unit from the motionless oarsmen.

"To the rear, left swing," he bellowed…it was the last order he would ever give.

The Empire Sergeant's head rolled from his shoulders and his lifeless body toppled over. Before the nine soldiers could turn, the oarsman with the long blade dripping the NCO's blood attacked.

The oarsmen in front jumped forward and from the street and alleyway between the warehouses, another wave of oarsmen assaulted the Empire troops from the rear. In nine heartbeats, the nine Qart Hadasht soldiers died.

Captain Frigian stood near a wall in his polished Greek armor.

"Drag them to the dock and dispose of the bodies. But keep the armor and weapons, they have value," he ordered before walking back into the deep shadows.

Chapter - 27 Over the Rails to Glory

Alerio's first instinct was to swim out and cut the transports free. They would drift away, opening the channel for the boats hauling the Legionaries. He expressed the idea in a group meeting earlier.

Captain Milon Frigian, after settling down the men in the meeting, explained the transports were prize ships seized by the Sons of Mars. Not only were the transports valuable, they were owned by every member of the crews that had captured the cargo ships. Simply cutting them free was not an option.

***

Alerio guided the six unarmored Sons and four more to the point. Stacking the Legion shields so they faced the open water, he instructed, "Light a fire and keep it burning. Do not allow it to go out even after the first Legionaries have landed."

"We understand, Lieutenant," one of the armored men whispered. "You can depend on us."

Now with the signal to launch lit, another fire marking the Strait side of the harbor, and Adiona's flame to guide the boats down the center of the channel, he'd done almost everything to help with the Legion's attack on Messina. There was one more task.

The Legionary yanked off his armor. While the remaining sixteen oarsmen stripped off their armor, Alerio and the six unarmored Sons, waded into the water and swam for the Corbita in the center of the blockade.

***

The Strait flowed northward causing the roped together transports to bow outward. This worried Alerio as the Legion boats could reach Messina rapidly but they might over shoot it again. Had the flow been southward at a different time of night, this part of the mission would have been easier. The transports after being untied would drift into the harbor on the current. A northbound current meant special handling once the transports were untied. And there was another issue. The current was attempting to suck Alerio out of the harbor and into the Strait.

Steady strokes the Legion instructors during Recruit training had advised. Crossing water silently required slow controlled motions with your arms and legs. Alerio took in a mouthful of saltwater and spit it out as a mental response to the instructions. His motions were rushed and almost frantic as he fought the current. And to add to the problem, he and the swimmers needed to approach the middle transport as silently as possible.

He passed the first two transports with room to flounder unheard. Masked by the creaking of the wood at the bow and stern from tension on the hemp ropes, the distant splashing was indistinguishable from fish breaking the surface.

As the dark hull of the second ship fell behind and he neared the center of the channel, the current increased. Alerio, despite his powerful underwater strokes, began to drift between the transports. If he went to an overhand stroke, he could fight the flow. But he might as well hail the Qart Hadasht archers on the transport and invite them to use him for target practice.

Suddenly, an arm linked through his right arm and another his left. The oarsmen swimmers turned him and he realized the power of three pairs of legs. When two more joined on either side, the seven pairs of legs kicking below the surface easily propelled them. Silently, they swam as one entity back towards the harbor then turned and headed for the center Corbita.

***

Riding the water empty, the transport's rails loomed six feet above Alerio and the swimmers' heads. From the dark waters of the harbor channel, the hull appeared to be an unscalable cliff. And there was noise from above and below. The tension of the ropes connecting the ship to those tied to her stern and bow, fifteen feet away, tugged and twisted the frame creating groaning and creaks. Above, they could hear the Qart Hadasht archers talking. It seemed there had been action on the docks and the soldiers were concerned.

Alerio, after studying the ship, assumed they would dive deep and come up fast. Then leap out of the water and grab the rail at midship. Being the lowest point from the water, it might be possible. It would also be loud and alert the archers. While he pondered the suicide action, a swimmer pulled his arm. He followed and they paddled to the bow.

Above them, the curved bow and the bow beam seemed to arch into the night sky. Although not as high as the stern with the steering and observation deck, the front of the transport towered above the water. Then an oarsman placed his hands on either side of the bow beam. Three feet above the water, the beam emerged from the hull and flared out as it rose roughly following the curve of the bow.

The oarsman pressed his hands together on either side of the beam and pulled himself up. By bending his knees, he lifted his feet and placed the soles on the beam. Then he jumped his hands higher and lifted his feet to a new position. After three more clamps on the beam, the oarsman reached out and got a hand on the rail. He swung free but managed to grip the rail with his other hand. When the oarsman vanished from sight another oarsman kicked, emerged from the water and pressed his hands together on either side of the beam.

Alerio marveled as all six oarsmen climbed the bow beam in that odd manner. Alone in the water, he gritted his teeth in determination and kicked with his feet. As his upper body emerged from the water, he reached up and clamped onto the beam. To his surprise, the beam was rough. Although it took pressure to hold on while he lifted his body and legs, his palms didn't slip. With his knees thrusting to the sides, he placed the flat of his feet on either side of the beam. He climbed, not as rapidly as the oarsmen, but he reached a point where he could grab the ship's rail.

His first attempt almost found him falling and splashing loudly into the water. Then, he pressed harder with his feet and flung his right arm out. When his palm slapped the rail, he curled his fingers and held on tightly. He had to. The movement towards the rail pulled his body off the bow beam and he hung suspended by one arm. With a powerful pull, he rose enough to get the other hand on the rail. Pulling up, he peered over the rail at the deck.

In the dark, he made out six archers standing on the steering deck at the stern. Three held lit candles over their heads. A cooking brazier glowed with hot embers behind the cluster of men. Below him on the deck and against the rails were his six swimmers. Alerio eased over the rail and took a position with the Sons' oarsmen.

***

It wasn't unusual in combat situations for men to rush towards the enemy over great distances then stop before engaging. Legion instructors drilled Legionaries to attack instantly. Training involved running ten miles, forming ranks and, before the Legionaries could catch their breaths, running shield and sword drills. Even after training some men still held back in the face of the enemy.

The Sons had braved dark waters with strong currents, scaled an imposing obstacle and worked their way in close - all with bravado and creativity. Then, with the enemy in sight, they froze. Maybe it was the fear of death or a hesitation to purposely take another man's life. In either case, Alerio's six swimmers hugged the boards as if their job was done.

How to break the apathy? Leadership, the kind where one man's actions acted as a catalyst to inspire others or to get himself killed. Alerio pushed off the rough wooden boards of the transport and, alone, crept across the deck towards the archers.

The Legionary drew the long-curved dagger from its sheath. As the only weapon he carried, it seemed small and inadequate compared to the mission. Staying low and hugging the rail, Alerio traveled to midship in small light steps.

Equipment belonging to the Qart Hadasht archers was placed in individual spaces. As if being assigned to guarding a barricade ship wasn't remote enough, each soldier claimed a separate area of the deck. Close to Alerio, an archer's bedding appeared darker than the deck and his skirmisher's shield glowed lighter than the weathered boards.

After snatching up the shield, Alerio increased his pace. Better to attack and surprise the archers than to continue sneaking up, hoping none turned around. If any of them spotted him, they'd have time to prepare. He didn't want them prepared.

***

From cat like steps, Alerio accelerated to a full sprint for the last low section of the transport. Vaulting to the steering and rowing deck, he ran five steps and slammed the shield into the backs of two archers standing to the side of the unit. They stumbled forward and their thighs hit the rail. The momentum carried their torsos out over the side of the ship and, despite reaching for the rail, they flipped over and fell screaming until they splashed into the harbor. Their cries ended as they sank and the water closed over their heads.

The other four drew short-curved swords and spread out in a semicircle. The glowing embers in the brazier reflected off their blades.

One stabbed out and Alerio deflected the blade with the shield. Another blade he parried with his dagger. But a dagger, no matter how well-crafted, lacked the length to be effective in a sword fight. And a swordsman, no matter his skill, was only as good as his weapons. And to compound the situation, Alerio was mostly naked while the archers wore armor.

Alerio moved to his left, sliding his feet for balance and keeping the shield between the four blades and his bare skin. A sharp pain stabbed into the ball of his left foot. He ignored the pain although he lifted the foot as he circled.

An idea to kick over the brazier and spread the embers on the deck crossed his mind. But two things stopped the idea before it was fully formed. He was barefooted and hot coals would hinder him more than the soldiers. And he'd suffer the wrath of the Sons should he burn their prize ship to the waterline.

Now with his forward foot balanced on the heel to keep pressure off the ball, and his right supporting most of his weight, the smooth circling of a master swordsman, became lurching movements. The soldiers noticed and all four stepped forward to end the fight. Alerio limped back and his calf muscle touched the lower board of the rail.

Die or swim, the thought flashed in his mind. Either move would end his mission as the barricade remained in place and the Legion ships couldn't enter the harbor. And the Qart Hadasht troops would massacre the Sons of Mars on the dock. Alerio inhaled, set his shoulders, and gathered his legs for a final assault. Just before he committed to the reckless attack, the four soldiers were clubbed to the deck.

"Sorry it took so long," one of the swimmers apologized as he swung a club back and forth. "It took us awhile to locate the weapon's locker."

"Good timing," Alerio complimented the man as he sank to the deck and pulled his left foot around. A finger long splinter ran under the skin of the ball of his foot. Taking the end with two fingers, the Legionary eased the little spear free. Blood gushed from the hole and his entire foot throbbed.

"Experienced oarsmen lift their feet," one of the swimmers advised him. "Never slide your bare feet on a deck."

"Thanks, I'll remember that," Alerio said as he squeezed and rubbed the foot.

"Over the side with them," another oarsman ordered.

As the four soldiers were lifted, Alerio studied the feet and shoulders of the unconscious men.

"Wait. Not that one," Alerio said as he stood with most of his weight on the right leg. "I want to save his shoulder and chest armor. And, I need his sandals."

"You heard the Lieutenant. Strip him. Someone, go below and get a couple of ballast stones," an oarsman advised. "We don't want the Qart Hadasht scum to wake up and start swimming."

While the oarsmen pulled off the sandals and armor, Alerio picked up two swords and limped to the aft rail. He began slashing the thick hemp line.

A shout from the next ship in the barricade was followed by several arrows. But it was dark, and Alerio dropped his profile by bending down. Fifty cuts later, the last few fibers unraveled and the rope fell into the water. Free from the tension, the ship with the active archers drifted to the north still attached to the ship anchored on the western shoreline.

"Cut the bow line. Everyone else, secure an oar," a swimmer directed. "Then we row across the harbor and straight to the dock."

"No dock," advised Alerio. "We need to keep it clear for the Legionaries. You'll have to run her aground in the shallows."

"We can do that, Lieutenant Sisera," the oarsman replied.

***

Without the necklace of ships holding each other in place, Alerio's transport drifted on the northbound current pulling the other two ships with it.

It got quiet as the five men lowered oars through leather lined holes in the rail boards. The only sound was the chopping of the bow line. Alerio slipped on the right sandal and laced it up. Then slowly, he eased on the left sandal and winced as he tied it on. With most of his weight on the right foot, he stood and glanced down at the armor. It was unnecessary for the trip to the other side of the harbor but having it nearby made him feel better.

When the line fell, the man cutting it turned and shouted, "Standby oars. Stroke, Stroke.

Running sure footed down the deck, the man hit the ladder and rushed to the rear steering oars.

"Stroke, stroke," he instructed. Then, as the transport began moving, he looked in Alerio's direction, "They're having trouble on the other ship."

"Which ship?" inquired Alerio.

"While I was cutting us free, I heard the sounds of fighting," the oarsman explained.

Alerio looked down at the armor. As he bent to pick up the chest piece, he ordered, "Row alongside her. At least get close enough for me to board."

"Stroke, stroke," instructed the man as he adjusted the steering oars.

***

Alerio strapped on the shoulder pieces taking longer with the strange Qart Hadasht armor than he liked. Once dressed, he pondered the swords and shields laying on the deck. A few heartbeats later, he snatched up two swords and limped towards the bow of the transport.

As he reached the fore section, he heard the man at the stern call out, "Port side, standby to ship oars. Ship oars!"

The other transport's rail appeared in the dark. As Alerio stepped up on his rail, he heard the men in the rear shout, "Go with Mars, Lieutenant Sisera."

Then the rails glided by as the ships passed each other. The Legionary pushed off and flew over the gap. Below, the water, dark and deadly for an armored man, passed and he touched the rail on the other ship.

Six archers stood with bows raised firing arrows down the length of the transport. The shadowy outline of barrels and cargo hole covers marked their targets and the location of the Sons' boarding party.

Alerio jumped down and charged at the archers. Two fell off the steering and rowing platform, bleeding from neck wounds as they crashed to the cargo deck. One realized the danger and twisted to sight at the Legionary along his drawn arrow. But the Qart Hadasht armor confused him and he hesitated.

With no hesitation, Alerio shot his right foot forward, bent that knee and straightened his left leg. Leaning far over the bent knee, he thrust his sword into the man's belly. The arrow flew harmlessly over his head as the archer folded up, holding his stomach.

To recover, Alerio pushed off with the right foot and twisted. His intention was to pivot on his left foot to face the next closest archer. Pain, as the skin over the puncture wound ripped open, caused his left leg to spasm and involuntarily buckle.

Down on one knee, Alerio glanced up as the final three archers spun to face him. Looking at the barbed iron tips of the arrows and the solid horned encased war bows, he felt as if he was a red deer at the end of a hunt. In a desperate act of self-preservation, Alerio fell to the side and rotated on his shoulders towards the edge of the steering deck. Three arrows struck in the boards marking the passage of the rolling Legionary.

The archers notched another arrow and stepped to the edge looking to finish off their attacker. As they sighted down their arrows…

Alerio hit hard on his back and he exhaled violently from the impact. As if holding his breath, he ignored the pain and leaped to his feet with bent knees. While the left foot hurt, he was prepared for the throbbing and able to ignore it. Straightening his legs, he shot up slashing the front legs out from under two of the archers. With their legs spewing blood and folding, the archers fell over Alerio. The third archer's arrow hit one of them below the armor in the lower back saving the Legionary from the iron tip.

The archer shuffled back while pulling another arrow. He slipped the notch over the bowstring and drew the arrow back. As he raised the bow seeking his target, a sword spinning through the air passed the tip of his arrow and smashed into his face. The impact from the side of the blade did no more damage than forcing his head back. Jerking his head down, he tried to regain the sight along the arrow. Instead of finding a target, a fist found him first.

Alerio stood over the archer for a moment before bending down and punching through the opening in his helmet, again. Confused as blood exploded from his nose and his vision blurred, the soldier didn't understand the sensation of floating then flying. That was before he splashed into the harbor and he forgot about his nose and vision as he held his breath while sinking into the water.

Chapter – 28 Surprise Attack

Multiple candles from the blockade ships caused an alarm when the lookout reported them to the duty officer and the duty NCO. They both went to their superior officer. According to the sub-commander, who woke up angry at the disturbance, it wasn't important.

"It's more likely to be pirates attempting to take the ships. We have, and correct me if I'm wrong, a squad in the town, guards on the docks, a full squad patrolling the hook, and archers on the ships," he grumbled. "I don't see any reason to mobilize the entire garrison."

Three squads were bounced out of their beds and ordered to arm up. By the time Alerio and the oarsmen took control of the blockade ships, thirty Qart Hadasht heavy infantrymen stood in front of the Citadel. They weren't happy at being woken up in the middle of the night and then left standing around waiting.

Eventually, a young Lieutenant appeared. The NCOs called the squads to attention.

"What are our orders, sir?" one asked.

"We'll march to the docks and display Empire might," the Lieutenant replied. "March them out."

The Qart Hadasht infantry hoisted their shields and spears and marched down the hill towards the dock. No one thought the situation was important enough to notify Admiral Hanno.

***

A young man peered around the corner of a wall and counted the troops. Then he sprinted away, turned at the next corner and ran all out for six blocks. At the warehouses, he slowed down through the alleyway. Once on the dock, he sprinted until he reached the man in the shiny Greek armor.

"Captain Frigian. Thirty of their infantry are coming," he reported between deep breaths.

"Only three squads? Our luck is holding," Frigian ventured. Then to the men lounging around the dock, he ordered, "Sons of Mars. Grab your sword, shield, and adjust your mentula. Company is coming. Let's give them a warm welcome."

Moments later, high up on the street, movement appeared between the pools of light. As the Empire troops drew closer, they resembled a herd of deer running through the woods. Some details flashed as they entered a light then vanished until more were visible. Eventually, they solidified into two lines of marching troops.

"Shields up," ordered Frigian and a hundred shields lifted. They didn't click together as a well-trained Legion unit but there were enough to form a formidable wall across the street.

Seeing the crowd of shields, the Lieutenant held up a hand and the NCOs called the squads to a halt.

"In the name of the Qart Hadasht Empire, what is the meaning of this display?" demanded the officer. "Disperse now, Sons of Mars, or taste Empire justice."

A more experienced officer would have retreated and sent a runner for help. The Lieutenant's NCOs would have told him. But the officer was an aristocrat, young and not open to suggestions.

A man in Greek armor sauntered up behind the loose rows of shields.

"We can't do that," Frigian informed the officer.

"And why not?" bristled the Lieutenant.

"The Sons of Mars are defending the harbor with pirates," replied Frigian.

Misunderstanding what the man said, the officer explained, "The Empire will defend the harbor. You can leave."

While the officer got the meaning wrong, one NCO didn't. He marched to his Lieutenant.

"Sir, we should assume a defensive formation," he suggested.

"Sergeant, when I need your advice, I'll send my man servant to elicit it," scolded the Lieutenant.

"Yes, sir," the NCO replied as he marched back and resumed his place beside the files of troops.

"As I was saying before the interruption, the Empire will defend your dock and harbor," the Lieutenant assured the man.

"We seem to be at a stalemate," observed Frigian. "Maybe you should go back to the Citadel and ask Admiral Hanno."

"And what should I ask the Admiral?" sneered the Lieutenant.

"Ask him why you are so stupid," announced Frigian. Then he whistled two sharp notes and yelled. "Charge!"

Suddenly, the hundred shields ran forward. Swords appeared between the shields and the Empire NCOs shouted for a defensive formation. But another group of shields and swords rushed out of a house to the squads' rear.

In the first flurry, the Lieutenant fell to three blade slashes. Being shocked by the audacity of a bunch of pirates defying the Empire, he neither drew his sword or fell back to his troops. He simply died with his nose in the air and the assurance that fear of the Empire would protect him.

One NCO managed to rally six men and they fought back to back. They made it a few steps up the main road before the circle of pirates hacked them to death.

"What are our losses?" shouted Frigian.

"A couple of minor cuts," his lead oarsman replied. "They didn't have time to level their spears."

"We learned that lesson last time," admitted Frigian. "The next time, I'm afraid they'll be ready for us."

"Do you want me and the crew back in the house?" the oarsman asked.

"No. That won't work against a bigger force," explained the Captain. "Spread your men out along the alleyways and streets. I have a feeling the Empire is done with coming at us down the main road. Next time, we'll need to defend the entire warehouse district."

"Any sign of the Republic forces?" the oarsman asked as he began sending his men to other positions.

"We've moved the transports. I saw them rowing for the beach," Frigian said as he turned his head in the direction of the dark harbor. "But no signs of the Legion."

"Remember the time we tried to board that Greek merchant?" the lead oarsman inquired. "That was bad. Do you think this will be that bad?"

"You mean the merchant ship with a cargo of Greek Hoplites heading home from war?" confirmed Frigian. "Yes. This will be that bad."

***

The nineteen relief Guards stood outside the Citadel rubbing their eyes as they shook off the sleepy feeling. The fourth watch, besides being woken in the middle of the night, also meant patrolling until after dawn. It was the most boring watch in the dull port town of Messina.

In the Citadel, the relief Sergeant of the Guard paced. The S.O.G. he was to relieve hadn't reported in and hadn't advised the Officer of the Guard of any disturbances.

"Maybe he's tied up in that business with the three squads," the officer suggested.

"Sir, we have forty-nine men in town. Why has no one sent a runner with a report?" asked the Sergeant. "I'm going to patrol the town down to the dock. When I find the Sergeant of the Guard, I'll relieve him. If there is trouble, I'll send a runner."

"Fine with me," the officer said as he yawned. "I don't think you'll discover anything unusual. Even the candle signals from the blockade ships have stopped."

***

Outside, the Sergeant called his troops to order.

"The hairs on the back of my neck are standing up," announced the Sergeant. "When we find the Sergeant of the Guard, we'll relieve his people. Until then, I want a combat patrol. Shields off your backs and on your arms. Spearhead formation. Forward march."

With a man at the tip of the spear, then two behind him but close, the patrol descended the hill and entered the town. North to south and back, they crisscrossed Messina, dropping onto lower streets with every crossing. They found nothing in the upper sections of the town. Not the Sergeant of the Guard and his four escorts or the roving patrol. And most peculiar, no citizens lounging on the streets or people returning from visiting acquaintances.

When they completed the middle section and still hadn't located any Empire troops or civilians, the Sergeant called a halt.

"You four," the NCO stated pointing out the men who were to serve as his escort. "Return to the Citadel. Inform the Officer of the Guard that most of Messina is unguarded. We'll continue to patrol the lower section to the dock. But, I need an officer's advice. Go"

The four jogged to the center road and pounded through the dark town. They slowed a little once out of the Sergeants view. At the base of the hill leading to the Citadel, they started walking. It was too late at night or too early in the morning to be breaking a sweat.

***

161

The lower section was as empty as the upper areas and just as barren of Empire troops and citizens. They patrolled to the northern end of the town several streets from the base of the steps to the Temple of Adiona. The Sergeant halted his troops. Peering down the street, from five blocks away, he thought he saw shapes moving around in the dark by the last warehouse.

He marched the patrol on to the fourth street from the avenue at the warehouses and called another halt.

Selecting one of his fastest men, the Sergeant had him take off his armor and distribute the armor pieces, his shield, and spear to troops around the formation.

"We're marching south, just like we've been doing," advised the Sergeant. "I want you to take an alleyway down one block and shadow us. If anyone runs, follow them and let me know where they go."

Once the man had vanished into the deep shadows, the Sergeant ordered the unit to move out.

***

The young man from the Sons of Mars watched the Qart Hadasht patrol cross the main road. After being sure he knew there were fourteen, although he thought there were fifteen when he first started tracking them, he ran back to the next street and headed down for the docks.

He was stopped by four men in armor with shields at the alleyway between the warehouses. After a few quick words, the young man disappeared into the shadows.

162

Across the avenue, the Qart Hadasht soldier waited for the armed men to settle down. Then, he backed up the street staying in the shadows. At the fourth block, he turned and ran to catch up with the Sergeant.

Chapter – 29 Blood on the Dock

"One hundred eighty Qart Hadasht infantrymen should handle the rebellion," announced the sub-commander. "Two squads down each street and forty men straight at them down the main road."

"Yes, sir, that should be sufficient," an officer replied.

"Of course, it is. We'll test their resolve but wait for dawn to break their lines," sub-commander Gisco explained. "By midday, I want the rebel leaders crucified."

***

"What happened to the roving patrol?" Frigian wondered.

"None of our watchers have seen them since they crossed the road," his lead oarsman replied. "I don't like it."

"Like what? That the Qart Hadasht infantry is about to run their spears down our throats. Or that the Republic hasn't arrived?" Frigian inquired.

"Both Captain, both," the oarsman responded.

Seven young men burst from the streets and alleyways between the warehouses. They turned and, on the run, converged on Frigian.

"Qart Hadasht infantry, Captain," they all shouted. "From up the street I was watching."

"Hold on," pleaded Frigian. Then he pointed at each and asked, "All the streets?"

"Yes," came a unified reply.

"There's a tidal wave about to wash over us," Frigian shouted to the crewmen. "Just like on the deck of a ship, hunker down behind your shields, and let them come to you."

He sent the messengers off to alert those between and on the ends of the warehouses. Then, he addressed the oarsman near him, "Messina is our home. Many of us have known no other. We invited the Empire in and we have paid dearly for that mistake. Today, we evict the Empire. Today, we stand in a battle line as our forefathers stood. Strong, united as one, fearless and determined. We are the Sons of Mars!"

Most of the crewmen cheered. A few grumbled and some turned to Frigian.

"Isn't that the talk you gave us when we were rowing away from those Syracusan Triremes a few months ago?" several inquired.

"I changed a few words," admitted Frigian.

"Still, it's a good speech," one acknowledged as those questioning turned to look at the dark and empty streets.

***

The main road and the streets weren't empty for long. Marching boots, shields and spears held high soon covered the pavers at the entrances to all the road and streets intersecting with the avenue. Only the long warehouses and the guarded passageways between the buildings prevented the Qart Hadasht troops from marching straight to the dock.

"I am sub-commander Gisco," announced an Empire officer. "You will bring me the rebel leaders. Then you shall be permitted exodus through our lines to return to your abodes."

"Our Captains are elected," one oarsman shouted from behind his shield. "We'll need to gather and draw stones."

The sub-commander brightened at the prospect of the pirates surrendering their leaders. Then, he'd have his infantry cull the herd before allowing a few to live. He was elated until another oarsman responded.

"Does anyone have stones?" asked a voice from the massed rebels.

"We all do," another voice called out. "We're standing in this shield wall, aren't we?"

Laughter rolled over the sub-commander and his face flushed. Almost losing composure, he came close to displaying emotions in front of his troops. Instead of replying with useless harsh words, he turned his back on the rebels.

"Front ranks!" he shouted.

The words were repeated by Lieutenants stationed at all seven streets facing the warehouses.

"Front rank, forward!" the sub-commander bellowed.

Again, his words were repeated. Spears dipped and armored men marched onto the avenue.

The Sons of Mars advantages were the Qart Hadasht infantrymen had to come at them at an angle. None of the city streets lined up with the alleyways between the warehouses. This protected the Sons to their left and right as they braced their shields along the mouth of the alleys. They were vulnerable in only one direction and the infantry had to adjust before bringing their spears into play.

Captain Frigian stood behind his last rank feeling helpless. As if it was a heavy rain, the spearheads pounded the shields. One slipped into a gap, an oarsman cried out and fell back. The spear withdrew dripping the oarsman's blood. Others fell but were replaced by crewmen and their shields. It was purely defensive and the oarsmen were holding but, at a high cost.

Then the Empire sub-commander added to the Captain's worries.

"Second rank, forward!"

***

Alerio limped to the end of the dirt path and adjusted his pace. With his right foot, he stepped down onto the dock. From the shadows in the alleyway between warehouses, he made out the shapes of shields at the end of the passageway. Beyond them, Qart Hadasht soldiers stood in a semicircle jabbing with their spears. He hobbled swiftly into the alley.

"Pull back four steps," the Legionary shouted, "Pass the word. Four steps, on my count."

Some of the oarsmen in the rear turned to see who was shouting orders. They saw a mostly naked man still dripping seawater with a bleeding left foot. Then, one of them recognized him.

"Lieutenant Sisera has taken command," he bellowed. "Standby, four steps back on the Lieutenant's command."

"Step back!" shouted Alerio. The order, repeated through the ranks, was followed and the line moved inside the corners of the warehouses.

"Step back!" he called out again. When the rows moved this time, the spearheads from the soldiers on the sides could no longer reach the shields.

After two more steps, the Qart Hadasht soldiers hesitated.

"Douse the lanterns and fires behind you. Make them come in after you," Alerio told the oarsmen. "They'll have to bunch up in the dark. Hold here and if you can, grab a spear and drag the cūlus to your ranks. You know what to do with him."

"Are you staying with us, Lieutenant Sisera?" one asked.

"You've got this under control," Alerio assured them. "I've got to go check on less hardy oarsmen."

As Alerio limped away, an oarsman observed, "The Lieutenant isn't wearing armor. Why he's barely got anything on."

"That's because he wants to leave something for us to do," another crewman replied. "If he had armor and two swords, he'd kill the soldiers and leave us bored."

***

After pulling back another group of Sons and having the fires extinguished, so the walls forced the soldiers to enter a tight and dark space, Alerio limped up beside Frigian.

"Back four steps, Captain, and kill the lights behind your men," the Legionary suggested. "Use the walls to narrow their attack line."

Frigian snapped his head around at the voice. He'd been so focused on the fight, Alerio's arrival surprised him. Then he ran his eyes from the exposed chest down to the bloody foot.

"Didn't you leave undamaged with a nice set of Legion armor?" inquired Frigian. Before Alerio could explain, the Sons' Captain shouted, "Standby oars. Back one step."

The order was repeated and his line backed up. Three more times he called out and the oarsmen retreated deeper between the buildings. The Empire soldiers paused rather than march into the dark and guarded space.

"Went for a swim and picked up a splinter," stated Alerio. "A big splinter."

"Oarsmen know to lift their feet when walking on a deck," scolded Frigian.

"I'd love to stand here all night and learn the finer points of being a pirate," Alerio explained. "But you have two more lines that I need to pull back."

The Legionary reached down and picked up a dead oarsman's Greek shield and sword. With a nod, he hobbled towards the next alleyway.

***

"Recover your lines!" the sub-commander shouted. "We'll dig the rats out of their holes at daybreak."

Shortly after the soldiers retreated, Alerio limped back to Frigian's position and sat down on a crate. He lifted his left foot.

"We held them," gushed the Sons' Captain.

"At dawn, I'll wager you'll find my bloody footprints all along the dock," proclaimed Alerio.

"We usually cut the loose skin and bandage the raw meat," Frigian explained as he examined the foot in the light of a lantern. "It's like a blister. Open it up to saltwater and it'll heal in a day."

"I've had blisters on my feet and this hurt way more," replied Alerio.

"You'll never be a good pirate, Lieutenant Sisera," the Captain teased him. "You're too delicate."

Then the splashing of oars rowing in rhythm reached them. Holding the lantern out over the water, they saw nothing. But their eyes were looking for the bow of a transport ship. The noise came from lower, near the water level.

A Legion patrol boat eased into the light with a taunt tow rope attached behind the coxswain. At the end of the rope came a transport.

"Back it down," shouted Sergeant Martius from the coxswain position.

The patrol boat jerked to a stop but the transport drifted forward.

"I said, back it down!" the rowing instructor yelled. "Have you forgotten all of your training."

Curses came from the six rowers on the transport as well as splashing from their frantic efforts to stop the bigger ship. Finally, it eased until the ship floated and lines were thrown to the dock.

"Sergeant Martius, any trouble with the crossing or the marker fires?" Alerio called down.

"Lance Corporal Sisera? Is that you?" the Sergeant asked gazing up from the boat. "You are out of uniform."

"It's been a busy night," replied Alerio. "Are the signal fires positioned properly?"

"Yes. Now if you'll excuse me, I need to go back to Rhégion and collect you another half Century of Legionaries."

Fifty fully armored Legion heavy infantrymen and a Centurion climbed over the rails and down to the docks. Soon javelins and shields were passed over the side and distributed.

"Lance Corporal Sisera. You're out of uniform," an NCO observed as he marched up.

"First Sergeant Brictius. It's been a busy night. This is Captain Milon Frigian, commander of the Sons of Mars on the dock," Alerio said introducing the men.

"Captain Frigian. Nice to meet you," the First Sergeant said briskly. "Where is the heaviest concentration of enemy forces. We'll get Legionaries there right away."

"The Qart Hadasht soldiers have retreated for the night but it'll get ugly at dawn," Frigian said.

"Ugly for them," promised Brictius. "Show me your defenses so I can have my lads relieve yours."

The two walked away with Frigian pointing out the locations of his oarsmen. Alerio sat down on the crate and tenderly touched the rip on the bottom of his foot.

"Do you need help?" asked a Legion Medic.

"Doc. I do," Alerio exclaimed. The Medic glanced at the foot before pulling out a honey, mint and salt salve. As he smeared it on the puncture wound, Alerio let out a sigh and said, "Doc that feels great. Better than a mug of fresh goat's milk."

The Medic glanced up with a quizzical look on his face before shaking his head and returning to the task of bandaging the wound.

Another transport arrived behind the first ship and fifty more Legionaries disembarked. The Republic had landed a full Century of heavy infantry, their Centurion and NCOs, a half squad of signalmen, and skirmishers. Not enough to take the town but certainly enough to hold the dock and warehouse district of Messina.

Act 5

Chapter - 30 Sunrise Surprise

Alerio found a better fitting pair of boots. As he slipped his bandaged foot into the left boot, a familiar voice greeted him.

"Lance Corporal Sisera. A Greek shield and chest armor, Legion shoulder rigs, an Egyptian pit fighter helmet and an Illyrian sword," Gerontius stated observing Alerio's scavenged equipment. "It must have been a busy night."

"It was First Sergeant. Glad you could make it," Alerio offered with a grin. "First Sergeant Brictius and the Sons' Captain are walking the defense lines."

"I'm sure they're up to the task," the First Sergeant of the Southern Legion replied. "What I need is your opinion of where to put Tribune Claudius' command post."

"We'll need to push the Qart Hadasht troops back across the avenue and up a few streets," explained Alerio. "From there you'll have access to the Temple of Adiona. Other than the Citadel, it's the highest observation point in Messina."

Gerontius turned and looked to the north. The Temple and hill were in silhouette against the starry sky. Before the First Sergeant could turn back, an oarsman walked up behind him.

"Lieutenant Sisera. The men want to know if they can light a fire," the oarsman inquired.

Gerontius spun around and watched the exchange.

"Keep it out of view from the alleyway," Alerio instructed. "Behind the warehouse works. Have the Sons rotate between the shield wall and the fire until relieved by Legionaries."

"Yes, sir. And thank you for pulling us back," the oarsman said as he turned to go. "It was getting a might rough. Glad you finally got dressed though, Lieutenant. A naked officer is unsettling."

"Naked and an officer?" exclaimed Gerontius as the oarsman vanished in the dark. "I guess it was a busy night."

***

Alerio watched as two more transports were towed to the dock. Tribune Gaius Claudius climbed over the rail and as soon as he touched the dock, the First Sergeants, two Centurions, plus a Corporal of the signal corps rushed to greet him.

With two Centuries of heavy infantrymen landed, the Sons of Mars were relieved from their five locations. In the dark between the warehouses, oarsmen in mismatched gear were replaced by Legionaries with their heavy shields and javelins.

Seven transports made the crossing before a crown of white light appeared on the mountains to the east. The last one hundred Legionaries didn't arrive. At the sight of four

174

Qart Hadasht Triremes entering the Strait, the signalman in Rhégion Tower waved the ships and patrol boats to stand down. In the coming daylight, the sea and Strait once again belonged to the warships of the Empire.

***

"First two ranks, on line," shouted sub-commander Gisco. As his orders were repeated by Qart Hadasht Lieutenants, the senior officer faced the warehouses. "This is your last chance to end the rebellion. Send out your Captains and save yourselves. Or else, face the swords of the Empire."

"We can't do that," yelled Milon Frigian from the deep shadows. "You'll have to come in and get us."

"First two lines forward," ordered the sub-commander. "No mercy!"

All along the western edged of the avenue, soldiers marched from the eight streets. They angled to lineup with the warehouse alleyways and lowered their spears.

"Forward!" the sub-commander shrieked.

The soldiers were marching to the alleyways in three ranks followed by their Lieutenants. Their officers couldn't see over the tall helmets when they repeated the command. And the first rank didn't have the authority or right to question their officer's orders. They marched into the alleyways.

The long spears should have found gaps in the loose formation of the oarsmen's shields. With holes punched in the line, the soldiers would assault through, breaking the Son's line and the second and third ranks would follow killing those knocked down or wounded. It was a standard Qart Hadasht military tactic used successfully against armies and rebellious tribes. Every adversary of the Qart Hadasht Empire had broken from this style of assault.

The spearheads of the first rank deflected upward on the tilted Legion infantry shields. As the rank closed in on the uniformed wall of shields, the second and third rank pushed forward. From over the Legion attack line, javelin thrusts struck and many of the soldiers on the front rank were wounded or killed. Dead, injured, or struggling to draw their swords, they were pushed onto the Legion shields by the mercenary ranks coming from the rear.

"Launch two," shouted the Centurion, Century's Sergeant and Corporal from different alleyways.

Heavy iron tipped javelins arched over the clashing front ranks. When the Qart Hadasht Lieutenants witnessed soldiers in their last two ranks fall from the air assault, they stepped back looking down the avenue at the sub-commander for directions.

Sub-commander Gisco, confident in the success of the assault, lingered at the side of the avenue. With a mug of wine in one hand, he washed his face with a damp cloth held in the other. Precious moments were wasted as he handed the cloth to his man servant and tilted the mug to drain it. When he finally glanced around, he was momentarily shocked to see all of his Lieutenants waving the distress signal.

He couldn't comprehend the meaning. A few without experience panicking was to be expected. But all of his officers at once overwhelmed him. While he pondered the significance of the distress signs, his soldiers died in the alleyways.

Where the Qart Hadasht's leadership failed, the Legion's command excelled.

***

Tribune Gaius Claudius positioned himself at the center of the dock. On his right was Centurion Valerian, the newly appointed Senior Centurion of his expedition. First Sergeant Brictius stood to his left. Both men faced away from the Tribune.

"Initial assault broken on the right, Tribune," announced Valerian after receiving positive signs from two signalmen.

"First Sergeant?" inquired Claudius.

"One positive and one holding, sir," Brictius explained the delay. A few heartbeats later, he reported. "Initial assault broken on the left, Tribune."

"Signal the advance," ordered Claudius.

With hand signs, the Senior Centurion and the First Sergeant unleashed the Republic's heavy infantry.

***

On the other side of the avenue, the next two ranks of Empire soldiers waited for orders. They could see the

Lieutenants signaling franticly but their Sergeants called for them to wait. Their feet shuffling nervously and their shields lifted in anticipation, they waited.

In the alleyways, the second and third ranks of the soldiers shoved forward. Not that they wanted to reach the unmoving shields and the javelins but to escape the falling javelin heads. There was a safe zone between the rear and the jabbing iron tips from the Legionaries. As men in combat who took time to think or pause for a moment, the survivors of the second and third ranks bunched up in the zone.

The sub-commander decided that all of his Lieutenants were cowards or unprofessional and lacking the fear and respect of their soldiers. After this was over, he'd ship them all back to Qart Hadasht in shame. There was always a new batch of nobly born brats to replace them.

"Third and fourth ranks, forward!" he shouted. Then under his breath, he whispered, 'I'd better replace the Sergeants as well. And have them whipped for dereliction of duty, to impress on the new ones the need for discipline."

As the Lieutenants repeated the sub-commander's order, Senior Centurion Valerian and First Sergeant Brictius' signs were passed from the signalmen to the Centurions or NCOs in the alleyways.

"Front rank, standby to draw. Draw!"

Javelins were hastily passed back and by the count of four, gladii were yanked from sheaths.

"Advance. Advance. Advance!"

The safe zone in front of the Legion lines vanished as the shield walls shot forward then retreated. In their place came steel blades. Again, and again, the progressing shields slammed into the soldiers and before they could recover, the blades stabbed out. None of the first three ranks that went into the alleyways marched out. Their bodies, hacked and stomped, were unrecognizable by the time the hobnailed boots passed over them.

***

On the streets, the next two ranks of Qart Hadasht soldiers stepped off briskly and angled towards the mouth of the alleys. They met and merged into three ranks. The leading ranks lowered their spears. Their Lieutenants stepped to the side to allow the ranks to enter the narrow space.

Suddenly, flights of javelins sailed from between the warehouse walls. With javelins hanging from legs and shields, the front rank faltered. Then, four ranks of Legionaries appeared. Without pausing, they smashed into the surprised Qart Hadasht soldiers.

***

"Contact on the avenue, Tribune," both Valerian and Brictius reported at almost the same time.

"Show the Qart Hadasht some depth," ordered Gaius Claudius.

Valerian and Brictius held up the hand facing the warehouses and motioned with the fingers of the other hand towards the upright hand.

Signalmen spoke to squad leaders, and the final twenty-six Legionaries marched into the alleyways. Instead of engaging, they stopped at the avenue holding their gladii low and their shields high.

What the Qart Hadasht sub-commander saw and feared were alleyways full of uniformed and ordered military ranks. Believing his troops were outnumbered and about to be slaughtered, he called out to his Lieutenants.

"Retreat. Back four blocks and setup defensive positions!" he bellowed as he pushed aside soldiers blocking his way as he fled up the town's wide center road.

"The right side Qart Hadasht forces are withdrawing, Tribune," reported Senior Centurion Valerian.

"They are withdrawing on the left side as well, sir," Brictius said moments later. Then he added, "Nicely played, sir."

Despite the cool morning air and the fresh breeze coming off the harbor, Tribune Gaius Claudius was sweating.

"I wonder if it would have worked if their commander realized we only had twenty-six infantrymen in reserve at the alleyways?" Claudius asked as much to himself as to the Senior Centurion and the First Sergeant.

"Should we pursue, Tribune?" Valerian asked.

"I don't want us stretched too thin," Gaius Claudius explained. "Get a forward squad patrolling on every street as if we owned Messina. We'll see how far they run."

Senior Centurion Valerian and First Sergeant Brictius marched off in different directions. Their signaling calling duties done, it was time they organized the expedition personally.

Chapter - 31 Hilltop Command

Sweat ran down the sub-commander's face and his ornate plumed helmet partially blocked his vision from where it twisted sideways during the run. At the top of the hill, he slowed and straightened the helmet. There was nothing he could do about the sweat because it was a result of the run and who he faced in the Citadel.

"Sun-commander Gisco, reporting," he announced as he walked into the Admiral's office.

"Sub-commander, are you well?" asked Hanno setting down a quill. "You seem feverish."

"Admiral. The rebellion by the Sons of Mars was a diversion for an invasion," Gisco stammered between deep breaths.

"An invasion?" inquired Hanno as he leaned back in his chair and stretched. His rib cage expanded and, under his robe, the muscles rippled across his chest. "And just who are these invaders?"

"The Republic, Admiral. They must have crossed the Strait during the night," ventured Gisco. "As uncomfortable as it was, I remained with our troops after an initial engagement with the Sons. I thought if I gave them until morning, they would surrender. When we assaulted, five hundred Legionaries countered. I ordered a retreat and we set up defensive positions."

"Five hundred Legionaries in Messina?" Hanno stated. He stood, walked out of his office, through the main hall and out the reinforced doors. At the top of the slope, he gazed down on the town. "I would think if there were five hundred of the dirt farmers, they would be marching up the main road by now."

"Well, maybe I over estimated, sir," Gisco offered. "They came out from between the warehouses and attacked. I could see more staged there and took the best course of action."

"And the best course?" Hanno asked with a tilt of his head.

"I pulled our forces back four streets and set up barricades," explained Gisco.

"A fighting retreat?" asked Hanno.

"Ah, no Admiral," Gisco confessed. "They didn't follow us."

"Let me see if I have all the details, sub-commander," sneered Hanno. "After one skirmish, you retreated and surrendered a quarter of Messina to a band of garlic eating savages. Is that right?"

"If you put it like that, Admiral," replied Gisco. "Yes."

"I do put it like that," Hanno said with exasperation. "Call out the garrison and pull two companies from the southern wall. Do it now, sub-commander. Do not stop for breakfast, a glass of wine, or to use the latrine. Understand?"

"Yes, Admiral. Right away," Gisco responded as he headed back into the Citadel to alert the duty officer and have him send out runners.

Admiral Hanno let his eyes roam over the town. From the hill, he could see details on the upper section. Further down, the houses blocked more of the streets and the lower section was a cluster of maze-like runs. Beyond the warehouses, the harbor reflected flashes of the morning sun and he observed Empire warships on the Strait. At least he didn't have to worry about more Legionaries crossing with the Triremes guarding the eastern approach to the town.

Then his eyes caught movement on the hill at the Temple of Adiona. He stood watching as men stretched something on the ground. Moments later, an ugly goatskin tent expanded blocking half the clay bricks of the temple building.

A group of men climbed the stairs and at the top, one turned. Even at a distance, Hanno felt as if the man was staring at him. The Admiral bared his teeth and growled at the man before realizing if he couldn't see details other than shiny armor and a hint of color on the man's helmet, the man couldn't see his challenge.

'Dirt farmers,' Admiral Hanno thought as he spit on the ground. 'Not in my town.'

183

"Who is the big guy at the Citadel?" questioned Tribune Claudius. He stopped at the top of the stairs to gaze across town at the higher elevation.

"I can make out two people, but I couldn't tell sizes other than one appears larger," confessed First Sergeant Gerontius. "You have good eyesight, sir."

"I have always been blessed by the Goddess Theia," admitted Claudius looking away from the hill. He took in the command tent set up beside the temple. "This location is excellent with a good view of the eastern sector of Messina. Although, I'd rather be on Citadel hill."

"That's why we're here, sir," Gerontius commented.

***

"Signalman, send two squads to reinforce the squad at the southern end of the street," Tribune Claudius ordered.

"Yes, sir," the man answered as he picked up two flags and started motioning with them

"What's going on, Tribune," Milon Frigian inquired. He squinted at the section of wall eighteen blocks away. To him, it was mostly haze with a few murky details.

"There is activity over the city wall," the Tribune explained. "Could be an assault from that direction."

"Tribune, without a doubt you are blessed by Theia. But there's no advantage to attacking the end of your line in a city," Frigian suggested. "It's probably a diversion."

"A diversion," pondered Claudius as he studied the town below him. While he enjoyed great vision, he couldn't see through buildings. So, he looked where he could see and that's when a flash caught the midday sun. Then another flash as a body ran between two large homes on the north side of Messina. "Signalman. Flag First Sergeant Brictius. Tell him to expect an immediate attack."

"What are you thinking?" inquired Frigian.

"I'll tell you, Captain. The Qart Hadasht are going to come over the south wall making a lot of noise and putting on a show," Claudius explained. "But the real show will be below us on the north side. I imagine they'll try and break through our lines. If they do, they'll head up the stairs directly for my command post."

"Cutting the head off the snake, so to speak, sir?" replied Frigian.

"Exactly. Can you put some Sons on our lines on the south streets to back up my Legionaries?" Claudius asked.

"Yes, Tribune, I can do that," Frigian assured him. "But any soldiers we kill, we keep their armor and weapons. Deal?"

"You really are pirates, aren't you?"

"Sons of Mars born and bred, Tribune," bragged Frigian.

"It's a deal, Captain Frigian," Claudius assured the pirate.

185

Frigian rendered a sloppy salute, grinned and ran down the stairs. His hundred or so oarsmen were lounging around the dock. Their Captain soon vanished behind a warehouse heading in that direction.

"Not a bad choice, sir," First Sergeant Gerontius commented. "We left a Century of skirmishers in Rhégion. Why not let the Sons of Mars take their place?"

"Tell me, First Sergeant. Which would you rather have?" inquire Tribune Claudius. "One hundred and twenty pirates or eighty Legion Velites?"

"The Legionaries of course," Gerontius replied.

"So, would I. But our Velites are across the Strait and the Sons are here," Claudius said. "My choice isn't good or bad, it's just convenient."

"I'm going down and help Brictius," announced Gerontius. "Any orders, sir?"

"Watch your flanks. In a town, the enemy can come through a compound and you won't see them until they're a blade's distance from you. Brictius taught me that," responded the Tribune. "Take care of my First Sergeant."

First Sergeant Gerontius saluted, turned on his heels and jogged down the stairs. Half way down, he smiled. Tribune Gaius Claudius, in a short time, had become a Legion combat leader. Always learning and always teaching. The type of officer all Legionaries hoped for and often didn't get.

***

"First Sergeant Gerontius, get bored being with the command staff?" teased Brictius.

"The Tribune spotted Qart Hadasht soldiers sneaking down on your side," Gerontius explained. "He's using the Sons of Mars to free up squads for your position."

"Good. Let's see how the Empire does in a face to face fight," replied Brictius.

The Lance Corporal of the first squad to arrive halted his men and walked over to the First Sergeants.

"Senior Centurion Valerian said you're in charge, First Sergeants," the squad leader informed the two senior NCOs. "He wants to keep the officers on the main road and on the south side to manage the Sons of Mars."

"Park your squad between the streets," Brictius explained. "If they hit us on more than one street, I want you available as a reserve."

Soon, nine more squads reported to their location. The fifty heavy infantry men stood between the streets with half facing First Sergeant Brictius at the intersection of one road and the other twenty-five facing First Sergeant Gerontius at the other. In addition to the ten squads, there were thirty-six infantrymen already guarding each street.

Brictius commented that one hundred and twenty-two of the Republics finest could hold the blocks against an army of Qart Hadasht soldiers. Later, he would come to regret the statement.

***

The tops of ten ladders popped up over the southern city wall.

"Standby javelins," ordered Senior Centurion Valerian. "Skirmishers, forward. Take them as they come over."

The seven Velites, who had made the crossing, ran between the three ranks of the squads. At the base of the wall, they placed five-extra javelins on the ground. Then with their right arms holding javelins, they waited.

Moments passed and Valerian began to think the ladders were just for show. Then the ladders shook and ten tall conical Empire helmets appeared. From over the wall, faces, shoulders, and arms rose into view. Spears, obviously passed up to the ten, were raised. As if to draw attention to themselves and to intimidate, they waved the shafts in the air.

They did draw attention but not from the heavy infantrymen. The Velites launched seven javelins and seven soldiers fell out of sight with iron javelin tips in their chests. Rapidly, three more were launched and the last of the Qart Hadasht soldiers fell away.

To the Legionaries surprise, the ladders shook as ten more soldiers climbed the ladders and hoisted spears. Again, the skirmishers swept the wall clear of the Qart Hadasht soldiers.

"They sacrificed two squads for nothing," one of the Lance Corporals said.

"Steady there," advised Valerian. "There has to be a reason to waste the lives of your men. I just don't know why. Be ready."

Then the ladders shook but, this time, soldiers started flowing over the wall. They came over hugging the top before dropping to the ground. Seven died as they were hit by javelins. Seven more were injured but the numbers scrambling over the wall outpaced the Velites' ability to throw. When the last javelin launched, the skirmishers drew their gladii preparing to engage the thirty uninjured Empire soldiers.

"Velites. Withdraw through the ranks," Senior Centurion Valerian ordered. Then he announced, "They may waste lives but the Legion doesn't. Squads standby. Front rank, draw. Squads Forward."

As the soldiers attempted to collect themselves into ranks, the Legionnaires marched at them. Left foot down then stomping with their right, the rhythm of the stomp caused the soldiers to look up. Shields locked together, moved towards them and, over the shields javelins waved in the air.

The Qart Hadasht Sergeants shouted for their men to form ranks and most did. But enough hesitated so when the Legion front rank approached, those soldiers left holes in their formation.

"Advance. Advance," called out Senior Centurion Valerian.

And the shields hammered forward rocking the Qart Hadasht front line. The gladii thrusts that followed dropped several and panic ran through the soldiers of the Empire. Some turned to the sides getting ready to run off.

"Third rank lateral right five steps," instructed Valerian. "Second rank lateral left five steps."

His orders were repeated by the Lance Corporals and repeated again by the squad's pivots. Almost as if they had planned the maneuvers, the squads shifted extending the front line to twenty Legionaries. It was more than enough to prevent any Empire soldier from escaping the deadly thrusts of the shields and the gladii.

***

The runner pounded down the street, hooked a right and raced through a gate. In the compound, he slid to a stop.

"Sub-commander, sir. Sub-commander Barca has begun the assault over the southern wall," the runner reported.

Gisco marched to where Admiral Hanno sat on a home's patio.

"Admiral. Sub-commander Barca's forces have begun their assault," Gisco reported. "Should we gather the soldiers?"

"Not yet, Gisco. Give the farmers a chance to rush reinforcements to defend their flank," the Admiral replied. "I've heard they overreact to everything like children playing. Well, the games end today because the Empire is about to do some mentoring. Once they've weakened the north side, we'll sweep the remaining clod busters from Messina and end this fiasco."

"Very good, Admiral," Gisco said before strolling over to where their Lieutenants lounged along a wall. There, the sub-commander explained how he and the Admiral had devised a plan to drive the Republic forces into the harbor.

The Lieutenants were tired of the sub-commander's bragging and the waiting around. But as officers in the Qart Hadasht military, they listened to their superior officer. Even if the knowledge he shared was thin on experience and long on theory.

"Sub-commander Gisco," Admiral Hanno called softly from the patio.

"Admiral, is it time?" Gisco asked as he walked across the compound.

"Split our forces," instructed Hanno. "Put a Company on one and another on the adjacent street."

"That's a hundred troops on just two streets," Gisco responded. "Shouldn't we split the Companies up. Then, we can open three or more fronts?"

"I prefer this not to become a battle of attrition," Admiral Hanno explained. "Concentration of force, sub-commander, dictates we employ a superior force to breach their lines. Once we've broken through, we'll split our forces to engage their splintered units."

"Yes, sir. I'll brief the Lieutenants," Gisco replied.

***

First Sergeant Brictius couldn't see what action was taking place on the south end of Messina. But he had a good view of Temple hill. The signalman at the top kept flashing the hold positions sign so he knew something was happening.

The street uphill from his Legionaries was empty. A quick glance at First Sergeant Gerontius let him know that street was also empty. So far, after the big rush to get him the reserve squads, nothing changed. The squads sat and talked, the birds sang, and the streets were peaceful.

Then from blocks away, faint and garbled shouts echoing off the walls and sides of homes reached him. He didn't understand the words but First Sergeant Brictius recognized commands when he heard them.

"Legionaries, stand up and gear up," he ordered. "We have visitors. Let's give them a Legion welcome."

"Standing up, First Sergeant," the infantrymen replied as they stopped sharpening and sheathed gladii, packed away half eaten pieces of food, capped water skins, and picked up their shields and javelins. On the other street, First Sergeant Gerontius' squads mirrored the preparations.

Brictius studied his Legionaries. Twelve shields wide, they stretched across the road in three ranks. Holding up a hand, he motioned over a Century's Corporal standing with the reserve squads.

"What do you need, First Sergeant," the Corporal asked as he marched up.

"Give me your opinion of our position and strength?" he responded.

"We're too close to the end of the houses," the Corporal replied. "If we have to step back, we'll be in the intersection and the Qart Hadasht can flow around our lines."

"You're right. And our strength?"

"Closed in on both sides, there's nowhere for the injured to go," the Corporal related. "If we have to push, we'll need more than three ranks to plow through their bodies."

"Good analysis," complimented the First Sergeant. "Call up a reserve squad and make them the fourth rank. They'll be short two but I don't want to break up a squad."

"Right away, First Sergeant," the Corporal said as he turned and went to speak with a squad leader.

"Squads stand by, forward ten paces," Brictius ordered.

***

The Legionaries had just reset when, far up the street, Qart Hadasht soldiers entered from a side road. Their front ranks marched into the intersection and turned towards the Legion lines. Five abreast, the columns stretched back and the tail's end vanished around the corner. More soldiers emerged until a full Company marched at the Legion lines.

"There must be a thousand of them," a Legionary remarked.

"You can't count, Private," his squad leader responded. "Five times twenty is one hundred. It's a standard infantry Company for the Qart Hadasht military."

"Maybe I don't count so good," the private observed. "But it sure looks like a thousand to me."

"How many men in a Century?" quizzed the Lance Corporal.

"Eighty infantrymen," answered the Private.

"See, only twenty more men than in a Legion's Century," explained the Lance Corporal.

"Still looks like a thousand to me," the Private insisted.

"First rank, stand by to draw," Brictius ordered from behind the ranks.

"Standing by, First Sergeant," twelve voices responded.

He waited as the Qart Hadasht columns closed to within fifteen paces. Then, orders rippled down from the Company's rear. Swiftly and professionally, the columns expanded to ranks ten across.

The Qart Hadasht soldiers and the Legionaries stared over their shields at each other waiting for the next order.

***

Tribune Claudius wanted to pace, yell or hit something. When First Sergeant Brictius repositioned the

Legionaries further up the street, he lost sight of the unit. Although he could still see the First Sergeants' four remaining reserve squads, he had no view of the enemy forces after brief glimpses of them passing through intersections. But he didn't pace. Instead, he scanned the town seeking clues about the Empire's positions or movements.

Most of Messina, at least on the eastern sectors where he could see, were stable. Then his eyes stopped scanning. At cross streets, about three blocks from First Sergeant Brictius, a man in a gold cloak and dressed in gold trimmed armor stood staring up at him. He wasn't positive but it looked like the big man he'd spotted on Citadel Hill.

Runners raced up to the man, talked and listened for a moment before rushing off down the streets. During the exchanges, the man never took his eyes off of Claudius.

Assuming the man was Admiral Hanno, the commander of the Qart Hadasht forces, Tribune Gaius Claudius brought his heals together and gave his opponent a crossed chest salute. He held the fist against his breast plate waiting for an acknowledgement.

Hanno, although Claudius couldn't make out the details, sneered and bared his teeth. What Tribune Gaius Claudius did see clearly was the Admiral spitting in his direction before marching out of view.

Gaius Claudius dropped his fist and rested it on the pommel of his gladius. Now, he neither wanted to pace, yell or throw something. What he desperately wanted was to run down the stairs, draw his gladius and kill the arrogant Admiral. But he didn't.

The Tribune returned to scanning the town searching for ways to gain an advantage. Revenge would come later, once he commanded Messina.

***

"Draw," shouted First Sergeant Brictius as the first rank of Qart Hadasht soldiers sprinted forward. "Brace! Brace!"

The front rank pulled their gladii and crouched down behind their shields. Behind them, thirty-four Legionaries bent their knees, leaned forward slightly, pushed their shields into the backs of the men in front of them and tightened their shield arms. When the soldiers collided with the Legion shields, they bounced off the inflexible wall.

The second and third ranks ran forward expecting to charge through holes made by their first rank. Confusion set in when the rank bounced back. The soldiers suddenly idled for a heartbeat.

"Advance, step back," ordered First Sergeant Brictius taking advantage of the situation.

The front twelve Legionaries lunged with their shields, plunged their blades into flesh and dropped back into the formation. It happened so rapidly, the Lieutenants standing beside their soldiers didn't understand why men fell to the ground.

Hesitation in combat kills - delayed response from their junior officers, from the survivors of the first three ranks, and from the overall Qart Hadasht Company commander proved it. Failure to adjust allowed First Sergeant Brictius a second opportunity.

"Advance, step back," he ordered.

Again, twelve shields shoved forward shocking those contacted. Before they recovered from the impact of the big shields, gladii blades thrust forward and more of them died.

"Second rank rotate forward," First Sergeant Brictius ordered.

All the Legionaries in the unit unfolded their left arms placing their shields perpendicular to their bodies. The first rank stepped back between the spaces and continued until they were in the rear of the formation. Almost as quickly as the shields opened to allow passage, they were pulled back across chests. Now Legionaries with fresh arms and legs manned the front rank.

Commands rippled down the Empire Company formation and the soldiers shuffled nervously. First Sergeant Brictius recognized the symptoms of men asked to perform a dangerous task. He decided to give them something to add to their misery.

"Stand by Javelins," he shouted. "Launch two!"

At close range to the opposing forces, the javelins flashed from hands to bodies in a heartbeat. Two launches and there were holes in the Company where wounded and dead fell out of formation. This got the Qart Hadasht commander's attention and he passed down orders. Suddenly, the entire company ran at the Legionaries.

"Brace, brace!" shouted First Sergeant Brictius just before a tide of soldiers washed over the Legionaries.

At first, Brictius couldn't see anything but the faces, helmets, and armored shoulders of Empire soldiers crawling on his Legionaries' shields.

"Push!" he yelled, to be heard over the grunts and cries of men struggling against enemies, their own sense of survival, and the mass of bodies pressed together. "Push!"

And Qart Hadasht soldiers rose into the air on rising shields. The higher the shields the more soldiers slid off and the straighter the Legionaries stood. One tilted back and a soldier tumbled behind the ranks.

A Private stepped up and drove his blade between the man's ribs.

"Advance, step back," ordered First Sergeant Brictius.

The shields shoved the leading edge of the Empire soldiers back and the gladii thrust helped to maintain the gap for a moment.

"Second rank rotate forward," Brictius ordered and, like sideways window slats, the shields opened and the front rank came off the line.

But only nine of the twelve made it to the rear. Three were down under the feet of fighting and scuffling Legionaries and soldiers.

The battle for the street became a blur of slashes, hacks, and jabs. Legionnaires and soldiers injured and killed each other. And First Sergeant Brictius was forced to feed his reserve squads into the meat grinder as the number of wounded and dead piled up behind the lines.

Even in the chaos of belly to belly fighting, the well-trained Legionaries responded to the call of rotating off the front line. While the Legion valued the ability to put fresh arms and legs into a fight, the Qart Hadasht military hadn't learned that lesson.

When the Empire Company commander passed the word to withdraw the remaining exhausted soldiers, First Sergeant Brictius had just rotated his ranks. As the Qart Hadasht attempted to retreat, the Legionaries received a different set of orders.

"Advance, advance," instructed Brictius.

The shields shot out downing soldiers who were stomped as the unit attacked. Gladii stabbed the stumbling and disoriented soldiers as they ran. And still, the Legionaries continued their assault.

"Corporal, on me," Brictius called out.

"Yes, First Optio," the Century's Tesserarius acknowledged. He was covered in blood with bags under his eyes from rotating to the front and fighting. He also sported a number of cuts and bruises.

"Get to First Sergeant Gerontius' position," Brictius instructed. "Tell him, we're taking five more blocks than setting up a barricade. Let me know if he's able to keep up."

"On it, First Sergeant," the Corporal replied before jogging away on rubbery legs.

***

Tribune Claudius watched as the Qart Hadasht soldiers ran in panic from Legionaries in perfect formation chasing them down.

"Signalman. All units to move up four, no wait, five blocks," the Tribune ordered.

As the flags waved, a weight lifted from Claudius' chest. With the harbor, warehouse district and half of Messina in Legion hands, he was close to victory. And completing his mission of supplying General Caudex a safe harbor on Sicilia for the Legion. The one remaining task, remove Admiral Hanno from the town.

***

Admiral Hanno strutted up the hill to the Citadel. While he had lost a battle, he was confident he'd win the war. One simply did not become an Admiral of the Empire and not believe in the destiny of the world's largest trading empire and naval power. No country could stand against Qart Hadasht. If need be, he'd starve them out. With a last glare at Temple hill, he marched into the Citadel.

Chapter – 32 War of Words

Tribune Claudius frowned as he wrote casualty reports from the day's actions. Too many men injured and far too many Legionaries died. A knock on the tent pole pulled him from the reports.

"Tribune. There is a Qart Hadasht messenger here to see you," a Legion Sergeant announced.

"Bring him," Claudius stated as he placed his quill in a holder.

A man wearing a white tunic with a thin belt was escorted across the command tent to the Tribune's work area. He clutched a scroll in his left hand. As he approached, the messenger extended his left arm. The Sergeant slapped it down.

"That's close enough," the NCO warned as he placed a hand on the man's chest. "I'll take the scroll."

The Sergeant examined the wooden end caps, sniffed it and partially unrolled it. Once satisfied the document holder was safe, he handed it to Claudius.

"Thank you," the Tribune acknowledged as he took the scroll.

After unrolling it, he began reading.

Tribune Gaius Claudius,

I greet you only out of necessity. You are an invader in Messina and have upset the balance of power in Sicilia. You and your killers will leave at dawn. Although distasteful to me, my magnanimous gesture of safe passage to Rhégion holds until the sun rests on high.

Should your arrogance exceed your senses, the outlaws who follow you will be put to the sword. You will suffer a cut for every soldier who died defending the town. After the blood sacrifice, your body will be crucified as a cautionary tale for the Sons of Mars, the upstart Republic, and any who defy the undying Empire.

Admiral Hanno of the Qart Hadasht Empire

"Sergeant take the messenger outside and hold him until I craft a response," Claudius ordered. "And find me Senior Centurion Valerian."

"Yes, sir," the NCO said as he guided the messenger out of the tent.

"What to say to you, Admiral?" Claudius whispered while rereading the message.

***

The messenger ran up Citadel hill and didn't break stride until he stood in front of the duty officer.

"Sir, a message from the Legion commander for the Admiral," he reported.

"Come with me," ordered the officer. He guided the messenger to a closed door, knocked, and opened it. "Admiral. The messenger has returned with a reply."

"Send him in and find me, sub-commander Barca," Hanno instructed.

The officer opened the door and the messenger bowed and scurried to the desk.

The Admiral held out a big hand for the scroll. Once in his hand, he broke the seal, unrolled the parchment and studied the words.

"I'll have a reply. Wait outside," instructed the Admiral.

"Tonight, sir?" the messenger asked.

Under the glare of Hanno's stare, the messenger nodded and backed out of the office. When the offending little man was gone, the Admiral reread Claudius' reply.

To the Honorable Admiral Hanno,

Greetings my worthy opponent. I write this with no malice or qualms. Messina is under the protection of the Republic. History tells the tale of the Sons of Mars connection to the Republic and, as such, they are under the protection of the Republic. And lest I remind you, not for embarrassment's sake, but to refresh your memory. My Legionaries freely patrol the harbor, the warehouse district, the Temple of Adiona, and half of Messina.

The Empire for all its vast holdings elsewhere, tenuously occupies the Citadel, the upper half of Messina and the southern wall. In balance, I suggest you accept my offer of safe passage to your two Triremes beached in the Republic's harbor.

Take them and go where you will, as long as you vacate Messina in its entirety.

Gaius Claudius, Tribune of Caudex Legion, Representative of Consul Appease Clodus Caudex, Consul Marcus Fulvius Flaccus, the Senate of the Republic, and Citizen of the Republic

***

"Halt," a Legion sentry ordered. "Who goes there?"

The messenger stepped forward into the flickering light of the campfire.

"I carry a missive from Admiral Hanno to Tribune Claudius," the man stated. Visibly nervous, his hands shook as he held them out showing they were empty of weapons. Clutched in his left hand was a rolled and sealed piece of parchment.

"Sergeant. We have a courier," the sentry called out.

Long moments passed before an NCO and two Legionaries, all three helmetless and without shields, materialized from the dark.

"Why are you so far south?" inquired the Century's Sergeant. "Temple hill is way north of here."

"I got lost," the messenger stammered. "This is where they, ah, I found myself crossing the Empire's barricade."

The Sergeant lifted his head and peered up the street. One block away, a Qart Hadasht campfire burning at that intersection marked the barrier.

"Take him to the Centurion. Let the officer find an escort to take him to the Tribune," the Sergeant advised. Then he yawned, reared back, arms extended and mouth open wide to fully vocalize the action before telling the

Legionary. "Off you go. And hurry back to your sentry duties."

The sentry ushered the messenger away from the fire and they vanished in the dark. Pausing to warm their hands around the fire, the NCO and two Legionaries stood wordlessly before they too walked out of the light.

"Go to our other positions and get four unarmored men for a little night reconnaissance," whispered the Sergeant. "Have them quietly check the walls. There has to be a reason they sent the courier this far south. I want whoever is watching us."

On the walls of the compounds bordering the street, two Qart Hadasht scouts watched the lackluster Sergeant. On opposite sides of the street, each had scurried over compound walls and crossed four courtyards just before sundown. When darkness fell, they climbed onto the tops of the last walls and used overhanging branches as cover. Both smiled when they observed the Legionaries' relaxed response to the arrival of the courier.

The evening passed and the scouts couldn't believe no one had come to guard the street. What Admiral Hanno said about the dirt farmers being undisciplined and lazy must be true.

A light breeze off the harbor blew up the street ruffling the branches of the trees. Using the sounds of moving leaves and scraping branches as cover, two Legionaries sprinted forward five paces. Then they both jumped, one grabbing an arm, the other a leg and they pulled the scout off his perch. On the other side of the intersection, that scout also slammed hard into the ground. Both were stunned as the Legionaries dragged them away.

***

"Tribune. A courier from the Qart Hadasht," the duty NCO announced.

"Come," Claudius said as he got off a camp bed and moved to his desk.

The NCO prevented the messenger from getting close to the Tribune. Only after the duty Optio took the message and examined, did he hand the parchment to the senior officer.

"Why do you do that, Sergeant?" asked Claudius. "I've served with Legions for over five years and have personally taken hundreds of messages directly from couriers. Why the caution here?"

"Combat zone, sir," replied the NCO. "First Optio Brictius gives a talk to every Legionary assigned to you and the command post. Tribune Claudius is to be protected at all times and at all cost. We are engaged with a ruthless Empire who will do anything, employ any method to harm the Tribune. If Tribune Claudius is stabbed or falls ill, the men guarding him will be executed. We face a cunning enemy and our shield against them is the wit of our Tribune. This Legionaries, and don't forget it, is a combat zone."

"I had no idea First Sergeant Brictius was so eloquent," commented Claudius.

The Sergeant squinted and his mouth twisted to the side as if pondering a difficult question. Finally, his face brightened and he explained, "No, sir. The First Optio is really serious about it."

"Dismissed, Sergeant," ordered Claudius as he unrolled the parchment.

Tribune Gaius Claudius,

Mortem Tuam Eminet

Globus Tuus Mortuus es

Admiral Hanno of the Qart Hadasht Empire

Senior Centurion Valerian marched into the tent and crossed to stand in front of the desk.

"Another message from the Admiral?" he inquired as his fist dropped from the salute. "Anything interesting, sir?"

"It seems, I am dead as well as my followers," replied Claudius. "I don't feel dead. How about you Senior Centurion?"

"Sir, I am pleased to report that I am alive. As are the Legionaries standing posts tonight," Valerian responded. "But in light of the Admiral's premature announcement, I'm ordering fifty percent watch tonight."

"An excellent idea," Claudius exclaimed. "I want to walk the lines tonight and reassure the men. Assign whatever guard detail you think I'll need."

"Let me consult with First Sergeant Brictius," Valerian said. "He'll want to know because this is…"

"A combat zone," Tribune Claudius interrupted with a wave of his hand dismissing the Centurion. "Find the First Sergeant and let me know."

Chapter – 33 Night Terror

Before sunset, sub-commander Barca strolled to his defensive positions beyond the southern wall. Usually, he moved alone among his soldiers talking to them and building them up. With four phalanxes of Hoplites, even more, Syracusan soldiers and horsemen cavalry units camped across the River Longanus, he needed his Companies sharp and their attention focused on the enemy. This afternoon, however, he walked between positions with two bodyguards.

Earlier today, the sub-commander assigned a Lieutenant he trusted with the diversion at the east end of the wall. Without realizing the young, nobleman's head was full of wine and his brain still addled from the night before, he gave the orders and sent the Company off to draw the attention of the invaders.

Barca waited at the city gate with another Company. With one eye on the Syracusans, who stirred at the movement of the Empire forces, he watched with the other for Admiral Hanno's signal. While the sub-commander waited for a signal that never came, the Lieutenant directed the ill-fated diversion.

***

"Ladders to the wall," slurred Lieutenant Maharbaal pointing at the wall. "Do it slow. The sub-commander wants the invaders to see the tops of the ladders and pull units from the north side to defend the wall."

As ten men rushed by to place the ladders, Maharbaal stumbled out of their way. Swinging his arms around as if to fend off an attack, he tripped and had to quick step to regain his balance.

"Sir. Let me handle the attack," suggested a Sergeant.

"Remember your place, Sergeant," scolded the Lieutenant as he lifted his hand as if to strike the NCO. "The sub-commander chose me to command the task. And by the gods, I'll complete the mission."

"Yes, sir," the Sergeant replied as he backed away to stand with his section.

"First rank, to the ladders. Show yourselves," he ordered when several of the ten soldiers stayed low. "Spears, they need spears. Hand them spears. Wave the spears. We need to draw the northern units to us."

The ten standing on the ladders dutifully hoisted spears and waved them in the air.

"Second rank. To the ladders," shouted Maharbaal enthusiastically.

The Lieutenant was looking at the formation and didn't see the first seven topple off the ladders with javelins imbedded in their chests. When he turned, the last three fell back but he was looking at the top of the wall.

"Why are there no men on the wall?" he shouted in anger. "Climb the ladders. Hand them spears. Wave the spears. We have a mission. Wave them higher!"

Seven fell back with javelins protruding from their chests. The last three tumbled off the ladders and lay crumpled with the first seventeen. Maharbaal's mouth fell open at the dead and dying soldiers. The remaining soldiers in the Company assumed their Lieutenant was shocked at the loss.

"Third rank to the ladders," Maharbaal screamed. "Over the wall. Make the invaders pay. Fourth rank to the ladders. Over the wall."

The Lieutenant also sent the fifth, sixth and seventh ranks over the wall. When the ten men of the eighth rank reached the top of the ladders, they noticed the street was empty. No units of invaders were running to defend the wall. But below, ranks of men with big shields chopped into the few living soldiers still standing.

"No! No! No!" one soldier on the ladder cried out. His words were picked up by the other members of his rank.

"Over the wall, you cowards," Maharbaal screamed while drawing his sword and swinging up at the closest ladder.

The blade sliced and blood spurted from the back of the man's legs. He fell off the ladder.

As the wounded soldier crashed to the ground, Maharbaal raised his sword preparing to cut the man again. A soldier in the ninth rank snatched up a spear and swung the butt end. It slammed into the Lieutenant's helmet and Maharbaal crumbled to the grass. Two men jumped from their ladders, ran to the Lieutenant and began kicking him. Soldiers from the ninth rank stepped up and joined them.

By the time a Sergeant and two of the tenth rank shoved the soldiers back and reached the Lieutenant, the nobleman was curled into a ball and crying. They picked up the officer and dragged him to the command post.

One Sergeant climbed the ladder and peeked over the wall. None of the soldiers who had gone over the wall lived. He climbed down slowly.

"Return to your camp positions," he ordered the last three ranks of the Company.

The other Sergeant walked up to him. Neither spoke, but the NCO who had climbed the ladder shook his head, no.

"None?" asked the Sergeant of the tenth rank.

"None are alive and the invaders haven't reacted," the NCO reported. "Except for those standing and waiting for more of us to die on their blades."

The Sergeant of the tenth rank walked to where Maharbaal's sword rested on the grass. He picked it up and headed for the command post.

Doctors had the Lieutenant stretched out as they searched for broken bones. A rag covered his nose in an attempt to stop the bleeding and the nobleman moaned in pain.

Sub-commander Barca reached the command post just before the Sergeant of the tenth rank.

"What happened?" inquired the sub-commander looking from the injured officer to the approaching NCO.

Wordlessly, the Sergeant marched up and stopped so he stood over the injured nobleman. Lifting the officer's sword to the center of his chest, he slammed the hilt into his chest plate. Then he slapped the blade into the palm of his left hand. A slight pull and blood dripped from the hand. Placing his knee in the center of the blade, he pulled until the steel gave and the sword folded in half.

The Sergeant of the tenth rank dropped the ruined swords beside Lieutenant Maharbaal. Then he turned and marched away. He hadn't said a word but the meaning was clear.

***

It was bad enough that seventy soldiers were killed for no reason, thought the sub-commander. If the remaining thirty of the Company were the only ones angry and suspicious of their officers he could deal with them.

Barca walked over to a different Company area. His two bodyguards lagged behind but stayed close enough on his flanks to help if any soldiers assaulted him. It wasn't just the thirty survivors of Maharbaal's Charge, as it was being called. Every soldier in the southern area knew about the senseless sacrifice. And now, late in the afternoon, the news had spread among the soldiers in Messina. To protect officers from any disgruntled men, the Lieutenants had one bodyguard, the two sub-commanders rated two, and Admiral Hanno only allowed himself three.

The sub-commander approached a defensive position. While the Sergeant and soldiers stood when he entered their campsite, none seemed happy to be visited by their commanding officer. Before he could speak with the ten men, a messenger ran up.

"Sub-commander Barca. The Admiral requests your presence," the messenger stated.

"I'll be back to listen to your complaints," promised Barca.

Then with his guards trailing behind, he headed for the Citadel.

***

"I want them pushed into the harbor and drowned," Admiral Hanno growled. "Tonight. By morning, I want Messina fully back in Empire control."

"Another drive on the north side?" asked Gisco. "We would have breached their lines if the diversion had been adequate. But what can you expect from a Maharbaal's Charge."

Blood rushed to Barca's face and he almost stood up to confront the other sub-commander. He settled for words.

"If I ever hear you use that term again, Gisco," threatened Barca. "I'll beat you to a bloody pulp."

213

Gisco blustered and huffed but he didn't address the fiery combat officer's comment. It was the reason Barca commanded the troops over the wall facing the Syracusan advance force. And if they arrived, do battle with the Army of Syracuse and their king, Hiero the Second. Gisco was very happy in the town, inside the walls, performing administrative duties.

"I have enough issues, I don't need dissent between my sub-commanders," warned Hanno. "No, we will not attack the north side. It's too close to their command post and too well defended. I want to hit them on the south side. Wrap around and roll them up."

"Syracusan command took notice of our losses this morning," Barca advised. "If we do an all-out push, in the morning, we'll find them waiting at our gates."

"Wait till it's dark and pull half your forces," instructed Hanno. "Join with Gisco's units from the town. I have scouts watching the street. They'll report any shifts in the invader's units. Let me show you the street on the map."

***

Tribune Claudius stepped carefully down the dark stairs. Once on the street, he headed for a roaring fire and First Sergeant Brictius.

"Good evening, First Sergeant," Claudius greeted him while pointing back with both thumbs. "Is this enough security to satisfy you."

A tall, thick Sergeant and a short, beefy Corporal hovered behind the Tribune's shoulders.

"Almost, sir," Brictius replied. "The Sergeant is an expert at escape and evasion tactics. And the Corporal is the wrestling champion of his Legion. But I want one more element before you go wandering across a dark combat zone. Lance Corporal Sisera, front, and center."

"You're the Legionary who organized Messina for our crossing," Tribune Claudius ventured as Alerio walked into the light. "You did an excellent job. But First Sergeant, why Lance Corporal Sisera."

"Our Lance Corporal is a master swordsman," Brictius replied. "I don't expect trouble. But if it finds you, I'm confident these three Legionaries will see you safely back to the command post."

"This is an inspection tour, not a combat patrol," The Tribune informed his First Sergeant. Brictius saluted but didn't say anything. Claudius having received the top NCO's meaning, ordered his bodyguards, "Let's get moving."

At each barricade on each street, the Tribune talked to the men. He asked about home towns, family members and promised better accommodations after Messina was captured. Alerio couldn't decide if Tribune Gaius Claudius was a caring Legion commander or a master politician. After he thought about it, he realized, there wasn't a difference.

The inspection team met Senior Centurion Valerian as the Tribune spoke with Legionaries at the wide road.

"You can see a light in the Citadel from here. It's faint. Must be in a back room away from the watch portals," Claudius informed the men.

"You can see the light, sir?" asked a Legionary. "I've been telling the squad about the light, sir. But no one believes me."

"You and I, Legionary, are blessed by Theia," pronounced the Tribune. "You keep watch here and I'll watch over you and your squad from Temple hill."

He left an excited young Legionary and an amazed squad as the inspection team moved further south. They had passed the first street and were headed for the second when Senior Centurion Valerian jogged up behind them.

"Tribune. The young Legionary with the good eyes. Were you serious about seeing the light?" Valerian asked.

"It's a rare gift. And yes, I was quite serious about seeing the light," replied Claudius. "Why do you ask?"

"The young man took you up on watching out for his squad. Since you left, he's been off to the side of the fire's light fixated on a point far up the dark road," Valerian explained.

"He's doing his job. Excellent," Claudius commented. "Morale is why we're doing this."

"Yes, sir. But he reported seeing units of troops crossing the road. No one else saw anything," Valerian informed the Tribune. "I wasn't sure whether to take him seriously or not."

"Senior Centurion Valerian. If one blessed by Theia mentions seeing something, it's not a vision or a trick of the mind. It's because he has witnessed reality," Claudius explained. "In what direction were the units heading?"

"South, sir," Valerian replied. "But we don't know what streets they'll come down."

"Tribune. I suggest you head back to Temple Hill," recommended the bodyguard Sergeant.

"Not yet," Claudius insisted. "I don't hear any Empire war cries. Let's do one more street."

As Alerio followed the tribune the guard Corporal leaned over and whispered, "I don't think the Qart Hadasht use war cries."

They were almost to the third street when a sentry challenged them, "Halt. State your name, rank, and unit."

Even in the dark, they could see the leveled javelin and shield.

"Gaius Claudius. Tribune of the Legion expeditionary force to Messina," replied Claudius. "Since when do you challenge behind the lines?"

"Since we caught two spies," the Legionary replied as he raised the javelin tip into the night sky. "The Sergeant and Centurion are questioning them in the shed just behind me."

Claudius rushed for the shed with Valerian right behind him. The bodyguards sprinted to keep the Tribune in their pocket of protection.

The entrance to the shed faced east and when Claudius opened it a little light spilled out.

"Light! Close the door," the Centurion snapped. "What's so important?"

"I could ask you that," Claudius replied as he stepped in and closed the door.

"Tribune, I didn't know," the officer began to explain but Claudius cut him off.

"You caught spies. Are there more?" he demanded

"After we pulled these two off the walls, we checked," the Centurion reported. "Just these two watching our squad at the intersection."

"Kill them and wake your men," Claudius ordered. "You have Qart Hadasht headed your way. I'll send all the help I can. But your squads are my spearhead."

The door opened and closed quickly. The Tribune called out.

"Senior Centurion Valerian. The third street is the target. Get as many Legionaries there as you can spare," Claudius commanded. "Lance Corporal Sisera. Can you rally the Sons of Mars to back us up?"

"Yes, sir. Once you are safely back at your command post," Alerio replied.

"Then let's get moving," Claudius said as he headed north.

Senior Centurion Valerian vanished in the dark as he sprinted away.

***

Sub-commander Gisco stood behind his one hundred and fifty soldiers. Down the street where the front of his Company and a half waited was a gap. A few paces away, another one hundred and sixty soldiers stood in columns. Further down the street at the head of his soldiers,' Sub-commander Barca waited.

"Down the street are the invaders," Barca said. "We are going to sweep them into the harbor. March silently until it's time."

"How do we know when it's time?" asked a soldier.

"When you gut the first rank of dirt farmers," he explained getting a laugh from the men at the head of the columns.

Barca smiled and waited for the exchange to be repeated back through the Companies. The farther back it went, the better he felt with each laugh. Then he had a bad thought. What if instead of gutting a dirt farmer, it got twisted to gutting a sub-commander?

He shook off the feeling and announced, "Forward!"

Turning with his bodyguards, he marched down the hill at the head of his men.

Soon the fire of the Empire's barricade came into view. Then the fire of the invaders appeared a block ahead.

Stepping to the side and marching slower, he let his Companies begin flowing passed him.

Barca ordered, "Form ranks. Form ranks. Form ranks."

By the fourth row, the soldiers were spreading into ranks by themselves. The lead rank passed the first fire. Barca kept up the pace, staying four ranks back and watching the fire in the intersection ahead. So far, there had been no cries of alarm. When the fire was a quick sprint ahead, Barca ran forward shouting.

"Charge! Charge!" he commanded and his soldiers responded.

The front rank lowered their spears, maintained spacing and alignment as they jogged towards the fire.

Than a voice called out in the dark from beyond the Legion barricade, "Brace! Brace! Brace!"

Act 6

Chapter – 34 Diplomacy

Barca couldn't separate the ranks of the invaders from the shadows. Had he time to think on it, the entire intersection appeared darker than the surroundings. But he was entering the intersection with the third rank. Once his soldiers cleared the cross streets, he'd order a flanking maneuver and turn the attacking ranks northward. They would sweep in behind the invaders' lines and decimate the upstarts…a sharp pain shot through his brain, his head snapped to the left, and he stumbled forward before falling into oblivion.

***

The leading ranks of the Qart Hadasht soldiers expected a quick smash, a turn and a hard, running fight to the edge of Messina. Instead, they slammed into ranks of Legion shields. As their bodies stopped as if colliding with a brick wall, the ranks behind shoved them onto the blades and javelins of the Legionaries.

By the fourth rank, the intersection was filling as soldiers attempted to flow around the logjam by moving off to the sides. The first charging to the left and right also died on Legion weapons.

The sixth rank didn't reach the intersection. They tripped over the bodies of their comrades. Lieutenants began shouting conflicting orders. Some calling for a retreat and others reinforcing the charge command. The attack faltered and the street leading to the intersection filled with confused, milling Qart Hadasht soldiers.

***

Senior Centurion Valerian wanted desperately to order an advance. But his two hundred Legionaries were arranged in a semicircle around the intersection. If he ordered it, they would attack and trip over the wounded and dead soldiers. That wasn't the problem. The issue was they'd end up converging and assaulting each other.

As a result, he waited as the shouting and cursing from up the street receded. Eventually, the sounds of Qart Hadasht soldiers faded and silence returned to the dark street.

"Stand down! Hold your positions," he shouted. "Pass the injured to the rear!"

***

Tribune Claudius paced the dark hilltop. Even though runners reported the success of his Legionaries, he couldn't rest. Not with Qart Hadasht units roaming the town and his lines thin. Even with the pirates backing up his men at the barricaded streets. Plus, he didn't completely trust the Sons of Mars and their brigand attitude.

***

Shortly before daybreak, sub-commander Gisco climbed Citadel hill.

"They were waiting for us, Admiral," Gisco reported to the silent shadow standing on the crest of the hill. "And sub-commander Barca is missing."

"Missing?" inquired the big shadow.

"He was at the front, prepared to turn the ranks," Gisco replied. "He never returned from the intersection."

"And, where were you?" demanded Hanno.

"I was with my Companies to the rear of his," Gisco responded.

"Don't go into the Citadel. Head directly to the south wall defensive positions," instructed Hanno. "If the Syracusans see we are weakened, we'll be fighting on two fronts."

"Of course, Admiral," Gisco said as he turned and started down the hill.

***

The sun had barely appeared above the eastern mountains. In the morning light, Captain Milon Frigian strolled up the steps. At the top of Temple hill, he was challenged by the command post guards. After waiting for a while, they ushered him into the command tent.

"Good morning to you, Tribune Claudius," Frigian said with a smile. "A very good morning as you broke the attack by the Qart Hadasht soldiers. With help from the Sons of Mars, of course."

"Thank you for your help, Captain," Claudius replied. "What can I do for you?"

"I have good news and a request," Frigian responded holding out his hands as if they were scales. He waffled them up and down each in turn.

"I could use some good news," Claudius suggested.

"Among the wounded prisoners from last night's activity, you have a Lieutenant," Frigian said as he raised one hand higher and paused. As he continued, he lifted the hand over his head. "And sub-commander Barca."

"Two Empire officers," Claudius replied flatly. "I wasn't aware, but what of them."

"Oh, my dear, Tribune. Barca is the number two officer in Hanno's detachment. That's if you don't count Gisco and nobody does," Frigian explained. "And the Lieutenant is the eldest son of an important family. Two, honey sweet, royal hostages. Now, Tribune, if you find them a nuisance, the Sons of Mars will gladly take the pesky officers off your hands."

"No Captain. I believe I'll hold onto them," Claudius explained than asked. "You have a request?"

"When armies battle, the fields will flourish after the trampling and the grass will regrow," Frigian began. "But in a town, the trampled are the women, children and the old."

"I wasn't aware of any civilian casualties," pleaded Claudius. "But, this is war. Have them stay inside."

"That's the problem, Tribune. They have been inside and are running out of food, water, and some require medical attention," Frigian informed the Legion officer.

"Those in areas controlled by the Republic are free to come out," offered Claudius.

"Unfortunately, the farms are beyond the west gate and many of the fishermen live in Empire sectors," explained Frigian. "If you could see your way to speaking with Admiral Hanno…"

Claudius held up the palm of his hand and exclaimed, "What makes you think Hanno will talk with me?"

"The Admiral is a nobleman and a military man, but his family are traders," Frigian informed him. "All the Qart Hadasht aristocrats are in business. Maybe you and the Admiral can reach an agreement? I'll be there to help in any way I can. As a matter of fact, the Sons have in our possession a large Egyptian tent. We will erect it on an empty lot between your two lines. See, I'm helping already."

Claudius thought silently before replying, "I'll send a message. And if Hanno agrees to a parley, you may attend on one condition."

"And, what would that be, Tribune?" Frigian asked.

"You don't say a word during the negotiations," warned Claudius. "One word, one whisper, or sound from you, and I'll walk out. Is that clear?"

"Tribune Claudius. My Lieutenant and I will be so quiet, you'll forget we're there," promised the Sons of Mars' Captain.

***

At the same time Frigian walked the stairs to Temple hill, Ferox Creon strolled to the top of Citadel hill.

"I am Captain Ferox Creon, the new leader of the Sons of Mars," explained Creon to the duty officer. "And by rights, the Magistrate of Messina. I'd like to talk with Admiral Hanno."

"Stay there," instructed the Lieutenant. He walked to a door, rapped, opened it and leaned inside. After a few words, he returned to his desk. "The Admiral will see you."

Creon strutted through the doorway and walked briskly to Hanno's desk.

"Admiral, good morning. I am Ferox Creon, the new leader of the Sons of Mars," he announced. "Before you say anything, the crews who have thrown in with the Republic are renegades. Disavowed by the Sons who are loyal to the Empire."

"You mean all the damage to my soldiers have been from a few dirt farmers?" sneered Hanno. "All right, let's say you represent the Sons of Mars and they are loyal. What do you want?"

"Our businesses and trade are suffering from the invasion," explained Creon. "Farmers can't get their produce to market, ships can't row into the harbor to barter, and local craftsmen are unable to ply their trade."

"And that is the Empire's fault?" inquired Hanno. "If you want Messina open for business tell the invaders to leave."

"Very astute of you, Admiral. That's exactly the reason I came to see you," Creon said with a smile. "The loyal Sons of Mars would appreciate it if you'd parley with Tribune Claudius."

"What makes you think he'll meet with me?" inquired Hanno.

"Claudius is a farmer as you've pointed out. What do farmers enjoy more than talking about the weather and haggling over everything?" Creon stated. "The Sons happen to have a fine Egyptian tent we picked up in our travels. Let's say we erect it on an empty lot between the Empire sector and the block temporarily occupied by the invaders. I would, as the Magistrate, make myself available to assist in any way you require."

"I will send an inquiry to the Tribune," Hanno promised. "But there is a stipulation."

"Please Admiral, name it," begged Creon.

"During the conference, you will not utter a sound," warned Hanno. "If I hear a resonance from your throat, I will walk out."

"Admiral, you have my word that my Lieutenant and I will say nothing," Creon assured him.

***

Tribune Claudius,

The merchants of Messina are greatly inconvenienced by your presence. I propose we discuss your withdrawal at the apex of the sun. The Sons of Mars will provide a tent for our talk.

Admiral Hanno of the Qart Hadasht Empire

***

Admiral Hanno,

The people of Messina suffer from your continued resistance to the inevitable. If you are agreeable, I suggest we meet in the tent provided by the Sons of Mars and celebrate a midday repast.

Gaius Claudius, Tribune of Caudex Legion, representative of Consul Appease Clodus Caudex, Consul Marcus Fulvius Flaccus, and the Senate of the Republic, and citizen of the Republic

***

The sun lingered high overhead. While most of Messina sought shade to enjoy the midday breeze, the wide center road hosted two small military parades.

Tribune Claudius and Senior Centurion Valerian marched up the grade. Behind them came a squad of Legionaries in perfect step with their equipment cleaned and polished. They represented excellent examples of the Republic's finest.

Admiral Hanno and Lieutenant Maharbaal marched down the grade. Close behind and moving in unison, followed a squad of Soldiers. Their equipment also shined and oiled to display the best of the Empire.

From opposite directions, the small displays of military pride converged on the billowing tent of Egyptian cotton. Layered with overlapping sheets of blue and yellow, the tent allowed air flow while providing privacy for the occupants. As the military participants approached the lot where the tent was pitched, two other parties emerged from buildings to the west and east. Unlike the men in armor with swords and gladii, the Sons of Mars wore loose tunics without blades.

Ferox Creon and Gallus Silenus angled to reach the tent's entrance flaps before Admiral Hanno and his contingent. Across the lot, Milon Frigian and Alerio Sisera moved diagonally to intercept Tribune Claudius and the Senior Centurion.

"Admiral Hanno, my I present my Lieutenant Gallus Silenus," Creon said as he held the flap back so Hanno and Maharbaal could pass to the interior.

"Tribune Claudius, may I present my Lieutenant, Alerio Sisera," Frigian said with a knowing smile. As Claudius and Valerian entered the tent, the Senior Centurion twisted his head when he was inside to stare back at the Lance Corporal.

A large table sat in the center of the space with two chairs on either side and one chair on each end. Small tables with covered dishes took up the four corners of the tent.

"Gentlemen, the food will come from all the dishes and be served by our Lieutenants," explained Creon. "The wine on the table is also communal. Please sit."

Hanno and Claudius took chairs and sat glaring at each other. A bruised Maharbaal settled across from Valerian but refused to look at him. Frigian and Creon selected chairs at the ends of the table. They also didn't look at one another. Mistrust, prejudice, and hate permeated the atmosphere in the tent.

Alerio and Gallus picked up plates. They went to each food station and placed slices of lamb, a pile of olives, pieces of goat cheese, a dollop of honey, and chunks of bread on the plates. After setting the dishes in front of the officers of the Republic and the officers of the Empire, Gallus filled three mugs with wine before handing the pitcher to Alerio. He filled three mugs and the two honorary Lieutenants stepped away from the table.

Tribune Claudius reached out, ripped off a piece of bread, dipped it in the honey and bit off the dripping edge. A satisfied smile creased the Tribune's face as he chewed. Maharbaal's hand lifted towards his bread but a sharp turn of Hanno's head froze the young nobleman.

"I am here to talk. Not to dine with my enemy," Hanno stated shifting his eyes back to Claudius.

"Is there anything preventing us from doing both?" inquired the Tribune as he plucked an olive and a piece of cheese from his plate. With the food held just in front of his mouth, he commented, "I don't know about you but I've missed meals and haven't had a good night's sleep in days."

"I sleep as if I were a baby in the arms of my nurse," Hanno bragged. "It's your disrespect to the Empire that troubles your sleep."

"Actually, it's the attacks led by your brave officers, like your young Lieutenant there, that keeps me up," admitted Claudius. "They are quite persistent."

Maharbaal dipped his head in acknowledgement of the compliment. Again, Hanno jerked his head to the side, silently chastising his Lieutenant.

"I command the forces of the Empire," Hanno said defensively. "And I will drive you from Messina."

Senior Centurion Valerian selected a slice of lamb and took a bite.

"That's wonderful," he gushed. "What spice is that I taste?"

No one replied for long moments. Then, Maharbaal mumbled, "Cinnamon from Egypt."

"Cinnamon? I've never had this cinnamon before," the Senior Centurion exclaimed.

"And, you never will again," Hanno observed. "It's rare and expensive. Fit only for Kings and Emperors. The Empire is widespread. We trade with many lands. And the navy and soldiers of the Empire protect the trade routes. Just as we protect Messina."

"Not to be too indelicate, but your forces only control half of the city," pointed out Claudius. The Tribune took a bite of lamb and nodded appreciatively.

"I will drive you back across the Strait," declared Hanno. "And perhaps, I'll bring in the fleet. Then, I'll sweep the coast on the other side free of the blight of your Republic."

Claudius had been pleasant trying to open a dialogue with the Qart Hadasht Admiral. But his patience wore out. He let the slice of lamb slip from between his fingers and the spicy meat slapped onto the plate. Squaring his shoulders, Claudius stared into Hanno's eyes.

"You might push us from the streets of Messina. It will cost you greatly," the Tribune acknowledged with his teeth clinched in anger. "And on the beach, beneath the flames and smoke of your burning Triremes, we will drain the blood of your soldiers. And not until my last Legionary is surrounded by dead Qart Hadasht noblemen, will the gladius fall from his hand. But, know this, you will never push us back across the strait."

Admiral Hanno's big hand slammed onto the tabletop and he jumped to his feet. Lieutenant Maharbaal rushed to catch up as the Admiral vanished through the tent's flap. Ferox Creon and Gallus Silenus hurried after them.

"You didn't mention sub-commander Barca, sir," questioned Senior Centurion Valerian.

"You don't display your best bargaining token unless you are negotiating," replied Claudius. "The Admiral never opened the table for ideas. Nor did he eat."

The Tribune picked up the piece of savory lamb and took a bite.

"Captain Frigian. And Sisera, whatever title you have today. There are two untouched plates of excellent food going to waste," Claudius noted. "Sit, eat, and keep up your energy. You'll need it. You're going to have a busy night."

"A busy night, sir?" inquired Alerio as he sat across from Valerian.

"Yes. You're going to cut the head off the snake, so to speak," replied the Tribune. After taking a sip from his mug, he declared, "This wine is excellent."

Chapter – 35 Bargaining Tokens

Nine Legionaries shuffled into position at the intersection. By feel, they settled into a line and their squad leader whispered, "Draw!" Ten gladii slid free and he commanded, "Forward." They started across the intersection. If it was daylight, other squads would have laughed as they lifted their feet and, as quietly as hobnailed boots would allow, moved out. High steps replaced the Legion stomp and soon, the squad filled the street between the compound walls. Behind the squad, five men in Empire armor also walked softly as they followed.

Whether it was the soft clap of boots on pavers, the jingling of armor, or simply shapes closing in from the dark, the Empire soldier on watch spotted the squad. Shouting a warning, he grabbed his shield, pulled his sword, and positioned himself in the center of his intersection. Standing alone, as an ancient hero in the tales of lore, he waited for the rush and the blades to cut him down. The charge never came.

The alert removed the need for stealth and the ripple of ten boots stomping loudly echoed off the walls. "Shields," the Legion squad leader shouted. But he didn't call for an advance or order a quick march. Instead, the squad moved forward at a pace giving time for Qart Hadasht troops to join the lone brave soldier.

In the campfire light that only illuminated the center of the opposing squads, the Legionaries and the Empire soldiers clashed together.

"Lateral left," ordered the squad's Lance Corporal. "Keep your end contained."

As the Legionaries' line wheeled left pushing the soldiers back and to the side, a gap opened. The five men in Empire armor slipped through the opening on the Legionaries right. Once beyond the skirmish line, they circled around behind the soldiers. They added their voices to the shouting, encouraging the soldiers and calling for reinforcements. And although their blades were clear of the scabbards, the only thing their five blades cut was the air over their heads.

"Wheel back, step back," the squad leader ordered. "Stay tight. Step back."

The big Legion shields protected the Legionaries but in the dark, a blade could sneak in and do damage. Two squad members stumbled. Fortunately, the embers of the scattered campfire provided enough light to see the injured men falter.

"Form two ranks," ordered the squad leader as he reached out and pulled one of the wounded to the rear. "Step back. Step back."

The other hurt Legionary was shoved to the rear by a squad mate. In a tight two rank formation, the squad hacked and chopped in a fighting withdrawal. Shadows in both intersections announced the arrival of additional fighters from both sides. Once the squad had moved a quarter of the way down the street, they were joined by more Legionaries. With the dark street full of invaders, the Qart Hadasht soldiers opted for setting a defensive line rather than pursuing the Legionaries.

As the distance between the warring factions grew, the tension lifted and the soldiers relaxed. With more Empire troops rushing to the intersection, the five men in the Qart Hadasht armor drifted against the flow and edged their way up the street and away from the intersection.

***

"That went better than I expected," commented Milon Frigian as he guided the other four through a gate and into a walled courtyard.

"But will he come?" Alerio asked while pulling off the high, conical helmet.

"You have Barca. And my sources tell me Gisco is with the soldiers defending the south wall," replied Frigian. "The Admiral, by his own admission, is in charge of the Empire

235

forces. How could he refuse the invitation issued by your Legionaries?"

"In the Legion, the commander would send a Centurion to investigate the skirmish," mused Alerio.

"Your Legion has a command structure that stretches down to the squad level," Frigian pointed out. "The Empire depends on mercenary troops. Don't get me wrong, the soldiers are loyal to the Empire. And they follow the orders of their Lieutenants. But command and control are from the top. Admiral Hanno will come to investigate the hostility. There's no one else with the authority to respond."

"I don't understand Captain Ferox Creon and Capitan Gallus Silenus being at the negotiations," questions Alerio. "Have they sided with the Empire?"

"Lieutenant Sisera, we are the Sons of Mars," Frigian said with a laugh. "We are on the side that wins. This is Captain Creon's courtyard."

"His courtyard?" asked Alerio looking around the black space as if he could see something. "What does he have to say about our mission?"

"If we pull this off and get away, he'll curse us," advised Frigian. "If we fail, he'll turn you over to the Qart Hadasht to be crucified."

"And that's why you volunteered you, and your men, for the mission?" inquired Alerio although he already knew the answer.

"Don't worry Lieutenant. The Sons owe you and we'll do our best to get you back to the Tribune unstretched on the wood," Frigian assured him. Then, to the side, he talked to the three huge rowers that accompanied them. "Someone, climb on a box and watch over the wall. The rest of you get some sleep."

Alerio leaned his back against the wall and sank to the ground. He wanted to rest, but the new cost of failure kept him awake. It would have been a short nap anyway. Boots running on the street carried over the wall and he tried to get a feel for the size of the force.

A voice from near the top of the wall spoke from the dark, "The Admiral has graced us with his presence."

Moments later a door opened, a light flashed as someone stepped quickly through. The door shut and darkness returned to the courtyard. Alerio jumped to his feet and pulled a sword. Frigian must have heard him draw the blade.

"Relax, Lieutenant. He's one of my crew," Frigian advised. "Are we ready?"

"Yes Captain," a new voice replied. "Are you ready to launch?"

"We are and good luck to you," Frigian assured the man. Then the door opened, light splashed out and the door closed. "It won't be long now. That's if the Admiral doesn't order an all-out attack."

"And if he does?" inquired Alerio.

"We wait until dawn to see which side we're on," Frigian admitted.

***

"Admiral Hanno. A moment of your time," a voice spoke from over the wall.

"Stand aside, Son of Mars," a gruff voice ordered.

"Admiral, Captain Creon has important news for you," pleaded the man. "It has to do with the plans of the invaders."

"Let him through," Hanno told his bodyguard. "What's this news your Captain has?"

"He has yet to return with the details," the man explained. "He bid you wait in his Villa. He should return shortly."

"What news?" Alerio whispered.

"Why, the details of your mission, of course," Frigian stated as of it was obvious.

"And where is Captain Creon?" asked Alerio.

"He's several blocks from here with ten or fifteen of his rowers," Frigian reported. "Waiting for my runner to alert him to the Admiral's distress."

"Have Captain Creon come to the Citadel," Hanno's voice carried to the courtyard.

"The Captain said the news is urgent, Admiral," the man advised. "His Villa is right here. And the Captain has provided refreshments for you while you wait."

Alerio listened but no one over the wall spoke for long moments. All the Legionary could hear was his heart beating in his chest. Finally, Hanno spoke.

"I'll avail myself of one mug of wine," he explained. "If Magistrate Creon fails to appear, he'll need to come to the Citadel with his report."

"Very good, sir," the man replied. "This way, if you please."

Boots and sandals crunched gravel as the unseen group moved off the street and onto the path leading to the front of the Villa.

"Hide in the shadows on either side of the doorway," ordered Frigian.

Alerio and two of the large oarsmen put their backs against the wall of the Villa. Frigian and the third crewman moved to the other side. As they waited together, Alerio became acutely aware of the rowers' size. If the Sons' Captain decided it was in his best interest to turn on the Republic, Alerio wouldn't stand much of a chance. With no other option, he waited.

"What's out here?" demanded a gruff voice of one of Hanno's bodyguards. The door opened and light spilled onto the courtyard.

"The cook shed, a storage building and Captain Creon's lemon trees. He's partial to lemon on his greens and fish and..."

"I got it, he likes the taste of lemon," the bodyguard said trying to shut the man up.

Alerio leaned away from the wall. A short man stood in the doorway. Towering over him hovered a big man who easily looked over the shorter man's head.

"Oh, it's more than taste," the short man babbled on. "Come with me. Let me show you the medicinal uses for the lemon juice and the peels. Most of..."

"No," the bodyguard said sharply. Then turning his head, he announced to someone in the Villa, "There's no one in the courtyard."

"Stand guard by the door," came a response from a different voice.

"I've got to go to the cook shed for the Admiral's ham," explained the short man.

There was a scuffling of feet before the little man stepped into the courtyard. He carried a large candle in a holder with a curved back plate behind the flame. The plate reflected and amplified the candle light. He walked to a shed in the pool of light and vanished inside. Moments later, he reappeared holding the candle above his head.

As the petite man neared the doorway, one of the rowers beside Alerio peeled away from the wall. His shadow circled around and he came up behind the man with the ham. The candle holder passed to the big oarsman and the little man tripped.

"Oh Gods, I almost dropped the Admiral's ham," he cursed. Then he called to the guard in the doorway. "Come here and take this candle from me. Come on, you don't want me to serve the Admiral dirty ham."

With the candle held over the short man's head, the light shown directly into the bodyguard's eyes. Blindly, he stepped into the courtyard. The giant rower holding the candle brought his fist from below the flickering candle and plowed it into the bodyguard's chin. As the soldier fell back, another of Frigian's large oarsmen stepped up, caught the unconscious man, and clubbed him again.

"Should I put the ham back in the shed, Captain?" asked the man.

"No coxswain, keep it as a reward for a job well done. Send a man and tell Captain Creon there's trouble at his Villa," Frigian answered. Then to the oarsmen, he ordered, "Lieutenant Sisera will take one bodyguard, we'll take the other one and Admiral Hanno. Go!"

The order of attack came so fast Alerio hesitated trying to figure out why he was assigned to take out a bodyguard. But he didn't have time to question Frigian. A big oarsman shoved him in the back and he stumbled towards the doorway.

***

Alerio caught a glimpse of shelves and bins along the walls of a small room. Then he raced down a hallway passing doorways before he burst into the Villa's great room.

"Protect the Admiral," growled a big soldier as he drew his sword.

Alerio brought his blade to a high guard and lunged at the soldier. Before the blades crossed, someone kicked him in the side of his hip and he tumbled over a couch. He hit hard landing between the overturned couch and a wall. The tip of a sword snaked around the overturned piece of furniture seeking the Legionary.

Sprawled on the decorative tiles and stunned, Alerio, through half closed eyes, saw the tip, a foot, then the forward leg of another bodyguard. Reaching out, he placed his hands on the side of the couch. Then he kicked back against the wall with his left foot and shoved the heavy couch. It clipped the rear leg of the bodyguard and the man paused to catch his balance.

Alerio glanced around for his sword. Not seeing it, he pushed off the tiles with his arms, lifted and placed his right leg on the edge of the couch, and launched himself at the bodyguard. In midair, he got two hands on the man's shield. Once his feet touched the floor, he applied torque and twisted the shield. Bending his upper body and rolling his torso, Alerio flipped in a complete circle.

The bodyguard attempted to shake off the turning of the arms by stepping back. But the hands held firm and the rotating body spun his shield as if they were spinning a wheel. With his arm strapped in and his hand holding the cross strut of the shield, the bodyguard had no choice but to

242

bend in that direction to prevent a dislocated shoulder. When he reached the limit of his shoulder, the bodyguard lost his footing and flipped onto his back.

Alerio released the shield and pulled his curved dagger. As the bodyguard kicked with his legs to fend off Alerio and to regain his feet, the Legionary lashed out with the blade. The slash left a deep, gaping wound on the inside of the bodyguard's thigh. Despite the blood spurting from a severed femoral artery, the man crawled to his knees.

The shield held high against his chest and the sword raised to strike, the bodyguard poised fierce and ready to continue his martial duties. Except he was on his knees in the center of an expanding pool of his own blood. Alerio wanted to grant the warrior a last few heartbeats of dignity. But there was a mission to complete, and he didn't know how Frigian and his rowers were doing with Admiral Hanno and the third bodyguard. Alerio kicked the shield. The light in the Empire soldier's eyes faded with a view of overhead beams instead of the sight over his shield of one last enemy.

Alerio stepped in the blood and snatched the sword from the dead but still warm hand. Turning, he relaxed slightly. The other bodyguard was a heap on the tiles. Not bloody, but certainly out of the fight. Admiral Hanno stood crouched in a corner of the room with a knife in one hand and his sword in the other.

"Now just give up Admiral," Frigian coached. "You're out numbered and we don't want to harm you."

"By morning, you'll all be bags of broken bones up on the wood," Hanno threatened. "Run while you can."

Hanno equaled the size of any of the three oarsmen. Armed, he posed a danger to all four of the Sons. Without speaking, Alerio raced across the room. Coming from behind one of the big rowers, he surprised Hanno and bashed the sword from the Admiral's hand.

The Sons stood shocked and their mouths fell open when Alerio stepped in front of Hanno. After kicking the Admiral's sword out of reach, he tossed his own sword aside. Frigian and his oarsmen weren't the only ones confused. Hanno glanced down at his empty right hand, at the knife in his left, and up at the unarmed Legionary. A sneer twisted his mouth and he jabbed at Alerio's stomach.

Trapping the knife hand between his palms, Alerio guided the blade harmlessly off to the side. Hanno jerked it back and attempted to slash the Legionary's face. But a wrist against the Admiral's wrist increased the arc and the knife passed over Alerio's head. Figuring the trouble with his attack had to do with the hand, Hanno brought his hands together to switch the knife to his right hand. As soon as the hands touched, Alerio clamped them together, shoved them to the side, stepped up, and head butted the Admiral. As Hanno staggered and a lump rose on his forehead, Alerio snatched the knife free and stepped back. Two of Frigian's oarsmen rushed in and grabbed Hanno by the arms. The third vanished down the hallway.

"Truly amazing unarmed combat," acknowledged Frigian.

Ignoring the compliment, Alerio demanded, "What happened? How did Hanno have the chance to draw his blades?"

"We clubbed the second bodyguard while he was admiring your vaulting abilities," confessed Frigian. "Then my oarsmen and I forgot about the Admiral when you did the wrestling and gymnastic moves. Also, truly impressive."

"You forgot about the Admiral?" Alerio asked in disbelief.

As with all auxiliary troops, the pirates had a tendency to wander off mission as their dedication wasn't up to a Legionary's standards. As a young lad, Alerio learned the lesson from a veteran Sergeant and Centurion when discussing the use of native scouts and ally cavalry.

"But it all worked out fine," Frigian announced pointing at Hanno and Alerio. "No one hurt and the first part of our mission completed successfully."

The oarsman came back into the great room with a length of hemp rope. Hanno protested as the rower began wrapping the Admiral's legs together. Frigian reached into a pouch on his belt and pulled out a piece of colorful cotton cloth. He shoved it into Hanno's mouth as the loops coiled upward binding Hanno's arms to his side.

"When will Captain Creon and his rowers get here?" inquired Alerio.

"That's right, we need to be gone before he gets here," Frigian replied. "Can't have him freeing the Admiral."

Alerio noticed Hanno's eyes snap open at the pronouncement. The game being played by the Sons of Mars became clear to the Legionary. The Sons would win with the Republic if they spirited Hanno back across Legion lines. Or, they would keep the Admiral and the Empire's favor if Alerio failed and was captured. In either case, the Sons maintained leverage and trust with both sides.

"Take the Admiral," Frigian ordered. "Everyone out the back door. Hurry."

One of the rowers tossed Hanno over his shoulder and strutted down the hallway. The other two followed. Alerio hesitated.

"Captain Frigian. Aren't you worried if I'm captured, you'll be tried for murder as well as me?" inquired Alerio.

"Lance Corporal Sisera. You are the only one who has killed tonight," responded the Sons' Captain while pointing at the unconscious bodyguard. "The worst case for me is I row out of Messina for a year then when Hanno is replaced, my crew and I row back. Shall we go?"

***

The five kidnappers hustled through the courtyard of Villa Creon turned left on the street and moved deeper into the block. Behind them, they heard Ferox and his crew noisily approaching from the other direction.

Two blocks from the Villa, a rower opened a door to a storage building and they hurried through the doorway. After the door shut, a flint struck and a candle blazed to life.

246

Then Alerio and two of the oarsmen gagged and almost vomited.

"A death house?" Alerio inquired. "We're hiding out here in the stink with rotting corpses?"

"It would be worse if the Sons hadn't rubbed the departed with sea salt," Frigian offered. "Not as fine grained as eating salt, or enough to pack them for shipping, just enough to preserve the bodies."

"This is preserved?" groaned Alerio. "On a battlefield, the wind blows some of the odor away. Within these walls, there is no upwind side to escape the smell."

"But the aroma is in our favor," promised Frigian. "Place the Admiral in the cart, face down. We don't want him suffocating on a dead thigh or a sluffed off piece of back muscle."

The rustic wagon had dual cart shafts, higher sideboards than a typical vendor cart, and a layer of straw on the bed of the cart. Hanno was placed on the straw and an oarsman forked another layer over the Admiral. Then four cloth wrapped bodies were tossed on top of the straw.

Frigian handed out rough woolen robes, old floppy felt Phrygians, and squares of cotton fabric.

"The cloth doesn't block out the smell," observed Alerio as he placed the fabric over his face and tied the ends behind his head.

"It's not there to filter out the aroma. It's there to hide our faces and thin enough so people can hear our chant," explained Frigian. The Captain adjusted Alerio's hat so only a little of his face was visible between the top of the mask and the Phrygian low on his forehead. "We will pay our respects to the departed with full voice and stately steps. Open the door and let us proceed."

"Were the departed Sons, friends of yours?" inquired Alerio as he lifted one of the cart shafts. Another of the oarsmen took hold of the other shaft.

"Them?" asked Frigian indicating the bed of the cart by jerking a thumb over his shoulder. "I don't know them. Three are Empire soldiers and one, I think, maybe a Republic Legionary, but I'm not sure. We would never treat our dead like this."

***

The door opened and the procession filed into the street with the Captain in front and two oarsmen walking beside the cart. Alerio and the other rower followed Frigian as he turned northward on the street. Then Frigian and the oarsmen began to chant.

> *Let all who grieve, chant the Sons of Mars Elegy*
> *An empty bench, an idle oar, our brother's passed*
> *he'll row no more*
> *Walk me through Messina dears*
> *A final view of the town I fear*
> *Of the beautiful harbor at sunrise*
> *And the high Citadel at sunset*
> *As I recall good days of cheer*
>
> *Let all who grieve, chant the Sons of Mars Elegy*

An empty bench, an idle oar, our brother's passed
he'll row no more
Beg my pardon of the Goddess sweet
Adiona's light the mariner greets
She'll guide my shipmates homeward
My journey, however, is but outbound
Never again her blaze to meet

Let all who grieve, chant the Sons of Mars Elegy
An empty bench, an idle oar, our brother's passed
 he'll row no more
Launch my ship one final time
Let me taste the salty brine
Let me feel the power strokes
Sing to me the rowing notes
Row me out with lusty rhymes
Let all who grieve, chant the Sons of Mars Elegy
An empty bench, an idle oar, our brother's passed
he'll row no more

***

The five hooded and masked chanters and the reeking cart of corpses crossed the main road and moved loudly into the northern blocks. All the while they chanted the verses. Citizens and soldiers stepped back from the feeling and smell of death surrounding the procession.

On the second block past the wide road, a Lieutenant and his bodyguard waved for them to stop. Frigian ignored the Qart Hadasht officer's challenge until they were beyond a lantern's light.

"In the name of the Empire, I order you to halt," he screamed trying to be heard over the chant.

Let all who grieve, chant the Sons of Mars Elegy
An empty bench, an idle oar, our brother's passed
he'll row no more

"Excuse me, Lieutenant, I can't hear you over the elegy," Frigian had to shout to be heard over the chanting.

"What is this and where are you going?" the officer demanded as his chest heaved and he gagged. The closer to the cart he moved the slower he walked and his cheeks puffed out as he attempted to hold his breath.

Walk me through Messina dears
A final view of the town I fear

"We're giving our dead a last tour of Messina," Frigian yelled back even though they were only a couple of feet away from each other.

Of the beautiful harbor at sunrise
And the high Citadel at sunset

"We will search the wagon," called back the Lieutenant. "Soldier, dig into the cart. See if the Sons of Mars are hauling weapons."

As I recall good days of cheer

The soldier reluctantly approached the side of the cart. Up close, the sweet and poignant odor of rotting flesh overpowered his senses and he hesitated.

"Do it! Search the cart," shouted his officer.

With fingers holding his nose and his eyes watering, the soldier stuck his other arm over the sideboards and shoved his hand into the straw.

Beg my pardon of the Goddess sweet
Adiona's light the mariner greets

The oarsman on that side of the cart struck out slamming the soldiers head on the top of the sideboards. He staggered back and the oarsmen punched him in the groin below the armor. Then, the rower punched the soldier on the chin below the helmet.

She'll guide my shipmates homeward
My journey, however, is but outbound

Alerio spun away from the cart shaft bringing the back of his elbow around. It crashed into the side of the Lieutenant's helmet.

Never again her blaze to meet

The officer, dazed and stumbling, crossed his legs trying to move laterally. Alerio hooked a leg behind the officer's ankles and pushed. The Lieutenant crashed onto the road.

Let all who grieve, chant the Sons of Mars Elegy

Alerio brought his elbow down and smashed it into the officer's face.

An empty bench, an idle oar, our brother's passed

he'll row no more

"Put him in the cart," Frigian ordered two of the oarsmen.

As they moved the wrapped bodies to make a hole, they continued to chant.

Launch my ship one final time
Let me taste the salty brine

Once the Lieutenant was buried under the bodies, the procession moved down the block.

Let me feel the power strokes
Sing to me the rowing notes

The cart reached the third street and tuned east towards the Empire lines.

Row me out with lusty rhymes

***

"What's this?" demanded a Qart Hadasht Sergeant. His voice, seasoned from years of issuing commands in the heat of battle, carried over the chant.

Let all who grieve, chant the Sons of Mars Elegy
An empty bench, an idle oar, our brother's passed
he'll row no more

"Giving our dead a final stroll through town," replied Frigian. "Then to the dock and a burial at sea."

Walk me through Messina dears
A final view of the town I fear

After years of war, the Empire Sergeant had developed immunity to death, the cries of the wounded, the plight of his enemy, the stink of unwashed bodies, and the paralysis of fear. While those issues didn't bother him, others he found revolting. His sensitives included eggs prepared in any fashion, sweet fruit with small seeds and the smell of rotting bodies.

Of the beautiful harbor at sunrise
And the high Citadel at sunset

"Move along," the Sergeant ordered as he moved far out of the campfire light and spit on the street. Death hovered and rot emitted from the cart and he wanted it gone.

As I recall good days of cheer

The cart and robed chanters moved down the street. With the raised voices echoing off the compound walls, the Legionaries further down assembled and waited.

Let all who grieve, chant the Sons of Mars Elegy
An empty bench, an idle oar, our brother's passed
he'll row no more

***

"Halt!" ordered the Legion Corporal. "We will search your wagon."

Frigian guided the cart northward on the street before stopping. Once around the corner and out of view from any sharp eyes at the Qart Hadasht barricade, Alerio brushed back the Phrygian and pulled down the cotton mask.

"I am Lance Corporal Alerio Sisera of the Southern Legion. And yes Corporal, you will check the cart," Alerio stated. "As a matter of fact, you'll unload the cart and send a runner for Senior Centurion Valerian."

"And why would I do that?" demanded the Corporal.

"Because we have the Tribune's bargaining tokens," reported Alerio. "They're in the cart."

Chapter -36 The Reality of Brutal Negotiations

Tribune Claudius' first orders included bathing and finding clean tunics for the Admiral and the Lieutenant. Then, he sent the Lieutenant off with Legionaries and had Hanno escorted up the hill to the Legion command tent.

"Seeing as I couldn't get you to speak with me during our meal," Claudius said as a Sergeant bound the Admiral's hands and ankles before settling the Qart Hadasht commander in a chair. "I thought this environment would be more favorable to a conversation."

"You have me at a disadvantage," Hanno replied holding up his hands. "I am unable to kill you with my hands tied."

"Or I could kill you," Claudius shot back resting his hand on his gladius. "But when my Legionaries were shipwrecked on your shoreline, you spared them. It's one of the reasons you're still alive."

"What is the other reason?" inquired Hanno.

"I don't want to start a war with the Qart Hadasht Empire," responded Claudius. "By murdering one of their Admirals."

Hanno burst out laughing.

"That Tribune Claudius is ironic," Hanno said when he stopped. "When I spared your Legionaries and the Greek sailors, I did it because I didn't want to be responsible for starting a war with the Republic."

"And yet, here we are looking at war over Messina," Claudius summed up. "In the final analysis, it won't be you or me who decides on war. It'll be our rulers."

"What is to become of me?" questioned Hanno. "Will you ship me, by night, back to your Capital to display a captured Qart Hadasht Admiral for your people? Or complete the task and murder me?"

"I was hoping you would order your men to leave Messina and row away with them," suggested Claudius. "That would take the decision out of my hands."

"I am Hanno, an Admiral of the Qart Hadasht Empire," he stated with pride. "Kill me, torture me, but I will never surrender Messina."

"Right now, I believe we should breakfast," the Tribune ventured as he watched the first rays of sunlight stream into the command tent. "Optio. Bring rations for the Admiral and me."

Claudius paced and thought as they waited for the food. Hanno settled on glaring at the Tribune. When the

Sergeant brought in two bowls of cooked oats sweetened with honey, a camp stool was placed in front of Hanno.

"If you don't eat, you'll be hungry and weak," offered Claudius when he saw the Admiral turn his nose up at the bowl. Lifting a small ladle, the tribune took a mouthful. "Delicious. It's a shame you're missing out."

"Suffering your presence is torture enough," Hanno complained. "Ingesting your common soldier's fare is insufferable."

"Explain something to me, Admiral," inquired Claudius as he took another mouthful. "Your officers. Are they all nobility from royal houses of Qart Hadasht?"

"There are no kings or queens in Qart Hadasht. Only aristocrats from the finest families are allowed to serve as officers of the navy and army," bragged Hanno.

"What about your sub-commanders, Gisco and Barca?" Claudius asked. "How important are their families?"

"Both are directly related to the current Suffetes," Hanno informed the Tribune. "In a few years, Barca would have become a great general of the Empire. Had you not killed him."

"I didn't kill him. You sent him on a night time suicide mission against my Legionaries," explained Claudius. "But you didn't tell me about sub-commander Gisco."

"Gisco will become one of the Judges and be a fine administrator for the Empire," Hanno stated. "He's only here for some military experience. Much to my detriment."

There was a rustling at the tent flap and Senior Centurion Valerian entered. He slammed a fist into his chest. Both Hanno and Claudius turned to look at him.

"Tribune Claudius. All is in readiness," Valerian announced.

"Bring them up and have the Sergeant escort the Admiral," Claudius instructed. Then ignoring the puzzled look on Hanno's face, the Tribune walked out with his Senior Centurion.

***

"They're going to come against us soon," guessed Valerian. "Once they figure out their Admiral isn't in the western half of the town. Do you think sub-commander Gisco would be agreeable to surrendering?"

Below them, they could see squads of Qart Hadasht soldiers racing up and down streets and in and out of Villas and craftsmen's compounds.

"From what I've learned, Gisco is an administrator," replied Claudius. "He'd rather wait in the Citadel until all his troops are dead before discussing the terms of his surrender."

Far off on the other side of the city, Claudius noticed movement. Lines of unidentifiable men marched. After watching for a time, he decided the men were marching towards Messina.

"Sub-commander Gisco must have pulled soldiers off the defensive line. Probably to aid in the search. He's left big

257

holes in his lines as an invitation," suggested the Tribune. "And the Syracusan commander has taken him up on the offer."

"We could always wait and let Syracuse remove the Qart Hadasht soldiers," advised Valerian.

"They'd begin crucifying Sons and we'd have to advance to protect the citizens of Messina," responded the Tribune. "If there's going to be woodwork, I'd rather it be me deciding who gets stretched. Not the Syracusans."

They strolled around to the back of the temple. Behind them came a hobbled Admiral Hanno with just enough rope between his ankles to shuffle.

***

"Admiral, I'm glad you could join us," Claudius said pleasantly as if Hanno had a choice.

In front of them, Legionaries were digging in waist deep holes. Behind the lip of the excavation, large stones were stacked. It wasn't the men, the holes or the rocks that caused the Admiral to flinch. Laying in front of each hole were heavy beams, notched and lashed together to form crosses.

"Five? Are you putting me up with some of your Legionary criminals?" Hanno asked. "I am not afraid."

But it was a weak attempt at bravado as his lips quivered.

"Of course not, my dear Admiral," Claudius assured him. Then the Tribune pointed at the steps. "Here come the attendees to your sunset viewing party."

On the steps leading to the top of Temple hill were four men in new tunics. Two displayed clean bandages on their wounds and their pace and posture told the tale of recent injuries. The other two climbed with stiff backs as if they were in charge rather than being prisoners. Four Legionaries walked behind with the points of their javelins inches from the captured Empire officers' backs.

"I'm sure you know these men," advised Claudius as the four reached the top and were herded towards the back of the Temple. "Sub-commander Barca, I'm sure. Hopefully, you recognize the others as three of your Empire Lieutenants."

Hanno's empty stomach sickened and bile rose in his throat. The four represented four powerful houses of the Qart Hadasht Empire. Two were eldest sons and two were second sons. All had bright futures ahead or short painful deaths. It was up to him and he didn't like the options.

"I thought you didn't want to start a war with the Empire, Tribune," said Hanno.

The Tribune motioned for the Legionaries in the post holes to stop digging.

"I don't. But with your soldiers deserting the south wall and Syracuse troops closing in, it seems I don't have a choice," replied Claudius. "Your soldiers will be trapped between two forces and they will die anyway. Why not

259

march out with your officers and men? It's not as if you're leaving me a pacified town."

Hanno glared at the Tribune before shifting to Barca. His sub-commander, although slumped from an injury, stared back at his Admiral with trusting eyes.

"I have two Triremes and rowers," Hanno said softly as if embarrassed by his words. "But not enough ships for my soldiers and officers."

"The Sons of Mars have transports in the harbor," pointed out Claudius. "We'll work something out, however…"

Tribune Claudius let his sentence end unfinished. As a commander, he didn't want to put words in the mouth of another commander making a hard decision.

"No!" shouted one of the healthy Lieutenants. "We are Qart Hadasht Empire. We do not surrender to dirt farmers."

Everyone froze. Standing silently, Claudius, Barca, and the two other Lieutenants seem as statues, no one wanting to move or even breathe hard.

Then Valerian with his arms hanging at his side lifted a finger and pointed it at the Legionaries in the holes. Unseen by the officers, the Senior Centurion jerked his finger up and down as a signal to dig.

The first shovel burrowed into the clay, sand, and pebbles. As the iron scraped into the gritty soil, it created a screech. As if a mythical night creature had escaped into the daylight, the hairs on the backs the officers' necks bristled.

Hanno glanced down at the shovels of dirt thrown from the hole and up at the Lieutenant who spoke out.

"Lieutenant Bomilcar. You are young and arrogant. Perhaps someday, you'll understand," Hanno whispered. Then to Claudius, in a loud commanding voice, he announced. "Tribune Gaius Claudius. As commander of the Qart Hadasht forces in Messina, I propose an end to hostilities. My only condition is that you allow the unmolested passage of my officers and soldiers to the dock. From there we will row away and leave the Sons of Mars and the Syracusan situation in your hands. Do you agree?"

"Admiral Hanno. By the authority invested in me by the Senate of the Republic, and as a staff officer of the Legion, and commander of Caudex Legion detachment in Messina, I accept your surrender," replied Claudius. "Sergeant, kindly untie the Admiral."

Act 7

Chapter – 37   The Inherent Dangers During Rotation

"Captain Frigian. I'm of two minds," confessed Claudius. "One is to disarm the Sons of Mars until just before you row out and need weapons and armor to protect your trade."

"That's a better deal than we had with Qart Hadasht," pointed out Frigian. "What's the other thought?"

The Tribune raised an arm and indicated the south side of Messina.

"Admiral Hanno is pulling his troops from the south wall and marshalling them for a march to the dock," Claudius explained. "I need all of my Legionaries to watch for treachery. Once they are stretched from the dock to our lines, they could easily turn on us."

"Like a wounded wolf," ventured Frigian. "Even if you beat it off, it might turn on you at the last moment. Or it might trot off into the woods."

"Yes, like a wounded wolf. I don't want Admiral Hanno turning on my Legionaries when he is behind my lines," agreed Claudius. "I need the Sons to man the south wall defenses until I can free up Legionaries."

"And what's in it for the Sons?" asked Frigian.

"You know, it's a bad idea," commented Claudius. "Maybe I'll let Syracuse have the western half. I only need the dock and beach for General Caudex and the rest of the Legion."

"Hold on, hold on Tribune," Frigian begged. He knew if Syracuse troops made it into Messina they would begin killing Sons. "We can hold them off until your Legionaries arrive. But I need one thing from you."

"And what is that?" inquired Claudius.

"I need Lieutenant Sisera," Frigian replied. "Rather, Lance Corporal Alerio Sisera to command my heavy infantry."

"The Sons of Mars have heavy infantry?" Claudius asked while squinting and crunching up his face. "Did you say Sisera commands your heavy infantry?"

"In truth Tribune, according to Lieutenant Sisera, the Sons' heavy infantry is like gold leafing on a Tribune's armor," Frigian explained. "It's safe and looks good because it's not made for real combat. It just looks pretty on the battlefield."

"Senior Centurion Valerian. Find Lance Corporal Alerio Sisera and tell him he is assigned to Captain Frigian until released," ordered Claudius.

***

Three hundred Legionaries lined the wide road. From behind their shields, they watched five hundred Qart Hadasht soldiers and their officers march by. In the western sectors starting with the Citadel, pairs of Legion skirmishers searched the town. They were looking for soldiers. Hidden units that could attack from the rear as the Legionaries collapsed to follow the last column of soldiers out of Messina.

Two pairs of the Velites came out of compounds on the opposite sides of a street and stopped. From the north marched columns of heavy infantry. Big shields, shoulder rigs, breast plates, javelins, spears, helmets and the infantrymen marched mostly in step. The skirmishers started to run and raise the alarm when they noticed something odd. All the equipment was from different city states. Egyptian, Legion, Greek, Macedonia, Qart Hadasht, and some that were so obscure in style and markings, they couldn't identify the origins.

A man riding a big horse and outfitted in shiny Greek armor rode beside the columns.

"Left, stomp, left stomp," the Greek commander called out the cadence.

As the infantrymen passed, the Greek turned on his horse and did a cross chest salute. Not knowing what else to do, the Legion Velites returned the salute.

***

"What's the hold up now?" demanded a frustrated Tribune Claudius.

"The soldiers wanted to stop for a meal before boarding," Senior Centurion Valerian replied. "Short of reigniting hostilities, our Legionaries are stuck with standing and watching."

Admiral Hanno had a tent on the beach where he could observe the loading of his soldiers. Other than a few runners, he sat in a chair doing nothing to hasten the departure. With only about a hundred soldiers loaded on transports, there was a real likelihood the Qart Hadasht could reengage.

"The wolf is delaying for one of two reasons, or both," reflected Claudius. "He wants to the Syracusans to come in and make us fight for the town again. Or he's changed his mind. With four hundred soldiers, he could hold the dock and warehouses until we are worn down. Then retake Messina."

"Do you think he'd go back on his word, sir?" asked Valerian

"I don't know. What's an aristocrats word to a dirt farmer worth?" pondered Claudius.

***

South of the wall and across the field, Syracusan units mustered. In the center were Hoplites with big shields and long spears. Squads of soldiers flanked the elite fighters. Farther out, on each side of the ranks of foot soldiers, cavalry mounts pawed and stomped the sod.

A rutted road stretched through the Syracusan troops, traveled across the grassy field and threaded between Messina's defensive line. It ended at the main gate to the port town. South of the wall, on either side of the road, Qart

Hadasht soldiers had dug wide, shallow pits and piled the dirt behind the dips to create hills. Two rows of misaligned pits composed the defensive line.

The pits were there to break up the Hoplites' phalanx formations. The Greeks could come up the road but only one phalanx at a time. While the single formation moved smoothly, the soldiers protecting its sides would be up and down pits and hills. If the phalanxes came across the field they would need to weave their tightly packed formations between the pits and hills. All in all, it was a good defensive line. However, like all good things, it came to an end – actual ends where the field flattened.

"Cavalry, port and starboard," announced a Sons of Mars runner.

Alerio, atop the big horse, lifted his eyes from the ranks of his infantrymen slowly forming up across the road. Looking left then right, he cringed.

Mounted Syracusan troops charged the ends of his line. Where he had heavy infantry at the center, on the ends were his irregulars. Half armored rowers, organized by boat crews, they fell back as the cavalry charged them. Bunched up and unable to defend themselves, several of the irregulars fell dead or wounded to the grass.

As the horsemen rode off and circled for another pass, Alerio called to his Sergeants.

"First and second squads, fall out and get to the port end," he shouted using the nautical terms familiar to the

Sons of Mars oarsmen. "Eleventh and twelfth, hustle to the starboard end."

Alerio would have preferred to be in the shield wall. But, Captains Frigian and Creon had appointed him overall commander. The leaders of the Sons were on his left and right trying to rally their men to defend against another cavalry charge. They were failing.

More oarsmen flew back, arms, heads, and shoulders slashed by fast moving mounts and swift sword strokes. Soaring splatters of blood, like rooster combs, marked the falling bodies while sprinkling the other irregulars. On the front ranks, oarsmen checked to see if the red drops were theirs or that of a fallen crew member.

Then, the first and second squads of the Militia's heavy infantry reached them. As if an armored glove had been slipped on a bleeding hand, the squads curled into two ranks. The bleeding appendage at the end of the Sons line had become an armored fist.

The Syracusan cavalry kicked their mounts and came about. They laughed and howled at the ease of the killing. With savage joy, they bore down on the irregulars for another round of whack-a-pirate. Except now their horses galloped towards tightly linked shields bristling with iron tipped javelins.

Realizing the enemy had changed, the mounted troops veered off and guided their mounts to the rear of the heavy infantrymen. But they swung wide and the irregulars, who had been fixed targets, turned the table. Now, the oarsmen raced towards the cavalrymen throwing javelins, and spears. Two mounts stumbled and the cavalry troopers fell as their mounted unit turned and escaped back around the heavy infantrymen. Angry oarsmen swarmed the wounded Syracusan soldiers before racing back to their place in the defensive line.

On the starboard side, the leader of the cavalry recognized the danger of heavy infantrymen. He turned his mounted unit and trotted them back to the Syracusan line.

"They didn't turn our line," commented Captain Creon as he rode up.

"But they did draw off some of our infantry," replied Alerio indicating the six remaining squads at the road.

"Sixty shields are still impressive," added Creon.

"They use thirty-two Hoplites in their phalanx formations," explained Alerio. "Even if we break it up, the Hoplites are better trained. We'll be lucky if our men can hold the line after the phalanx breaks up."

"You don't have much faith," observed Creon.

"Captain. My faith is founded on Centuries of Legionaries coming through the gate," Alerio said glancing at the empty opening in the south wall. "Until then, I believe a lot of us will die if Syracuse attacks."

***

The sun had passed its zenith and Tribune Claudius had worn a slight trench in the hard soil of Temple hill from his pacing. Below in the harbor, another hundred Qart

Hadasht soldiers had boarded transports and rowed into the Strait.

"They're down to three hundred," announced Valerian as he reached the top of the hill. "At least now we're evenly matched."

"But we're not," Claudius replied lifting an arm and pointing southward. "There's movement at the Sons' position."

"I could sneak away a Century and send them south," offered the Senior Centurion.

"And if one of those transports returned and Admiral Hanno changes his mind," reflected Claudius. "Those eighty Legionaries will make a difference here. Over the wall, I'm not too sure. Hold what we have."

"Yes, sir," Valerian replied while looking down on the dock and beach at the inactivity of the Qart Hadasht soldiers.

Then, Admiral Hanno raised from his camp chair, arched his back and put his hands over his head. Claudius and Valerian stiffened focusing on the figure in front of the tent on the beach.

"Signalman. Stand by," Valerian called without taking his eyes off the Admiral.

"Standing by, Senior Centurion," the Legion signalman responded.

But Hanno didn't signal an attack. He opened his mouth and yawned. With a wave at a servant, the Admiral strolled to a ramp and boarded one of the Triremes. After his baggage was carried aboard, crewmen pushed the Empire warships off the beach. With uniformed strokes, the Triremes powered across the harbor and entered the Strait.

"You've cut the head off the snake, sir," Valerian said congratulating the Tribune. "Do you want to send units to the south wall now?"

"Bomilcar and Gisco are still on the dock," Claudius warned. "Those two have had their heads together for most of the morning."

"Bomilcar? The officer who challenged the Admiral?" inquired Valerian. "Do you think he's irrational enough to order an attack?"

"While Lieutenant Bomilcar is, I believe his rashness is being tampered by Sub-commander Gisco," surmised Claudius. "I'm afraid Lance Corporal, or should I say, Lieutenant Sisera will have to make do with his Sons of Mars heavy infantry for a while longer."

Chapter – 38 An Unheroic Welcome

Two and a half days later, the two Triremes rowed into the Empire port of Zis. They had crossed two thirds the width of northern Sicilia and passed all the troop transports. As the warships ground onto the sandy beach, an Admiral and a squad of soldiers rushed to greet them.

"Admiral Hanno. We sighted the ships expecting news," Admiral Yutpan, the commander of all the Qart Hadasht forces on Sicilia, explained. "I didn't expect to find you. What's the status of Messina?"

"Admiral Yutpan. We need to have a conversation," replied Hanno.

"Come. We'll go to my office," Yutpan urged.

The two Admirals and the squad marched off the sand, up granite steps and took a winding path to Yutpan's office.

***

"And with the Syracusan's forces closing in from the south and four of our families' sons in danger," Hanno related softly ending his long explanation. "I withdrew our forces and left Messina to the Republic."

"That is disheartening. But from what you described, I can't imagine you'll have any problems with your decision," Yutpan guessed. "Let me have my staff assign you quarters. Get some rest while the remainder of your command rows in. I'm sure we can find you a new posting soon."

Admiral Hanno didn't relax for the two and a half days it took for the last transport to row into the docks at Zis. He roamed the beach during the day and the halls of his quarters at night. All the while questioning his actions and especially the final decision concerning Messina.

***

A knock at the door dragged Hanno out of a restless sleep. When he opened it, a messenger handed him a rolled parchment. Stripping off the band and seal, he read.

Admiral Hanno,

Your presence is demanded in the naval hall at first light.

Admiral Yutpan

Hanno dressed rapidly and rushed from his room. He strutted down the hallway, and out a back door. Across a courtyard, he entered another doorway, marched down another hallway and stopped in front of a set of large ornate doors. There, he paused and took in a deep breath before shoving the doors open and walking into the naval hall.

***

It was a mid-size room with a long candlelit table on one end. Three men sat on one side of the table - Admiral Yutpan and two Empire staff officers. Although they faced the room, none of the three looked up when Hanno entered. They were occupied with pieces of parchment they passed back and forth. They'd silently read a section by candle light, point out specific words, hand the missive to another of the trio, and repeat the process. Brief whispered discussions followed each sharing of the parchments.

Braziers cast weak, shadowy light around the room. A line of five chairs had been placed several feet from the table. Men occupied four of the chairs and Admiral Hanno knew all of them.

Sub-commander Gisco, Lieutenant Maharbaal, and Lieutenant Bomilcar sat in the first three. Over a short divide was an empty chair. Sub-commander Barca occupied the fifth chair which was also separated from the empty one. Admiral Yutpan glanced up, indicated the center chair, bent his head, and returned to the discussion.

Hanno walked by Gisco and Maharbaal, who didn't raise their eyes or acknowledge him in any way. Beside them, Bomilcar jutted his chin out and tracked Hanno's passage with malice in his eyes.

As Hanno reached the empty chair, he received a sad smile and a nod from Barca in the last chair. He returned Barca's greeting and sat with his back rigid in the empty and isolated chair. Placing his hands on his knees, Hanno faced the three judges without expression.

The windows behind the judges' table lightened as dawn approached. But the three continued to use the illumination of the candles until sunlight passed over the table and crept the several feet to the line of five chairs. Only when Hanno's face was clearly visible did Admiral Yutpan and the two staff officers cease their examination of the documents and their discussions.

Admiral Yutpan blew out the candles on the table and announced, "Charges, horrible and dark, fit only for the black of night, have been levied against Admiral Hanno. We have reviewed them seeking enlightenment with the rising sun. Now with the morning light shining on the accused, we are prepared to also shine the light of Qart Hadasht justice on Hanno, an Admiral of the Empire."

As Yutpan finished and sat, another of the judges stood.

"Admiral Hanno, you have been charged with desertion in the face of the enemy, disgracing the Empire," listed the staff officer. "Actions unbecoming of an Admiral of the Qart Hadasht military, showing a lack of judgement and cowardice."

The officer sat down and the third member of the panel stood.

"Hanno has an exemplary record as a military leader," the officer stated. "Coming from a good but moderately successful house of Qart Hadasht, his talents and strength of character allowed him to rise to the exalted level of Admiral. Maybe it was the struggle to climb and the self-preservation necessary to advance that caused him to act as he did in Messina. Or possibly, he had risen too far above his abilities to make sound decisions concerning the Messina incident."

"Messina incident?" cried out Bomilcar with scorn in his voice. "When faced with death and honor, Hanno chose to save his own life with dishonor."

"And he saved your life, and my life," Barca reminded Bomilcar.

"I'd rather die than give up land to the Republic or any other rogue government," Bomilcar bragged. "Maybe my honor and my love for the Empire are stronger than yours."

"Lieutenant Bomilcar. Do you challenge my honor? My commitment?" Barca asked in a low and threatening tone. "Because while you were running errands for Admiral

Hanno and sub-commander Gisco, I was beyond the wall facing Syracusan soldiers. If you want to test my courage, open your mouth one more time!"

"Now see here, sub-commander Barca. There is no need to chastise a young Lieutenant for speaking his mind in a court," Gisco exclaimed. "And certainly, no reason to make it personal and threaten violence."

"What did Bomilcar promise you, sub-commander Gisco?" inquired Barca. "A trade deal with his family? Or, maybe his sister and a fat dowry as payment for bringing down a fine Admiral? Or maybe you think you will be promoted to Admiral in his place?"

Gisco opened his mouth but nothing came out. In the glare from the combat officer, he decided not to respond.

"The panel of judges has read the reports and heard the opinions of witnesses both for and against the Admiral," Yutpan stated. "Admiral Hanno do you have anything to add before the panel renders a decision?"

Hanno raised slowly and straightened his shoulders. With his eyes level and clear, he spoke.

"I have served the Empire for fifteen years. During that time, I have endeavored to protect the interest of Qart Hadasht at all times. Against all foes in battles at sea and on land, I have been successful. In Messina, I faced an adversary I was not prepared for, not emotionally or militarily," explained Hanno. "By retreating, I saved the lives of my junior officers so they could share the experience. Hopefully, they will help mold the Empire's forces so the next time we face the Republic, our soldiers and officers will be prepared. For that reason, the future of the Empire, I ordered the surrender."

Hanno sank into his seat as if all the air had left his body. As a military commander, he was accustomed to being in control and deciding the fate of others. Now, his was in the hands of three judges.

Mercifully, the panel didn't take long to decide.

"Admiral Hanno. It is the unanimous decision of the court," Yutpan stated. "That you have been found guilty of lack of judgement while in command of a strategic shipping port, and cowardice in the face of an enemy of the Empire. For these charges, and to impress upon all Qart Hadasht officers the need for perseverance in the face of opposition, you shall be taken to a high hill so all may witness the justice of the Qart Hadasht Empire. On the hill, at the sun's zenith, you will be crucified and remain on the cross until death takes you."

***

With the sun high overhead, a squad of soldiers marched with Admiral Hanno to the crest of a hill. Before Hanno laid down and spread his arms out on the wooden beam, he looked upon the rolling waves and the ships of the mighty Empire rowing across Zis bay.

After lashing his arms to the cross piece and his ankles so his heels touched the wedge piece, the soldiers hoisted the beam. Its end slipped over the edge, dropped into the hole, and slammed into the bottom. The jolt dislocated

Hanno's shoulders and he fought to fill his lungs. As the soldiers filled the hole with stones and packed rocks around the beam to keep it upright, Hanno pressed with his heals, rose up on quivering legs, and sucked in air. But his heals slipped off the wedge and he dangled strangling until he could locate the sloped wedge with his heels. Again, he rose up, breathed and slipped. It was a struggle he would repeat until sundown when his strength failed and he hung fully stretched on the wood. As the sunset over Zis bay, Admiral Hanno jerked violently as he suffocated to death.

Chapter – 39   Motivation in Question

The soldiers rushed down the hills on either side of the rutted road. Ahead of them, the phalanx moved too fast and the spacing of the soldiers became uneven. In a ragged line, they hit the solid shields of the Sons of Mars heavy infantry while the phalanx surged ahead.

"Why are they suddenly in a rush to kill us?" asked Frigian.

"I don't know Captain," Alerio replied. "Are you ready?"

"Give the order, Captain," Frigian responded.

The two leaders split apart. One running to the left, the other to the right. Each joined two ranks of differently armed men. In the front rank, the heavy shields and swords of infantrymen dominated. Behind the infantry, oarsmen stood gripping long poles with thick shafts. Another difference, the second rank was noticeably larger.

***

This was the third charge by the Syracusans. All afternoon the soldiers and Hoplites came at the Sons' line. Each time, the Sons broke the assault but gave ground and left bodies of dead crewmen on the trampled grass.

During the second beating, as Alerio thought of the punishment the Sons suffered, he noticed one section of his line held. The heavy infantry wasn't any better than the other squads. Their advantage was behind them. The second rank had poles and spears wielded by large oarsmen. Each time they slammed the poles or spears into the Syracusan soldiers' shields, the powerful strikes delivered by the massive shoulders of the oarsmen drove the soldiers back a couple of steps and, in some instances, knocked them to the ground.

Alerio called Creon and Frigian to him during a lull in the killing.

"Captains. Of your oarsmen, who are the strongest?" Alerio inquired.

"All the machina locus and et mallei crewmen," Frigian replied with pride. "Our center rowers who provide the power for our ships and the few who have the most strength but lack technical ability. Because, well, they have no rhythm. They are by far the strongest men on this battlefield."

"Captains, I'd like you to pull all your machina locus and et mallei," advised Alerio. "Put them on the second rank and arm them with poles or long spears."

"Poles against armored soldiers?" questioned Creon.

"Captains…" Alerio began to explain when Creon interrupted.

"I've decided it's impossible for a Lieutenant to order Captains around, even on a field of battle," Creon interjected. "As the leader of the Sons of Mars, I bestow upon Alerio Sisera the rank of honorary Captain of the Sons of Mars. If we live though this and you want to leave the Legion, you can always get a ship and row with the Sons, Captain Sisera."

"Thank you, Captain," Alerio replied.

"Captain Sisera. Now that we've made you a Captain and held a very informal ceremony, what were you saying about our machines and our hammers?" asked Frigian.

"Spread them out in the second rank, even if they are currently in the front," ordered Alerio. "Let's take advantage of their power and have them pound the shields and keep the soldiers back. Maybe it'll make up for the undertraining of our infantry and irregulars. It may be our only advantage."

***

The first two phalanxes were broken by logs placed across the road. But the logs were gone, toted away by Syracusans soldiers as they retreated to regroup. Now the

279

road lay open and the third phalanx began to outpace the soldiers protecting the formation's flanks.

"Close it off," shouted Alerio while making a chopping motion with his hand.

The surviving Sergeant on his side, as well as Frigian and the NCO on the other, peeled back the infantrymen from where the phalanx would breach their line. Then the pole men shifted towards the opening and pounded the Syracusan solders backwards.

With the concentration of pounding poles, the soldiers rushing forward to protect the flanks of the phalanx found themselves flying back into their second rank. Soldiers attempting to untangle were clubbed with the blunt end of a shaft from over the infantrymen's shoulders.

The end of the phalanx moved through the Sons line. Instead of their soldiers following the formation through the line, the pole men and the Sons' infantry closed the hole. Realizing they were cut off, the Hoplites, like ants from an ant hill, streamed from their formation. Irregulars and infantrymen swarmed in and it became vicious individual combat.

Now, there were two distinct battles. The surrounded Hoplites in the center of the Sons' formation and the fight along the shield wall.

Two Hoplites battered aside irregulars and ran at Alerio. Their aim was to kill the Sons' commander. With the big Greek shields and swords bearing down on him, Alerio drew his sword and cursed his lack of a shield. He'd been too busy directing the flow of the battle to think about his own defense. Suddenly, it became paramount to his survival.

He shuffled to the side trying to isolate one of the Greeks and keep the other away for a few heartbeats. But the Hoplites knew their business. Together they pivoted staying one shield forward and the other beside the lead but a half step behind.

Alerio circled and the Hoplites shifted, maintaining the two-man attack formation. All around them, Syracusan soldiers and Sons' oarsmen and infantrymen sliced and hacked at each other. From what Alerio could tell, the Hoplites in the center were dropping Sons three to one. Along the shield wall, the odds were more even.

With a yell, Alerio sprang forward then spun, his sword whipping around towards the Hoplite. It connected with the shield as the Greek shifted and blocked the backhanded slash. Ducking, Alerio let the other Hoplite's blade pass over his head. But the Greeks stepped forward, rapidly pressing their advantage. Needing to put space between him and the Hoplites, Alerio dove backwards preparing to do a neck roll and come up on his feet.

Alerio's helmet smashed into a shield and he flopped to the ground. Looking up, he saw a big shield lift and a foot raised to stomp down on his head.

"Not him!" shouted a familiar voice that Alerio couldn't place. "Kill the cūlus Hoplites."

The shield and hobnailed boots passed over Alerio. Then the face of a bent over Legionary peered down at him.

"Well Lance Corporal Sisera, are you going to lay there all afternoon looking up my skirt?" First Sergeant Gerontius inquired.

"No First Sergeant," Alerio replied as he rolled over and gathered his arms under him.

Pushing off the ground, Alerio stood and glanced over the First Sergeant's shoulder. Through the city gate, jogged Legionaries. By threes, they burst between the posts and formed a moving line. The Legion ranks grew wider as more heavy infantrymen joined.

"Where did you come from?" asked Alerio.

"I brought a squad and came looking for you," explained the First Sergeant. "I was going to ask where you needed us. But I'll just assume you need us everywhere."

The rank of Legionaries reached to where the Hoplites and Sons of Mars fought. From three to one, the odds shifted and the Legion heavy infantry nudged the Sons aside and cut into the remaining Greeks. Once the center fight dissolved into a few isolated duels, they marched towards the shield wall.

The pole men found themselves yanked back and then the irregulars and the Sons' infantry at the wall were shoved aside and flung back. None of the deposed fighters complained about the rough treatment.

After taking their place on the line, the Legionaries locked shields. Then from the rear, a Centurion shouted, "Stand by to advance." All down the line echoed a repeat of the order from Sergeants, Corporals, squad leaders and pivots. "Advance, advance, advance." In three heartbeats, the Legion line thrust their shields forward and followed up with a stab of their gladii.

Syracusan soldiers and Hoplites went from fighting an outclassed band of half trained pirates to facing a professional fighting force. As the troops from Syracuse fell back in the face of the advances, Captain Frigian and Captain Creon staggered up.

"We held them again, Captain Sisera," an exhausted Frigian stated.

"What took the Legion so long to get here?" asked Creon. Everyone could tell he wanted to be angry. But from the slump of his shoulders, they could tell he was too spent to press the issue.

"The Qart Hadasht soldiers stopped for a meal," First Sergeant Gerontius answered. "We're here now and Tribune Claudius wants to meet with you on Temple Hill. After you see to your wounded and dead."

The First Sergeant scanned the section of the battlefield exposed as the Legion line moved forward. He couldn't tell the wounded from the exhausted except for the cries of pain from the injured. Both categories had the same bent and fatigued postures.

***

"The Syracusans had the opportunity to attack when Qart Hadasht command pulled squads from the defensive positions," Creon pondered. "But they didn't."

"Then this afternoon, they launched three assaults," Alerio added. "I don't understand, sir."

Alerio, Milon Frigian, and Ferox Creon sprawled in camp chairs with drooping eyes and mugs of wine resting on their thighs. None had the energy to hold the mugs up except for quick sips. Then the mugs returned to rest on their thighs.

"There must be a reason for the aggressive tactic," commented Tribune Claudius. "From a strategic stand point, it made sense to test the Sons. After the rotation from Qart Hadasht soldiers to the Sons of Mars, I would have ordered one or two to test your defenses. However, as Lance Corporal Sisera put it, I don't understand why they pressed for the third."

"Maybe they didn't know about the Legionaries in Messina," ventured Frigian.

"Unlikely. There are enough spies and farmers traveling to and from town to warn them," Claudius pointed out. "Something was driving the Syracuse commander. And it wasn't to draw out the Legionaries."

A hush fell over the men in the command tent. It was deep in the night and they'd all had a busy day. Finally, Creon broke the silence.

"I assume Tribune, you didn't summon us to Temple Hill to discuss the motivation of the Syracusan commander," offered the Sons' Captain.

"We need to show a strong Legion presence at the south wall and in town," Claudius explained. "To do that, we'll be thin at the docks."

"You need the Sons to guard the harbor for you?" guessed Creon. "Seeing as the only two forces likely to row in are angry Qart Hadasht soldiers and equally rabid Syracusan soldiers. I believe it's in our best interest to assist you."

"Thank you, Captain Creon. I'll give you a day or so to rest and organize your troops," Claudius exclaimed. "Once the Sons have the harbor secured, I'll move my command post to Citadel Hill. It'll give me a better vantage point to observe the Syracusan forces and to watch over the harbor."

"Good night, Tribune," Creon said as he, Alerio, and Frigian stood to go.

"Lance Corporal Sisera, a moment of your time, please," ordered Claudius.

While the two Sons' Captains pushed aside the tent flap and left, Alerio waited. Long after the crunch of the Captains' sandals on the gravel faded, the Tribune called out.

"Sergeant. Are they gone?" he asked.

His personal guard stuck his head through the flap.

"They're on the steps and headed down, sir," the Optio reported.

"Thank you. Sisera we can speak freely," Claudius announced with a smile. "First, Captain Sisera, you did an admirable job commanding the defense of the south wall. I expect you'll be an excellent Centurion someday."

"Thank you, sir," Alerio acknowledged the compliment. And although exhausted, he brightened up at the Tribunes praise.

"Now about the Sons. I don't trust the Sons of Mars. I need you to remain with them and be my eyes and ears."

"Yes, sir. Are you expecting trouble from the Sons?" inquired Alerio.

"Not in the sense that they'll attack us," Claudius explained. "It's just, they aren't disciplined. Messina harbor is key to General Caudex and the Legion landing. If you think the Sons are failing or lacking in vigilance, I need to know. If required, I'll shift additional Legionaries to protect the harbor."

"I can do that, sir," promised Alerio. "Is there anything else?"

"No, Lance Corporal, dismissed," Claudius said releasing the tired Legionary.

Chapter – 40 The King Arrives

The old boar snorted, dug a rut in the soil with his tusks but didn't charge. Instead, he remained in the tangled underbrush.

"Think the old pig will ever come out?" Frigian asked holding a spear at waist level with the iron head pointing at the barely visible animal.

"Maybe if you ask him nicely," a crewman suggested. He also held a spear aimed at the boar.

"I don't think please come out so I can kill you is anybody's definition of nice," Alerio added. The Legionary grasped two javelins, one in each hand, poised at shoulder height.

"Left or right, Captain Sisera? You can't do anything with a throw by the weaker arm," commented another of Frigian's oarsmen.

To the crewmen, Sisera looked ridiculous holding two javelins. None of them knew he was ambidextrous and lethal with either arm.

***

After two days of rounding up pirates for guard rotations and exchanging Officer of the Guard duties at the dock, Frigian had recommended a pig hunt.

"Something to get your blood boiling," the pirate had promised. "And unlike the Syracusan troops who may kill you, the boars, while dangerous, are good eating."

As Tribune Claudius' staff packed his gear and carried it down Temple Hill to a cart, Alerio, Frigian and six

287

members of his crew set out from the warehouse district. Carrying spears, javelins, poles and hemp rope, they crossed Messina, circled around Citadel hill, and left the town through the small west gate. High in the foothills, they crossed a trail made by a sounder of swine.

Two of the oarsmen spotted a sow in the brush. A quick thrust with their spears and tense moments while they crawled in to drag out the boar, gave the hunting party their first wild pig.

"Not a bad size," exclaimed Frigian. "But we'll need a lot more meat if we want to return with any bragging rights."

That's when loud snorting, the snapping of branches and popping of roots came from deep in the thicket.

"That might be more meat than we can handle," commented an oarsman as a huge shadowy shape appeared in the thick brush.

***

"Left or right, Captain Sisera? You can't do anything with a throw by the weaker arm."

"Don't worry about Sisera's aim," urged Frigian with a hint of fear in his voice. "Keep your spears ready."

"I have two thoughts," another rower added. "One is I hope he doesn't come out. The other is, if he does, I hope seven spears are enough to bring him down."

"If you wanted fresh goat's milk, you should have stayed in Messina," another replied.

"I'm here. I'm holding this perfututum spear," shot back the rower. "So, you can…"

"Enough! Keep your minds on the task at hand," warned Frigian. "This is what separates men from little lads. The hunt, the bragging, and the eating. Or the stripping of flesh from your bones by sharp tusks."

"What is he waiting for?" inquired Alerio.

"The wise old boar is waiting us out," ventured Frigian. "See how he's settled. If we turn, he'll run and soon be lost in the hills."

"Then let's bring him out," suggested Alerio.

"How? You going to sneak in there and wrestle an animal ten times your size?" questioned an oarsman.

"No, I thought I'd nudge him with a javelin," Alerio informed the hunting party.

"Go right ahead," a rower said. "I'll stay right here behind this spear."

Alerio drew back his left arm and powered it forward as he released the javelin. The shaft crossed to the undergrowth, threaded between the thick bushes, creased the boney head of the boar before burying the iron head in the wild pig's back.

The great animal squealed an ear shattering wail and shredded the brush as he charged. Fully embedded, Alerio's first javelin flopped back causing the iron tip to rip the creature's lung. Mad with pain and furious with the two-legged animals invading his territory, the boar thundered across the clearing.

The second javelin struck at a steeper angle and the iron tip pierced deeper. The massive boar staggered but remained on his feet streaking forward. Seven spears sank in and still, the giant wild pig came at the men.

Frigian and his rowers leaped out of the way of the charging boar. All seven men hit, rolled and came swiftly to their feet. With knives in hand, they faced towards the boar. Then it stumbled, righted itself and stopped. With a last shake of the broad snout and sharp tusks, the wild pig fell to the ground.

"I pronounce the hunt a success and over," Frigian announced between shallow breaths. Like all the men, he was shaking from the close encounter with the fierce and muscular animal. "Lash him and the little one to poles and let's head back."

"Whose pig are you calling little?" challenged one of the oarsmen who had brought down the sow.

Frigian strolled to the sow and spread his arms to the length of the wild pig. While still holding his arms out, he moved to the boar. Laying his hands against the wide side of the huge boar, he displayed the size difference. Without a word, he turned his head and smiled.

"She's still a nice kill," protested the oarsmen.

"I never said she wasn't," Frigian replied. "Lift them and let's get back. We have a pig roast to prepare."

Two oarsmen balanced a pole on their shoulders with the sow dangling between them. The boar required two men on each end to lift the pole to their shoulders. Frigian and Alerio took the lead and the happy hunting party started down the hill to the first ravine. As the porters of the wild pigs slowed to navigate the gully, Frigian stopped to direct the crossing. Alerio surged ahead climbing the slope.

As he approached the top, the whinny and neigh of horses reached him. Raising up, he peaked over the crest. Below, four Qart Hadasht cavalrymen moved slowly, letting their mounts pick their way through the foothills. If they weren't already at the next shallow valley, Alerio might have engaged them. He scurried down to Frigian.

"Empire cavalry just over the hill," Alerio explained. "I'm going ahead to warn the Legionaries."

"A complete unit?" asked one of the oarsmen. He lifted a hand from the pole and, with a sad expression on his face, pointed to the wild pigs. "Do we have to leave them?"

"Only four and they have moved away," replied Alerio.

"The Goddess Diana is watching over our hunt," the oarsman responded.

"Let's hurry before she changes her mind," suggested Frigian. "Captain Sisera, we'll see you in town."

Alerio saluted and climbed to the top of the hill. After checking to be sure no more horsemen were there, he glanced back and waved the oarsmen forward. Then he vaulted over the top and ran for Messina.

Alerio rounded Citadel Hill and almost ran into Senior Centurion Valerian.

"Slow down, Lance Corporal," Valerian advised to the huffing and puffing and soaking wet Legionary.

"Qart Hadasht cavalry to the west moving south," Alerio blew out before inhaling deeply.

"How many?" demanded Valerian.

Alerio bent over with his hands on his knees, lifted one hand and displayed four fingers.

"Mounted couriers. If that's all, there's no threat," Valerian ventured. "If they are heading for the Syracusans, that's a tale yet to be told. Walk with me."

The two men strolled casually up the slope so Alerio could catch his breath. They glanced up to see the Tribune on the crest gazing to the south.

"Tribune Claudius. Let me be the first to congratulate you on seizing Messina," Valerian said as they reached the top of Citadel Hill.

"Thank you, Senior Centurion," replied Claudius. "Please express my appreciation to the Legionaries for their sacrifice."

The Tribune hadn't looked at them. His head was turned as he continued to stare off towards the south.

"Over the River Longanus, I see more Syracusan forces," Tribune Claudius reported while lifting an arm indicating the thin ribbon of water beyond the battlefield. "Based on the number of columns, I believe King Hiero II has arrived. And, with a sizable army."

"Orders, sir?" inquired Valerian. Then he remembered Alerio. "Lance Corporal Sisera reported a mounted Qart Hadasht courier detail of four riding to the south."

"Lance Corporal Sisera, please tell the Sons' Captains, I now understand the motivation of the commander of the Syracusan advance force. He was putting on a display because his King was coming. He didn't want to admit he let his soldiers sit idle for weeks," Claudius explained. "Ask the Sons if they will maintain their surveillance of the docks."

"Of course, Tribune," Lance Corporal Alerio Sisera assured him.

"Senior Centurion, I have two fears," exclaimed Tribune Gaius Claudius as he caught sight of the Qart Hadasht cavalrymen trotting towards the River Longanus and the King of Syracuse. "By capturing Messina, we have united two adversaries against the Republic."

"And the other fear, Tribune?" inquired Senior Centurion Valerian.

"We may have started a war that will either make or break the Republic."

The End

A note from J. Clifton Slater,

I appreciate you reading Brutal Diplomacy. The Clay Warrior Stories are a passion project for me and the success of the series tells me I'm not alone in my fascination with the Roman Republic.

Hopefully, the tension between Hanno and Claudius came through in this book. The actual events, which I attempted to reenact, gave me the bones for this story. And yes, Hanno was crucified by Carthage for surrendering Messina.

The other event I found interesting was the first public gladiator contest held as funeral games in 264 B.C. They took place in the stockyards between captured Etruscan warriors.

Alerio Sisera will fight again Fortune Reigns. But I have a lot of research to do on the First Punic War before writing the next installment of the Clay Warrior Stories.

My readers are amazing. To you, I send a cross chest salute and say, Euge! Well Done!

J. Clifton Slater

I like chatting with readers and I do read reviews on Amazon.com and Goodreads.com. If you have comments or want to reach me, I am available.

E-Mail: GalacticCouncilRealm@gmail.com

To sign up for my newsletter and to read blogs about ancient Rome, visit my website.

www.JCliftonSlater.com

Facebook.com/Galactic Council Realm

I write military adventure both future & ancient.

Books by J. Clifton Slater

Historical Adventure – 'Clay Warrior Stories' series

#1 Clay Legionary   #2 Spilled Blood

#3 Bloody Water   #4 Reluctant Siege

#5 Brutal Diplomacy   #6 Fortune Reigns

#7 Fatal Obligation   #8 Infinite Courage

#9 Deceptive Valor   #10 Neptune's Fury

#11 Unjust Sacrifice   #12 Muted Implications

#13 Death Caller   #14 Rome's Tribune

Fantasy – 'Terror & Talons' series

#1 Hawks of the Sorcerer Queen

#2 Magic and the Rage of Intent

Military Science Fiction – 'Call Sign Warlock' series

#1 Op File Revenge   #2 Op File Treason

#3 Op File Sanction

Military Science Fiction – 'Galactic Council Realm' series

#1 On Station   #2 On Duty

#3 On Guard   #4 On Point

Made in the USA
Coppell, TX
07 October 2021